CHRISTOPHER BUSH
THE CASE OF THE BURNT BOHEMIAN

CHRISTOPHER BUSH was born Charlie Christmas Bush in Norfolk in 1885. His father was a farm labourer and his mother a milliner. In the early years of his childhood he lived with his aunt and uncle in London before returning to Norfolk aged seven, later winning a scholarship to Thetford Grammar School.

As an adult, Bush worked as a schoolmaster for 27 years, pausing only to fight in World War One, until retiring aged 46 in 1931 to be a full-time novelist. His first novel featuring the eccentric Ludovic Travers was published in 1926, and was followed by 62 additional Travers mysteries. These are all to be republished by Dean Street Press.

Christopher Bush fought again in World War Two, and was elected a member of the prestigious Detection Club. He died in 1973.

CHRISTOPHER BUSH

THE CASE OF THE BURNT BOHEMIAN

With an introduction
by Curtis Evans

DEAN STREET PRESS

Published by Dean Street Press 2020

Copyright © 1953 Christopher Bush

Introduction copyright © 2020 Curtis Evans

All Rights Reserved

The right of Christopher Bush to be identified as the Author of the Work has been asserted by his estate in accordance with the Copyright, Designs and Patents Act 1988.

First published in 1953 by MacDonald & Co.

Cover by DSP

ISBN 978 1 913527 03 7

www.deanstreetpress.co.uk

INTRODUCTION

Ring out the Old, Ring in the New
Christopher Bush and Mystery Fiction in the Fifties

"Mr. Bush has an urbane and intelligent way of dealing with mystery which makes his work much more attractive than the stampeding sensationalism of some of his rivals."
—Rupert Crofts-Cooke (acclaimed author of the Leo Bruce detective novels)

New fashions in mystery fiction were decidedly afoot in the 1950s, as authors increasingly turned to sensationalistic tales of international espionage, hard-boiled sex and violence, and psychological suspense. Yet there indubitably remained, seemingly imperishable and eternal, what Anthony Boucher, dean of American mystery reviewers, dubbed the "conventional type of British detective story." This more modestly decorous but still intriguing and enticing mystery fare was most famously and lucratively embodied by Crime Queen Agatha Christie, who rang in the new decade and her Golden Jubilee as a published author with the classic detective novel that was promoted as her fiftieth mystery: *A Murder Is Announced* (although this was in fact a misleading claim, as this tally also included her short story collections). Also representing the traditional British detective story during the 1950s were such crime fiction stalwarts (all of them Christie contemporaries and, like the Queen of Crime, longtime members of the Detection Club) as Edith Caroline Rivett (E.C.R Lorac and Carol Carnac), E.R. Punshon, Cecil John Charles Street (John Rhode and Miles Burton) and Christopher Bush. Punshon and Rivett passed away in the Fifties, pens still brandished in their hands, if you will, but Street and Bush, apparently indefatigable, kept at crime throughout the decade, typically publishing in both the United Kingdom and the United States two books a year (Street with both of his pseudonyms).

Not to be outdone even by Agatha Christie, Bush would celebrate his own Golden Jubilee with his fiftieth mystery, *The Case of the Russian Cross*, in 1957—and this was done, in contrast with Christie, without his publishers having to resort to any creative accounting. *Cross* is the fiftieth Christopher Bush Ludovic Travers detective novel reprinted by Dean Street Press in this, the Spring of 2020, the hundredth anniversary of the dawning of the Golden Age of detective fiction, following, in this latest installment, *The Case of the Counterfeit Colonel* (1952), *The Case of the Burnt Bohemian* (1953), *The Case of The Silken Petticoat* (1953), *The Case of the Red Brunette* (1954), *The Case of the Three Lost Letters* (1954), *The Case of the Benevolent Bookie* (1955), *The Case of the Amateur Actor* (1955), *The Case of the Extra Man* (1956) and *The Case of the Flowery Corpse* (1956).

Not surprisingly, given its being the occasion of Christopher Bush's Golden Jubilee, *The Case of the Russian Cross* met with a favorable reception from reviewers, who found the author's wry dedication especially ingratiating: "The author, having discovered that this is his fiftieth novel of detection, dedicates it in sheer astonishment to HIMSELF." Writing as Francis Iles, the name under which he reviewed crime fiction, Bush's Detection Club colleague Anthony Berkeley, himself one of the great Golden Age innovators in the genre, commented, "I share Mr. Bush's own surprise that *The Case of the Russian Cross* should be his fiftieth book; not so much at the fact itself as at the freshness both of plot and writing which is still as notable with fifty up as it was in in his opening overs. There must be many readers who still enjoy a straightforward, honest-to-goodness puzzle, and here it is." The late crime writer Anthony Lejeune, who would be admitted to the Detection Club in 1963, for his part cheered, "Hats off to Christopher Bush....[L]ike his detective, [he] is unostentatious but always absolutely reliable." Alan Hunter, who recently had published his first George Gently mystery and at the time was being lauded as the "British Simenon," offered similarly praiseful words, pronouncing of *The*

Case of the Russian Cross that Bush's sleuth Ludovic Travers "continues to be a wholly satisfying creation, the characters are intriguing and the plot full of virility. . . . the only trace of long-service lies in the maturity of the treatment."

The high praise for Bush's fiftieth detective novel only confirmed (if resoundingly) what had become clear from reviews of earlier novels from the decade: that in Britain Christopher Bush, who had turned sixty-five in 1950, had become a Grand Old Man of Mystery, an Elder Statesman of Murder. Bush's *The Case of the Three Lost Letters*, for example, was praised by Anthony Berkeley as "a model detective story on classical lines: an original central idea, with a complicated plot to clothe it, plenty of sound, straightforward detection by a mellowed Ludovic Travers and never a word that is not strictly relevant to the story"; while reviewer "Christopher Pym" (English journalist and author Cyril Rotenberg) found the same novel a "beautifully quiet, close-knit problem in deduction very fairly presented and impeccably solved." Berkeley also highly praised Bush's *The Case of the Burnt Bohemian*, pronouncing it "yet another sound piece of work . . . in that, alas!, almost extinct genre, the real detective story, with Ludovic Travers in his very best form."

In the United States Bush was especially praised in smaller newspapers across the country, where, one suspects, traditional detection most strongly still held sway. "Bush is one of the soundest of the English craftsmen in this field," declared Ben B. Johnston, an editor at the *Richmond Times Dispatch*, in his review of *The Case of the Burnt Bohemian*, while Lucy Templeton, doyenne of the *Knoxville Sentinel* (the first female staffer at that Tennessee newspaper, Templeton, a freshly minted graduate of the University of Tennessee, had been hired as a proofreader back in 1904), enthusiastically avowed, in her review of *The Case of the Flowery Corpse*, that the novel was "the best mystery novel I have read in the last six months." Bush "has always told a good story with interesting backgrounds and rich characterization," she added admiringly. Another southern reviewer, one "M." of the *Montgomery Advertiser*, deemed *The Case of the Amateur Actor* "another Travers mystery to delight the most critical of a reader audience," concluding in inimitable American lingo, "it's a swell story." Even Anthony Boucher, who in the Fifties hardly could be termed an unalloyed admirer of conventional British detection, from his prestigious post at the *New York Times Books Review* afforded words of praise to a number of Christopher Bush mysteries from the decade, including the cases of the *Benevolent Bookie* ("a provocative puzzle"), the *Amateur Actor* ("solid detective interest"), the *Flowery Corpse* ("many small ingenuities of detection") and, but naturally, the *Russian Cross* ("a pretty puzzle"). In his own self-effacing fashion, it seems that Ludovic Travers had entered the pantheon of Great Detectives, as another American commentator suggested in a review of Bush's *The Case of The Silken Petticoat*:

> Although Ludovic Travers does not possess the esoteric learning of Van Dine's Philo Vance, the rough and ready punch of Mickey Spillane's Mike Hammer, the Parisian [sic!] touch of Agatha Christie's Hercule Poirot, the appetite and orchids of Rex Stout's Nero Wolfe, the suave coolness of The Falcon or the eerie laugh and invisibility of The Shadow, he does have good qualities— especially the ability to note and interpret clues and a dogged persistence in remembering and following up an episode he could not understand. These paid off in his solution of *The Case of The Silken Petticoat*.

In some ways Christopher Bush, his traditionalism notwithstanding, attempted with his Fifties Ludovic Travers mysteries to keep up with the tenor of rapidly changing times. As owner of the controlling interest in the Broad Street Detective Agency, Ludovic Travers increasingly comes to resemble an American private investigator rather than the gentleman amateur detective he had been in the 1930s; and the novels in which he appears reflect some of the jaded cynicism of post-World War Two American hard-boiled crime fiction. *The Case of the Red Brunette,* one of my favorite examples from this batch of Bushes, looks at civic corruption in provincial England in a case concerning a town counsellor who dies in an apparent "badger game" or "honey trap" gone fatally wrong ("a web of mystery skillfully spun" noted Pat McDermott of Iowa's *Quad City Times*), while in *The Case of the Three Lost Letters*, Travers finds himself having to explain to his phlegmatic wife Bernice the pink lipstick strains on his collar (incurred strictly in the line of duty, of course). Travers also pays homage to the popular, genre altering Inspector Maigret novels of Georges Simenon in *The Case of Red Brunette*, when he decides that he will "try to get a feel of the city [of Mainford]: make a Maigret-like tour and achieve some kind of background. . . ."

Christopher Bush finally decided that Travers could manage entirely without his longtime partner in crime solving, the wily and calculatingly avuncular Chief Superintendent George Wharton, whom at times Travers, in the tradition of American hard-boiled crime fiction, appears positively to dislike. "I generally admire and respect Wharton, but there are times when he annoys me almost beyond measure," Travers confides in *The Case of the Amateur Actor*. "There are even moments, as when he assumes that cheap and leering superiority, when I can suddenly hate him." George Wharton appropriately makes his final, brief appearance in the Bush oeuvre in *The Case of the Russian Cross*, where Travers allows that despite their differences, the "Old General" is "the man who'd become in most ways my oldest friend."

"Ring out the old, ring in the new" may have been the motto of many when it came to mid-century mystery fiction, but as another saying goes, what once was old eventually becomes sparklingly new again. The truth of the latter adage is proven by this shining new set of Christopher Bush reissues. "Just like old crimes," vintage mystery fans may sigh contentedly, as once again they peruse the pages of a Bush, pursuing murderous malefactors in the ever pleasant company of Ludovic Travers, all the while armed with the happy knowledge that a butcher's dozen of thirteen of Travers' investigations yet remains to be reissued.

Curtis Evans

Chapter I
QUESTIONABLE CLIENT

It was two o'clock on an afternoon of early May and I was in Norris's office at the Broad Street Detective Agency. Norris, an ex-Chief Inspector at the Yard, is general manager, and I appear on the billheads as chairman. When there's nothing doing for me at the Yard as what they call an unofficial expert, I put in quite a lot of time at Broad Street. I devil for Norris when he has to be away, and when we're particularly busy I don't mind putting in time as an operative.

We have contracts with two of the big insurance companies, and that morning Norris had been running an eye over an arson case. It was two o'clock, as I said, when Bertha Munney buzzed me from her office to say a possible client was on the line. She said he would give neither his name nor his business, and that he wanted to speak to one of the principals.

"Put him through, Bertha," I said, and picked up the receiver.

I wriggled comfortably in my chair and sat back to listen. There was a faint crackling at the other end of the line and then the rather turgid clearing of a throat.

"The Broad Street Detective Agency," I said. "Travers speaking."

"You're one of the principals of the firm, Mr. Travers?" the voice said.

"The chairman," I said, and I didn't see any point in adding that I was also the proprietor.

"My name is Chale," he said, and spelt it for me. "I live at 15 Meriton Gardens. You may know it. It's just off Sloane Square."

"Just one moment, Mr. Chale," I said. "I'll write it down. Just as well not to trust one's memory."

Chale's was a deep bass voice, inclined to the pompous. My mind's eye saw him as a man of about sixty, short and with a fifty-inch waistline.

"15 Meriton Gardens," I said. "And now what can we do for you, Mr. Chale?"

"Well," he said, and then cleared his throat again, "I'd like to be assured that everything is confidential."

"Secret as the grave," I said. "You need have no fears about that, Mr. Chale. You're as safe with us as you would be with your doctor or lawyer."

"Yes," he said, or he made a noise that was something like it. "And you do all sorts of work?"

"Everything except divorce work."

"This isn't that sort of thing," he told me quickly. "As a matter of fact it's something very different. I hardly—well, I don't know if you'll believe me. I'm a psychiatrist, by the way."

I don't know what he expected me to say, but I didn't say it. A moment, and he was speaking again.

"We deal with all sorts of queer people, you know."

"So I imagine."

"Yes," he said, "and it's to do with one of them that I want to consult you. I believe I'm in danger of my life."

"Uh-huh?" I hoped that questioning grunt had had in it nothing of the sceptical. It hadn't. He was talking on.

"Yes. And I was wondering whether you could supply some sort of bodyguard."

I gave another sort of grunt. From my end of the line I must also have given Mr. Chale a sheepish sort of smile.

"Let me be fair to you," I said. "That sort of thing would cost you money. A lot of money if the job lasted any considerable time, and we shouldn't feel too happy about it. On the other hand, why not go to the police? It's their business to do the job for nothing."

"I know," he said. "But I daren't risk the publicity. Also I can't divulge the name of the person. Professional secrecy, if you understand me."

"I understand," I said, and was just about as wise as I'd been before. "But why not come and see me here or let me come and see you? It sounds the sort of thing that needs a bit of private discussion."

"My own opinion entirely," he told me heavily. "Perhaps you could call and see me."

"At what time?"

"In the morning," he said. "There'll be no time this evening. I have an appointment in North London at six and I may be back rather late. Shall we say noon tomorrow?"

"That will suit me admirably," I said. "At noon tomorrow, Mr. Chale. I take it you're not anticipating trouble before then?"

"I hope not. In fact I think not. But wait a moment."

The bass voice had shot up a key or two as if at a sudden thought, and he cleared his throat again.

"I beg your pardon," he said, "but there was something I'd forgotten. May we change the appointment to your office at the same time?"

"Most certainly."

"That's excellent," he said, and seemed loth to hang up. "Tomorrow morning at twelve at your office. I shall be very relieved to see you."

If he wanted to be chatty, I didn't mind. I said I'd be relieved to see him too, after what he'd hinted.

"Queer people, these mental cases," he said. "It's impossible, even for me, to calculate what their actions will be. The whole thing is most disturbing."

"Well, don't worry," I told him. "I'll expect you in the morning. Oh, and by the way. If necessary you can ring here at any hour of the night. I mean, should you wish to make the appointment earlier."

"I'll remember it," he said, and hesitated for a moment or two and then rang off. I hooked up my receiver, stretched out my long legs and did some quick thinking. Then I buzzed through for Bertha Munney. She came in with pencil and notebook.

"Not that," I said. "Just wanted to know what you thought of our Mr. Chale—I beg his pardon—Dr. Chale."

Bertha's a good judge: she ought to be after best part of twenty years in that office of hers.

"Sounded a bit stuffy and fussy to me," she said. "Yet he didn't sound scared. Not enough to want a bodyguard."

"And what about that professional secrecy excuse for not going to the police?"

"Something fishy there," she said. "If you ask me, he'll be telling quite a different tale tomorrow morning. Probably got himself mixed up with some woman or other. Or blackmail more likely. Or up to his tricks with one of his patients."

I didn't disagree. In our job it pays handsomely to form a sound idea of an unseen client. Queer specimens turn up at times for appointments, and even a little previous deduction can provide a not unprofitable anticipation. And there were quite a few things about Chale that came under the heading of queerness. I wasn't even happy about his allusion to mental cases. That didn't strike me as the language of a psychiatrist, even if he were avoiding jargon for a layman's benefit. And while I was puzzling my wits about that, Norris came in.

"A tiring morning?" I said.

"Not too bad," he told me, and then, before he could tell me about it all, I reported the conversation with Chale. He seemed to take it as an ordinary matter of business. Norris is like that: imperturbable and not too imaginative. Good solid routine work is his forte, and maybe that's just as well. Agility of mind doesn't always pay dividends, and one harum-scarum brain in one office is more than enough.

We settled down to that arson case, and it was getting on for three o'clock when I got up to go. It was as I was at the door that he reverted to Chale. He had picked up the engagement pad and was looking at it.

"A funny name—Chale."

"I suppose it is," I said. "I don't know that I've ever run across it."

"Reminds me of something," he said, and was frowning at the pad. "Something just before the war. This Chale's a psychiatrist?"

"So he said. I unthinkingly called him Mr. Chale, but he appears as a Dr. Chale in the telephone directory."

"A psychiatrist," he said, and was still frowning. "The one I thought I remembered was just an ordinary doctor."

I came back. I told him one or two of the peculiar things that had struck me about that telephone conversation. Running a business like ours—the private client side of it, I mean—is like driving a car. If you want to go on living you have to drive as if a suicidal fool was round every corner. You may meet only one such fool for every thousand drivers like yourself, but it's that one who matters. And it's the same with the one rare tricky or hopelessly unreliable client. A plausible one has more than once made trouble for us with the police, and once we escaped a lawsuit by the skin of our teeth.

"What was this business about a Dr. Chale?" I wanted to know.

Norris couldn't remember. All he knew was that two cousins then living at Brumford—which, by the way, is not its name—had been involved in a blackmail case and one had been acquitted. He hadn't handled the case himself, but he knew the Yard man who had had something to do with it. The cousins had been in partnership: one a doctor and the other a psychiatrist. Only one, as far as he remembered, was called Chale.

"Be a good chap and get hold of this Yard friend of yours," I said. "I'll drop in again some time later and hear if he's given you the details."

Bernice, my wife, was out and I'd intended going to my club, but I changed my mind and hopped a bus at the near corner. Half an hour later I was getting off at Sloane Square and asking for Meriton Gardens. Another ten minutes brought me there.

It was a high-class backwater with late Georgian houses that gave it the look of a fashionable square, and it had escaped the bombing. Fifty years ago one might have seen a handsome carriage or two, and a butler or footman at a door. Now it was merely somnolent and primly refined.

I walked past No. 15. A brass plate was by its door, but too distant for me to read. The house itself had no sign of life, but some fifty yards on I crossed the road and stood for a minute or two watching its door. Somehow I was disappointed, and that was, at the least, a curious state of mind. I ought to have been relieved. No doctor with a plate in Meriton Gardens could be other than ultra-respectable, and then again I wasn't too sure. I wondered once more why a man like Chale, making enough money to live in so expensive a neighbourhood, should be afraid to apply for protection to his lawful guardians—the police. The police were tactful and discreet. There was, as I saw it, no possibility of the scandal at which Chale had hinted. And that made me think that Bertha had been right. Even the vague recollections of Norris seemed to bear out what she had hinted; that the bodyguard business was only a smoke-screen, and that the next morning's disclosures would be vastly different from the telephone conversation of the afternoon.

That was what I was thinking when a car suddenly came round the corner of Copley Street and drew up outside No. 15. Before I could move, a horn was sounded; and by the time I was twenty yards nearer, the door had opened and a woman was coming down the steps. She looked about thirty and was wearing a fur coat. I lengthened my stride, and I saw her open the near door and get into the car. I caught a glimpse of her from my six-foot three, and I knew her for a good-looking brunette. Then the driver moved the car on. He was a grizzled, elderly man with a heavy moustache and was wearing a chauffeur's blue coat and peaked cap.

I walked on towards Sloane Square, amusing myself with a few deductions, and the things at which I finally arrived were highly contradictory. The woman hadn't been a patient of Chale's, since no one had accompanied her to the front door. She hadn't been Chale's wife, for the driver hadn't opened the door of the car. She was well out of the domestic category, and that made her a secretary or a receptionist. But I'm something of an authority on fur coats, and the glimpse I'd had of her coat had made it cheap at four hundred. And the logic of all that was that she was something betwixt and between—a summarising that left me nowhere.

I caught sight of a telephone kiosk and rang the office. Norris was out, Bertha said, but Hallows was in, so I gave her the number of the car and wanted the ownership traced. Then I looked round for a taxi, caught one and made my club in time for tea.

*

At five o'clock I was back at the office, and Norris was there with what we wanted. I pass it on without the irrelevancies.

In 1939 there had been a blackmail case at Brumford and the Yard had been involved. The defendants had been two doctors: a Colin Morse, a psychiatrist, and his cousin, Arthur Chale, a physician and surgeon. Both men were highly qualified, with English and Continental degrees.

The plaintiff, X, was a woman patient of Colin Morse, and the information on which the blackmail had been based had, she asserted, been extracted from her while under hypnotic influence. The outcome, which is all that matters, was this. Morse skipped his bail and disappeared, presumably abroad. Chale was honourably acquitted.

Sequels were that Chale's practice deteriorated badly, his wife died, and he left Brumford early in the war. Morse, it was discovered, died in France just before the Germans left. X retired into the anonymity from which she had emerged for the purposes of the trial.

"Our client is A. Chale, and that's presumably Arthur," I said. "But he's now a practising psychiatrist. Surely you can't switch from general practice to psychiatry?"

"I don't know," Norris said, and with a kind of dogged insularity. "You learn all sorts of things at those foreign universities. I reckon each partner knew something of the other's job, you bet your life on that. And if Chale came to London for a fresh start, why shouldn't he have tried a new professional branch as well?"

"There was a shortage of doctors and surgeons. The ordinary run of work should have paid handsomely during the war."

"Not if you were employed by the Government," he said. "The other job paid better, if you ask me. What about people's nerves, with the bombing and all that?"

"Yes," I said, if a bit dubiously. And then I remembered the car number.

"Belongs to Arthur Chale, M.D., etc.," Norris told me.

"Well, there we are then," I said, and I had to laugh. "Staring us in the face. You were plumb right. Chale did switch from general practice to psychiatry. The trouble is, just where does it get us?"

"Don't know," he said. "All I know is I don't like that blackmail business, whether he was acquitted or not."

I said I didn't care a lot for it myself. Then I was wondering if there was anyone I knew in Brumford, and for the life of me I couldn't think of a soul. But that only led to a short cut. Bertha looked up the number of its daily paper and finally got it for me. I was put through to a news editor.

Five minutes later I was leaving the office. Brumford had told me that it might take an hour to look up the files, so I'd arranged for them to ring me back at my flat in St. Martin's Chambers. I hadn't been home more than half an hour when the call came. But meanwhile I'd had all sorts of ideas. As I've said before, I suffer from a far too agile brain. I hate an unsolved problem, and by hook or crook I have to find, and quickly, an answer that satisfies, at least reasonably, my too inquisitive self.

What I'd wondered was if Norris was right after all. Two cousins in partnership, and one so guilty that he'd bolted and the other so guiltless that he'd been acquitted without a possible stain. But had Morse been the scapegoat? Could one partner have acted without any knowledge whatever by the other?

And there was a thought still more intriguing. Arthur Chale, the physician and surgeon, had now become a psychiatrist. *Or hadn't he?* Had those cousins borne a close resemblance, and was it Morse, the psychiatrist, who was now masquerading as Chale, the doctor? And had Chale been murdered or otherwise disposed of?

That's the kind of brain I have, but, as I said, the telephone bell rang and I began talking to the very man who'd handled the case for the newspapers. What he gave me was merely an enlargement of the story Norris had received from Chief-Inspector Wale.

"Morse and Chale," I asked. "Did they resemble each other?"

"Can't say that they did," he said. "At least it never struck me so at the time."

"What was their age, Mr. Baker?"

"Nearer fifty than forty, I should say. Chale was the elder; I do remember that."

"And they didn't resemble each other at all?"

"Not that I remember. If they had I think I'd have noticed it. Perhaps they were the same height and roughly the same build: in fact I'm pretty sure they were, but that's all."

"Any difference in what I'd call personality?"

"Most decidedly. Chale was the quiet, professional type. Mind you, I don't mind telling you after all these years that I thought it a case of still waters running deep. The judge thought otherwise. The other chap, Morse, was quite a different sort: a regular man of the world; suave and smooth as they make 'em. A dam' clever chap too. President of the Brumford Arts Club and quite a good painter himself for an amateur. On the committee of the local repertory theatre and a few other things."

"You don't mind if I go on pestering you?"

"Not a bit," he told me. "Only too glad to be of help."

"Then this chap Morse," I said. "My information is that he's dead. If so, it affects the whole case."

I'd had to tell him that my enquiries were connected with a possible legacy. Had I been able to anticipate the decent, frank and helpful chap he'd be, I think I'd have ventured to tell him something nearer the truth.

"He's dead all right," he said. "We followed up the story—resurrected it, rather—because of local interest, and one of those queer coincidences had turned up. One of our men with a nose for a story happened to be in Paris with his regiment at the actual time of the liberation, and he happened to get hold of it. This chap Morse had been running a fine arts business in Paris in conjunction with another pal of the Germans, handling a lot of looted stuff and so on, and Morse must have been caught out in some double-crossing. At any rate the Germans shot him just before they left. He was calling himself Delorme, by the way. Supposed to be a Belgian."

There was nothing else I could ask and nothing more that Baker thought helpful, so I thanked him gratefully and rang off. But I wasn't feeling any too happy, and maybe because the whole business from the word go had developed from a mere uneasiness into something highly melodramatic and even turgid. My small researches had produced a story of blackmail, hypnotism, collaboration with Germans and a probable shooting against a wall—all the ingredients needed, in fact, for a popular thriller. And I was still obsessed by an idea that was as turgid as the rest—the wonder if there had been more behind that disappearance of Morse than a bolting from his bail. Had my client Chale been, in fact, as guiltless as the judge and jury considered him? Wasn't it at least something I should have to keep in mind when I interviewed Chale the following morning? And in any case, I was feeling more pleased with myself. Chale might turn out to be yet another tricky customer, but it would be I who would hold most of the cards. Quite a poker session it might be, with Chale unaware that the cards were marked.

Then Bernice came in and during the next five minutes I recovered some sense of proportion. I could assure myself that I was a fool to anticipate trouble. In the morning I'd be face to face with Chale and listening to his story, and, armed with what I knew, I'd be in a position to sum the man up, believe or disbelieve what he had to tell me, and then take whatever action might be best for the firm. And it was just as I'd somewhat reassured myself with all that, that the telephone bell rang.

Chapter II
BORDEN WALK

"That you, Travers?"

George Wharton was on the line. Before I could do more than open my mouth he was going on.

"Been trying to get you the last half-hour," he was telling me pettishly, and that was just like George Wharton. I've been working with him for over twenty years, and I suppose that in the course of the average year there haven't been more than two cases of the sort, at least, that needs the attention of a Chief

Superintendent of New Scotland Yard. And yet when one such case does emerge from the blue he expects me to be sitting at the end of a telephone.

"I must have been having a rather long conversation with a man at Brumford," I said.

He gave a snort at that, and I could see in my mind's eye that vast weeping willow of a moustache of his suddenly billowing like a tent in a tornado.

"Looks like a job," he said. "Some artist chap at Chelsea. May be straightforward, and then again it mayn't. You can be here in about ten minutes?"

I said I hoped to. I grabbed a hat and coat and made it with a minute or so to spare. George was waiting in a police car, and it moved on as soon as I got in. I hadn't seen him for best part of a month, and I was thinking that a ten-year-old photograph would still have passed muster. It was a coolish evening of May and his heavy bulk was well into the corner, with the velvet collar of the overcoat drawn up round his ears. Usually he looks deceptively and pathetically forlorn, but now he was looking a bit irritable. When I asked too casually how he was he told me belligerently that he thought he was in for a cold.

I tried to think of something sympathetic but had to fall back on Chelsea. What part of Chelsea?

"Place called Borden Walk," he said. "Know it?"

I said I didn't. That produced another snort. George, I was pretty sure, was being temporarily awkward. Putting on his famous old-master act for the benefit of the driver.

"Halfway along Cheyne Walk and down to the right," he told me. "An artist chap by the name of Sindle. A knife in his back and a fire started to blind the trail."

For once in his life he was quite communicative. The knife hadn't been left in the body, he said, and the idea apparently had been that the fire would so char the corpse that murder wouldn't be suspected. Fortunately it had been brought under control in a very few minutes. There had been some burning of the back, but the local police-surgeon had spotted the cause of death and had asked for our own man, Cave. And the upshot was Wharton and myself on the way to Borden Walk.

Then Wharton was peering out of the window, the car slowed, and we were there. We must have come in by a route I didn't know, for there'd been never a glimpse of the river. Borden Walk, as I saw, was a backwater like Meriton Gardens, but with very much of a difference. It was narrow, with room only for one-way traffic, and it looked precisely as it should have done—a stage setting for some corner of an operatic Bohemia.

But maybe that was only how my imagination saw it in that evening light, and yet it was a feeling which the next few days were not altogether to change. Its houses, for instance, were of different heights and had an artistic touch of the ramshackle. Two buildings short of No. 7 was an old-fashioned shop, its windows crammed with sketching-boards and blocks and paint-boxes, and even a couple of easels. No. 7 was three storeys high and looked in good enough condition in spite of its slight air of the maudlin. On the other side of the road was the back of what looked like a warehouse, and then a long stretch of high wall. A narrow passage ran back between Nos. 7 and 8, and I caught a glimpse of a uniformed constable at its far end.

The front door was wide open, and we went through to a bleak kind of hall from which a stairway led to the upper storeys. Sergeant Matthews was there. He's tall, very dark and always cheerful. He has to be devil for George Wharton.

"Got everybody?" Wharton said.

Matthews nodded at a door on our left.

"In there, sir. Mr. Ferndale had to go, but he'll be back later."

"Ferndale? Who's he?"

"The one who has the studio," Matthews told him, and nodded again at the door. "And I've got the address of the lady who was sitting to him."

Wharton grunted: the kind of grunt that tells me he's putting up a front.

"Well, keep 'em quiet another minute or two, then I'll be in."

I heard a confused sound of voices as Matthews opened the door, then the door closed on him and we were mounting the stairs. A plain-clothes man joined us on the first landing.

"Straight up, sir."

He went ahead and we followed. There was a strong smell of burning before we came to that last landing, and then on the left were the ruins of what had been a studio. Water and charred wood were everywhere. Plaster from the shattered ceiling made puddles of thick, whitish mud, and the slates from the broken roof and glass from the skylights cluttered the floor and the partly burnt table. There was a partly burnt easel and various small canvasses, and through a door, smashed from its hinges, the same indescribable filth and chaos had straggled through to what seemed a bedroom.

A man appeared from that room, shook hands and introduced himself. He was some kind of assessor who'd been rushed in from the insurance company.

"Well, Mr. Green, what's your considered opinion?" Wharton was asking him.

Green said he hadn't had a lot of time to look round.

"This tells the story," he said, and pointed to a darker heap among the filth of sodden plaster and charred wood.

"Paraffin?"

"Paraffin and kindling wood and God-knows-what. A regular bonfire started."

Wharton cocked an ear. Steps were on the stairs. Cave came in. He's elderly, disillusioned and grossly cynical. Maybe if I'd handled as many corpses as he I'd be that way too. Wharton greeted him with a grunt.

"Quite a nice little fire," Cave announced, and looked amusedly round.

"Might have been a mighty dangerous one if it hadn't been for these tiles," Green said.

I hadn't had time to notice the tiles, and the moisture still in the air had steamed up my horn-rims. The red tiles were the sort one sees sometimes in old Victorian houses, laid in waterproof cement on top of a wood floor.

"Yes," Wharton said. "If it hadn't been for them the floor'd have collapsed into the room below. What about time of death, Cave? Worked it out yet?"

"As near four o'clock as dammit," Cave said. "Pity they moved him."

"The firemen had to lug him out," Wharton said. "How were they to know he wasn't alive?"

"Alive!" Cave said, and seemed tickled at the idea. "With the whole of the face burnt away. And the hands. Even the dental plates had gone."

"Plates?" I said.

"That's it," Cave said. "That plastic stuff's as inflammable as hell. It's not even allowed to be sent by post. It has to go by train. Marked 'Highly inflammable'."

"Let's do a quick reconstruction," Wharton cut in to Cave. "Then you can get along back. My information is that he lay here with his feet to the door and his head and hands on that pile where the fire was started."

He picked up a piece of charred lath and drew a rough outline. He looked at Cave and he looked at me.

"Stabbed as soon as he entered the door," Cave said. "He didn't open the door to anybody or he'd have been stabbed in his chest and found on his back."

Wharton snorted.

"Dam' rubbish! The body was moved, wasn't it? The head and hands were laid on the fire, or where the fire was going to be. Then whoever did it just nipped through where that window was and down that fire-escape."

I hadn't noticed that fire-escape. There'd been too much talk and things had been happening far too quickly. And I was thinking I'd better cut in with my question.

"This face-and-hands-on-the-fire business. What was the idea? So that the corpse shouldn't be identified from finger-prints or by its face?"

"What else could it be?" Wharton told me impatiently.

"But didn't the man live here?"

"Of course he lived here."

"Then everybody knew him," I said. "So why trouble to conceal his identity?"

Wharton shrugged his shoulders. There was plenty of time to go into that. Then he was asking Cave for a description of the dead man's clothing and the contents of his pockets. Cave produced a sheet of paper.

"Anything else you want here?" Wharton asked him.

"Two or three teeth missing," Cave said. "Probably dropped out when they moved the body."

It was the false teeth, presumably, that he meant: porcelain teeth that had fallen from the vanished dental plates. It was a pretty grisly idea.

Wharton told the plain-clothes man to get busy on a light lead from one of the other rooms. Dusk was heavy in the sky and it was almost dark in that inner room.

"Look," Wharton said to me. "I'll be here a minute or two longer. You go down and run an eye over those people. Most of 'em don't know a thing in any case. I'll run my rule over 'em later."

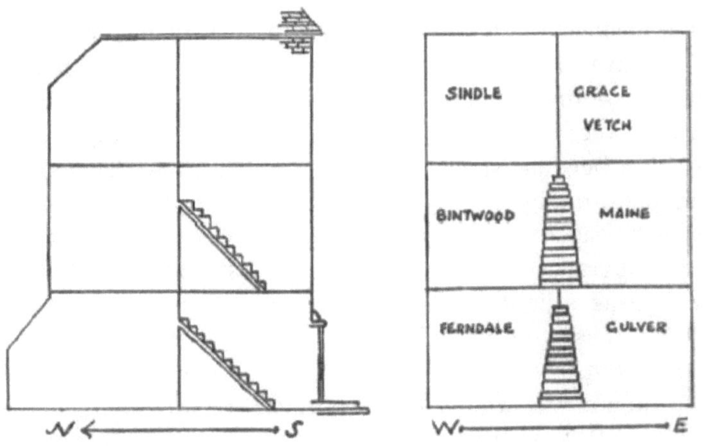

Before you meet, with myself, those people—as Wharton called them—you might like a rough plan of No. 7 Borden Walk and a list of the occupiers of those six sets of rooms or studios. One roughly drawn plan shows a section from south to north. The top north studio was that of the dead man, Sindle. The bottom studio was a much larger affair with a wall removed to allow of lights in the roof of the extension. That studio had behind it a tiny strip of grass which had once been a lawn, and then a wall separated No. 7 from the corresponding houses in Howe Street, which ran parallel to Borden Walk.

Beneath the rooms occupied by Gulver was a cellar with a boiler for the hot-water plant. Each set of rooms had a tiny bathroom-lavatory, a room used as a living-room or studio, a largish bedroom and a small kitchen. That ground-floor studio was rather different, though I wasn't aware of it when I first walked in. I wasn't aware of anything except that five people were sitting round an electric fire, and that the eyes of all five were on me when I entered. Matthews came across, and I told him I was holding the fort for Wharton.

"They just think it's a fire," he told me. "None of them knows anything about a murder. And if I were you, sir, I'd start with the old lady. Her name's Maine."

He switched on the light and I made a few apologies. Everything would be very formal, I said, though official statements might have to be made later. I was feeling my way, as it were, with an eye round the room. Just beyond the electric fire where the five were sitting was a heavy curtain that seemed to be a partition beyond which would be another room. That, I was thinking, would probably be the actual studio. The room where we were was a comfortable lounge. Pictures, portraits mostly and temporarily unframed, were on the walls, and mingled with the fug was a slight smell of paint and oil.

"May I ask your name?"

I was speaking to the woman whose name, as Matthews had told me, was Maine. Maybe because she was so much older than the other two women, and the two men were so lacking in personality, she seemed to dominate the small group that had swivelled round to face me. She was tallish and her age might have been anything in the late sixties. Her white hair was parted in the middle and coiled back above the ears. Her thinnish, clean-cut face was pale and the deep-set eyes amazingly dark.

The eyes were fixed on mine, and as she sat there, rigidly upright in her chair, there was something regal and vaguely tragic about her; a quality, a poise and a patience.

"Excuse me, sir, but you'll have to speak up. Miss Maine's a bit deaf."

That was the elderly man with the grizzled moustache. I raised my voice.

"Miss Maine, what can you tell me about this fire?"

She gave me a little bow, and somehow I felt that I had to smile in return. She had a beautiful speaking voice, and at once I was guessing that she must at one time have been an actress.

"I was in my room," she said, "and I was resting as usual when I smelt burning. That would be at about four o'clock. I looked out and saw the smoke. I didn't know whether to go up or down, but I went down and I began calling, 'Fire!' I thought Gulver might be there or Mr. Ferndale, and it was Mr. Ferndale who rushed out. He had a sitter, but he ran to the nearest fire alarm. When he came back he tried to put out the fire. He carried water up from my room. And then the firemen came."

"That's very clear indeed," I told her. "Did anyone else notice the fire? Either of you two ladies?"

They began to speak together, giggled, and stopped.

"You tell him, Helena," the shorter one said.

I asked her name and she said it was Helena Grace. She and the other girl, Viola Vetch, occupied the top rooms facing the burnt studio. Both she and Viola were at business and they weren't home till after five when the fire was out.

"What about you, sir?" I asked the man who'd been spokesman for Miss Maine. "Mr. Gulver, is it?"

He had the look of an old soldier, a regular who had served in the first world war. He had a ramrod back, and that unmistakable look and manner. His greyish hair was thin but brushed neatly across, and his moustache was neatly twirled at the ends. The face was red and the cheek-bones high, so that he had the look of a countryman out of his milieu.

"Gulver it is, sir." He had a crisp, economical sort of voice. "I was out too. Didn't get back till well after five."

"And you, sir?"

He was five feet eight or thereabouts, with the beginnings of a middle-aged spread. His reddish-purple face was plump, the nose rather squat and the rather narrow eyes a pale blue or grey. He was clean-shaven, with a blueness about his jowl. Of those five people he seemed the least interested and the least concerned.

"The name's Bintwood," he said. "I'm in the picture business. Henry Markov of Sloane Square. I didn't get home till just after six."

Then Wharton came in. He introduced himself, but we didn't have to begin all over again. What he wanted was a description of the dead Sindle. And as soon as he said so, something was happening in that room. People were looking at each other. There was a raising of eyebrows, a shrugging of shoulders. Vetch and Grace, the room-mates, began to whisper.

"Someone begin," Wharton told them amiably. "What about you, sir?"

It was to Gulver he was speaking, and there began a series of strange stories. Gulver, who was the handyman of No. 7, said the dead Sindle was a rum bird. On his taking over the studio Gulver had gone up to introduce himself. Sindle had opened the door just a crack, had listened without saying a word, and then had shut the door in Gulver's face. Later Gulver had found a note from Sindle pushed under his door. It said curtly that Sindle wanted nothing and would be obliged if Gulver would keep himself to himself as he, Sindle, proposed to do.

"Got the note?" Wharton said.

"I haven't, sir. It made me so dam' wild—begging your pardon, sir—that I chucked it on the fire."

"I see. And what was this Sindle like?"

"About medium height, sir. Slovenly-looking, if you know what I mean. Hair untidy and had a bit of a moustache and one of them little imperials. Had sort of rabbit teeth. Oh, and a fat, sort of unhealthy face, and wore glasses."

The two girls were whispering again. Wharton switched to them. It was Helena Grace again who did the talking. She was a brunette of medium height with hair beautifully coiled and a make-up that had a perfection of unobtrusiveness. She was twenty-five and a mannequin at Max Durance, the famous couturier of Richard Street, or so Bernice was later to inform me.

According to her, Sindle was a perfectly repulsive man. She and her room-mate saw him very rarely, and then he never spoke but merely scowled. The two were rather scared of him and saw that the door was not only locked at night but wedged with a chair. She confirmed Gulver's description, and thought Sindle would be about fifty.

"And you, Miss Vetch?"

Viola Vetch, a synthetic name if ever there was one, was a model. She confirmed everything that Helena Grace had said. I was watching her while she was talking and thought her out of the ordinary. She had a pinched sort of face with a mop of reddish-blonde hair and pouting pre-Raphaelite lips. There was something of the gamine about her, maybe because she looked so very much alive, and even when she frowned there was a kind of secret amusement in those blue eyes of hers. She was shortish but sturdy and compact.

I'd missed a question from Wharton. Apparently it had had to do with seeing Sindle anywhere outside. Helena Grace took up the story. She and Viola had twice seen Sindle at the Tabby Cat. Wharton raised his eyebrows.

The Tabby Cat, it appeared, was one of those smallish restaurants that spring up suddenly in the neighbourhood, become the rage and then lose popularity and as suddenly disappear. But the Tabby Cat, it appeared, was months old and still flourishing. Sindle had appeared there twice and had taken a far table and kept himself aloof.

Bintwood took up the story. Pictures were his line of business, and, as he told us, you never knew when you might have a find. Soon after Sindle's arrival he had gone up to his studio when he heard him moving overhead. Sindle had behaved with him as he had with Gulver and then shut the door in his face. As he did so he had uttered one sentence.

"All bloody dealers, keep out."

"I could have smacked him across the mouth," Bintwood said. "The way he sneered and showed those rabbit teeth of his. The room sort of smelt too, even if the door was only open a crack. I think he'd been drinking. If you ask me, that's how the fire started."

"As a matter of fact there were a few empty bottles up there," Wharton told him, and doubtless to give some harmless information in return and keep it one big family party. "And what about you, Miss Maine?"

Pamela Maine had seen Sindle once or twice and thought him surly and uncouth. She had spoken, but he had merely grunted.

Wharton switched to Gulver again. Sindle, we learned, had occupied that studio for just over a month. How he obtained possession we could find out from the owner, a Mrs. Oddfort who had a flat at Capron Court near the Tate Gallery.

"She's a very nice lady, sir. I was batman to her husband, the late Colonel. That's why she settled me in here."

Wharton whispered a something to Matthews, who left the room, and we could hear his quick steps on the stairs. Then Wharton got to his feet.

"I think that's everything for the moment. I may have to see you all again and I may not. You've been a great help. But just one other thing. I'd like you to give me an account of the clothes you last saw Sindle wearing. I'd prefer you to write it down. Please write your name or initials on the sheet of paper."

He passed the papers round and enough pencils were somehow mustered. Nobody seemed to realise that what he was after was fingerprints. Matthews came back, and he had a half-dozen small canvases that had come from the burnt-out studio above. Wharton collected the papers and was unctuous with thanks.

"I don't know that I need keep you ladies any longer," he said. "Or you, Mr. Gulver, though you might stay in your room in case I should want to pop in. You, Mr. Bintwood, I'd like to be so good as to run an eye over these pictures."

I moved across quickly to the open door. Miss Maine was walking with a slight limp and Helena Grace was gently holding her arm. The elder woman gave me a little bow and a smile as she went through: the other caught my eye and then looked away. Viola Vetch gave me a cheerful grin.

"Think the superintendent'll keep me long?" whispered Gulver. "I really ought to be out."

"Ten minutes at the most," I told him, and I wasn't to be far wrong.

I closed the door after him, and as I turned back something queer happened. Below the sloping roof, with its inset lights towards the back patch of grass, the one big window ran, and on to the studio beyond. The electric light, of course, was on, but the curtains had never been drawn, and all at once it seemed to me that I saw a woman's face moving quickly away from that window. It was there, and it wasn't there. It was as if someone had been peering in from the outside dark and had drawn away into that same impenetrable dark just as I turned from the door. I blinked my eyes and wondered if I'd been mistaken. Maybe I'd have spoken to Wharton if he hadn't been busy with Bintwood. And I didn't then know the lie of the land. For all I knew, neighbours might have to pass that window, and a looking-in had been a natural curiosity, especially after the fire. And just then I heard my name.

"Travers would like to listen to this," Wharton was saying. "He professes to know something about pictures."

Chapter III
MORE ABOUT SINDLE

"A queer bird," Bintwood was saying. "Didn't seem to have a mind of his own."

He held a canvas at arm's length, then handed it to me. It was a landscape, grossly out of perspective but with a certain garish attractiveness: the vivid red roofs of two cottages, splashes of colour for flowers, trees of a nightmare green and an intense purple distance.

"Matthew Smith," I said. "In one of his worst moments." That tickled him for some reason or other.

"You may be right," he said. "With a little Gauguin thrown in. And look at these tulips."

That was a still life, and, as we agreed, the devil of a way from van Gogh or Fantin-Latour. There was a head that showed traces of Cubism, and another still life of a collection of bottles that had in it something of Chardin.

"What're they worth?" cut in Wharton.

"Not a damn," Bintwood said bluntly. "Wouldn't mind risking a couple of quid on the landscape."

He picked up another unfinished landscape, grimaced, and dropped it back on the table.

"How'd he get his living then?" Wharton wanted to know.

"He didn't," Bintwood said. "Not if these are a fair sample. He must have had money of his own."

Wharton let out a breath. He said it was a pity.

"I hoped you'd be a godsend, Mr. Bintwood. You see, we're trying to get a line on him and his friends. I thought you might have known a dealer or two he could have dealt with."

"He may have called on dealers—I don't know. Mind you, he wasn't a tyro. He could paint. He could put the paint on, if you know what I mean. And he didn't mind colour."

He shrugged his shoulders.

"You haven't asked for my opinion, but I'd say he was a dope fiend or drinking himself towards d.t.s or both. Might have been a remittance man. Some sort of black sheep."

"If he received cheques he must have cashed them somewhere," Wharton said. "And the same with money orders." Bintwood shrugged his shoulders again. A solid, undemonstrative sort of chap, I thought him. And he knew his job.

"Well, there we are," he said. "I must say he was quiet enough for an overhead neighbour. I heard very little of him. Maybe he was generally tight by evening. And those tiled floors muffled sound a good deal."

"Yes," Wharton said gloomily. Then he switched the conversation.

"Ferndale, who has this studio. What's he like?"

"Portrait painter," Bintwood said, and smiled. "Been here three or four years now. Very well known. Exhibits a good deal."

"He doesn't live here?"

"Oh, no. He's got a flat—a very nice place—near Sloane Square. I've been there once or twice. A nice chap. Never a bit of side. Bit of a Bohemian too. And quite a good, workmanlike painter. Women mostly. Or children. He's quite good with children."

"That the studio through there?"

"That's it," Bintwood said, and drew the curtain slightly back. His hand went out to the light switch. "I'm sure Ferndale wouldn't mind you having a peep."

We had a peep. It was a fine airy studio with all the paraphernalia. There was a tiny kitchen beyond, Bintwood said, and a lavatory with washbasin.

We went back and Wharton began collecting the canvases. "If that's all I can do at the moment, I think I'll be getting upstairs," Bintwood said. "Some water's seeped through and there's a bit of a mess. You'll know where to find me if you want me again. Most nights I'm out, but I don't look like being so tonight."

He and Wharton went out together. Sergeant Matthews had a look at the canvases and reckoned the landscape was pretty good. I said I wouldn't mind having it myself. Then he told me Cave had found the missing teeth. Green had been grubbing about, he said, and was coming back in the morning. A tarpaulin was being put over the open roof of the burnt studio in case it rained. In the morning all the mess was going to be cleared up.

Five minutes went by, and I guessed Wharton was with Gulver. Then I heard voices outside and he came in with Ferndale.

I won't say there was something Bohemian about Ferndale, but there was certainly much of the artist. He was a man of medium height, thinnish in the face but with a colour that spoke of quite good living. He was clean-shaven, with side-whiskers that came just an inch or so along the ears, and his slightly greying hair was worn rather long. I put him in the late fifties. If he were older it was because the slightly retroussé nose gave him a look of the boyish or friendly. As for his clothes, his black hat was almost a ten-galloner, his tie was definitely flowing, and beneath the dark overcoat I could see corduroy trousers of a natty olive green. I winced when he shook hands with me. He had the very devil of a grip.

"You people would like a drink," he said.

Wharton mentioned duty and regulations. Ferndale damned the regulations, but Wharton still refused the drinks. Not even a sherry or a spot of gin and something.

"Besides, you look as if you're bound somewhere," Wharton told him, "and we don't want to keep you."

"Just a casual meal with a couple of old friends," he said. "Won't do them any harm to wait."

"Well, about this wretched man Sindle," Wharton said, "who died in the fire. You had a shot at putting it out, so they tell me."

"A dam' bad shot," Ferndale said, and grinned. "You could hear it crackling inside and smoke was pouring out under the door. I smashed the door in—"

"It was locked?"

"It certainly was." He rubbed his shoulder ruefully. "I ought to know. Soon as I had it in, the fire and smoke simply leapt at me. I chucked a bucket of water and hopped well out of the way. Got myself in the devil of a mess, though."

"You didn't even see Sindle?"

"Good God, no! I was half blinded by smoke and soot and heaven knows what. I must have coughed for five minutes: well, till the firemen came. Then I came down here. I had a sitter, and I had to explain and all that. Luckily she's a friend." He smiled. "It rather amused her to see the sight I was."

"You kept your head and you tried to do a good job," Wharton told him. "But about Sindle. You don't happen to know the name of any friend of his?"

"Never a hope. The chap was a lone wolf."

"Ever happen to see him with anybody?"

Ferndale almost said no. The moving lips became a slight gape. He frowned.

"Yes," he said. "Now you come to mention it, I did. Let me see now, Wednesday. Last Wednesday. About half-past four. I'd called in here for something, and I ran right into Sindle at the door. He was with a young chap: cheap-looking specimen of nineteen or twenty or so. Pansy sort of chap. I know because I had some rather dirty thoughts." His hand went up to check Wharton's question. "Don't ask me for any more because I can't give it you. I just saw this pansy-looking chap and no more. Sindle was the last person I wanted to run into."

"Well, thank you for what it is," Wharton said. "It ought to fit in with anything else we happen to pick up. But you never saw this chap Sindle anywhere outside here?"

"I saw him once at the Tabby Cat." He smiled. "I see you've heard about the Tabby Cat. Quite a decent little spot. I'm a bachelor and I often nip in for a meal. But, as I was saying, I did see Sindle there. I think it was early one evening about a fortnight ago. And, if it's any use to you, I heard he made himself objectionable there last week."

"How?"

Ferndale shrugged his shoulders.

"Nothing much. He had some soup, it appears, and Nancy—one of the two girls who run the place—asked him how he liked it, and he just chucked the money for it on the table and said it was muck, then stalked out. That's what Nancy told me. I told her I wouldn't serve him again."

"Might do worse than have a look in at this Tabby Cat place," Wharton said. "But what about letters here? The postman bring them up?"

"There're six lock-up boxes in the hall. Didn't you see them? We have our own keys. The milkman leaves his bottles on top of the particular boxes and we leave notes for what we want. Quite a good arrangement, that."

"And tradesmen?"

"They go up, I think. But Fred Gulver's always around in the mornings. He's a dam' useful chap. Absolutely reliable. I get him to do all sorts of jobs for me. We all do."

"Well, that seems about all," Wharton said. "If anything else happens to occur to you, perhaps you'll let us know."

"You'll be about here long?"

"Can't say. We might be in and out of the place for days. Not myself, perhaps, but someone or other. Strictly between ourselves, there're one or two highly suspicious things about this Sindle's death. I can't say any more at the moment, so don't ask me."

"Well, I'm not surprised," Ferndale said with a shake of the head. "Also between ourselves, he was a dam' funny bird. But about this room. Use it as much as you like. I shan't be here again till tomorrow afternoon."

"We'll be away long before then," Wharton told him. "But just one other thing. What clothes was Sindle wearing when you saw him last?"

"Clothes?" He frowned. "Don't rush me. This'll take some thinking about. Clothes. A pork-pie hat. Dirty olive green—I think. A brown frayed tweed coat. I'm almost sure a high-necked pullover. Once old gold, I'd say, with paint stains on it. I remember a reddish stain—Indian red. Very old and stained flannel bags. That's all I can safely say."

"Anything particular about his appearance?"

Ferndale laughed just a bit unpleasantly.

"Practically everything. He looked dirty and grubby and bloodshot and altogether repulsive. A real nasty specimen. Had some horrible protruding teeth. God knows why. I mean, they looked false to me."

He'd been moving towards the door. Wharton went out with him. Then he looked in quickly again to say good night to myself. A nice, unconventional sort of chap, and much as Bintwood had described him. Plenty of money, probably. I wondered what he paid for that quite handsome studio.

"*La vie de Bohème,*" Matthews said. The accent wasn't all it should have been, but he gave me a look that expected from me a surprise at the carefree display of linguistics. "This Sindle seems to have been a Bohemian all right. One of the lads. Dope and drink and a spot of painting, and then some more dope and another drink. Only one thing missing."

"And that?"

"No Mimi," he said, and winked. "Reckon he had a few in his time, though. Almost a pity someone did him in."

"And what're your own ideas about that?" I said.

"Some of it sticks out a mile," he said. "Even the old—"

He was going to say, 'The Old General', which is Wharton's nickname at the Yard, but checked himself in time. "Even the Super's got that much taped. I mean, Sindle was tight and a pal of his—perhaps that pansy—nipped up the fire-escape, shoved the knife into him, got the fire going and locked the door if it wasn't locked already, and then nipped down the same way."

I was just going to ask just how that helped, when Wharton came back.

"You, Matthews," he said. "You heard what Mr. Ferndale was saying about the Tabby Cat? Nip round there and get the story. And everything else you can on Sindle."

Wharton and I went upstairs. The plain-clothes man was still there, going methodically over the debris. The tarpaulin was in place and an electric-light lead hung from a beam.

Wharton and I tiptoed into the next room. A camp bed was there just as it had last been slept in. It had grey army blankets and no sheets and a greasy cushion for a pillow. A cheap chest of drawers was practically empty, and Wharton said the few contents—oddments of clothing—had gone to the Yard. The sooty ash of a fire was in the small grate.

"Thought they had electric fires here?" I said.

"This is the only grate," Wharton said. "The rest have been converted to electric fires. Have a look in here. Here's his kindling wood—the little that's left of it. Plenty of bottles. Must have done himself pretty well. Ought to be easy to find where he bought the stuff."

That kitchen was even tinier than I'd thought. It had a little sink with dirty plates and cups and a filthy frying-pan. On a small deal table were a couple of dirty enamelled saucepans. In the little corner cupboard were oddments of crockery and cutlery. An electric ring had a long flex as if he had plugged it into the light for cooking. There was a Primus, out of order, probably, and an empty paraffin tin. Everywhere was a smell of dampness and sourness, and I was glad to get back to the bedroom. That had a smell that at least could be stomached.

"No letters found at all?" I said.

"Never a personal thing," he told me, and scowled. "This is going to be a dam' tricky case, if you ask me."

"Fingerprints?"

"That's the queerest thing of all," he said. "I had a try myself where there ought to have been prints, and damned if there were any!

"Mind you," he went on, "we'll know more about that in the morning. All this rubbish is being bagged up and sent to the Yard, and then we can get around. First thing tomorrow I'll have everyone here. Plenty of time. We haven't even started yet."

"I'm betting you don't find prints," I said.

"You mean about the fire?"

"That's it," I said. "The fire. His hands were laid on the fire so that we shouldn't get his prints. No point in doing that if there were prints in the room."

"Then what the devil was he? A man with a record?"

"Looks like it," I said. "Whoever killed him was making pretty sure we'd never know who he actually was. It follows from that that once we know who he was we'll know who killed him. Or that's the way the murderer thought."

"Wait a minute," he said. "There's something wrong about that. You're jumping too far ahead. Let's assume there aren't any prints anywhere in here. The murderer couldn't possibly have wiped every one off. Therefore Sindle himself always took care not to leave any prints. Used gloves, and so on."

I said it didn't alter the logic of the general argument. Sindle knew he was a wanted man. So did the murderer. The murderer had to make sure. And if Wharton could look round for prints, so could the murderer. The murderer also didn't find any, but he made sure about everything by burning the prints from Sindle's fingers.

"Maybe you're right," Wharton said heavily. "We'll know for certain in the morning. But another thing."

He took out his notebook and had a look at that sheet of paper that Cave had given him. And he had those other sheets that he'd collected in the studio.

"The clothes he was wearing seem all right," he said. "Pullover and trousers and so on. But there wasn't a thing in his pockets except a beer-bottle opener, some small change, and about three inches of a stick of charcoal. No wallet, no letters, no nothing."

"It all fits in," I said. "The murderer cleaned out his pockets."

I happened to glance towards the studio.

"There's Bintwood," I said. "Wonder what he wants."

Wharton called him in. Bintwood stepped gingerly over the debris.

"Something I thought of," he said. "It mayn't be any good to you, but I thought I ought to tell it. It's about Sindle."

He'd been going out one evening about a week back and had just come out of his door when he saw Sindle going down the stairs ahead of him.

"Dam' fellow moved about like a cat," he said. "Wore an old pair of rubber-soled shoes—"

"He died in 'em," Wharton said grimly.

"Probably his only pair. But I saw him, as I was saying, and I said to myself, 'Damned if I won't find out where he's going.' So I kept the right distance behind and right along to the top of Howe Street, where he waited for a bus. I kept back and took the same bus. He went inside, so I slipped on top. At every stop I kept my eyes out, and when we got to Piccadilly I thought I'd try a look, but he wasn't there! The conductor said he'd nipped off while the bus was moving on again at Buckingham Palace Road. What do you make of that?"

"What do *you* make of it?"

"Well, I thought he knew I was following him, so he gave me the slip."

"That's what I thought myself. See him again when you got back that night?"

"I didn't actually see him. I heard him, though. About three o'clock in the morning, it was. He was sort of groaning in his sleep. Reckon he was tight."

"A queer business," Wharton said. "Let's hope it'll fit in somewhere. You ever go to the Tabby Cat, by the way?"

"The Tabby Cat—everywhere," Bintwood said largely. "I'm a bachelor and I nearly always go out. To a married sister at Pimlico sometimes, or anywhere for a meal."

"Did you ever see Sindle anywhere?"

"Once at the Tabby Cat. He was just going out as I came in."

"Bohemian sort of place, is it?"

"Depends what you mean by Bohemian," he said. "It's a nice clean little place. I don't say you don't get a bit of noise sometimes, but that's nothing. All sorts go to it. I've seen Ferndale there, for instance, and he could afford to feed anywhere."

"You can get drinks?"

"Lord, yes. A pub almost next door. A boy—lad, you'd call him—nips in and fetches them and you pay beforehand. The usual thing."

"That might help too," Wharton told him, and that seemed to me in the nature of blarney. "But something more confidential. You're a man of the world, like myself. So just what's your idea about the people here? Those two girls, for instance, across the way?"

"A couple of nice girls," Bintwood said. "Helena's a bit on the superior side, if you know what I mean. Keeps herself pretty smart and means to get on. The other one, Viola, is a bit of a lass. Mind you," he said, "I'm not hinting she combines business with pleasure or anything like that. I know 'em pretty well. Been out with 'em more than once."

"They been here long?"

"A couple of years or so. I'm the oldest inhabitant. Been here over five years now. Miss Maine comes next. She's been here four years or just over."

"Is she an ex-actress by any chance?" I asked him.

"Why, yes," he said, and looked surprised. "Be a bit before your time, though."

"But she isn't all that old?"

"You'd be surprised," he said. "She doesn't look it, but she's well over seventy. Suffers from arthritis a bit and"—he tapped his skull significantly—"has memory fits. Sort of gets mixed up with dates and people and things. Only at times, of course. That only came on after that business with her daughter."

"Her daughter?"

"Yes," he said. "Barbara Maine was her daughter."

"Good Lord!" I said. "And I had never an idea!"

Neither had Wharton, so I explained. Barbara Maine was rather late in making a name for herself, but at the time of her death she was more than established. Then there was mention of a nervous breakdown, and then, before one had hardly grasped that fact, she was dead. Committed suicide.

"I think I remember something about it now," Wharton said.

"Miss Maine came here soon afterwards," Bintwood went on. "She must have a bit of money from somewhere, but she makes lampshades. Vellum, and so on. Decorates them herself. Does fairly well at it, I believe."

"A handsome old lady," Wharton said.

"A very charming one too," Bintwood said. "Gives a sort of tone to the place. The girls are very good to her. So is Ferndale."

"And so," I said to myself, "are you." But Wharton was making a move to the still cluttered studio. He nodded at the few canvases that had been salvaged. Seven or eight, perhaps, in addition to those we had downstairs. Not one was undamaged, and two were little more than shreds of discoloured canvas.

"Like to have a look at those?" Wharton said. "They might tell us something. You're the one who'd know."

I began putting them on the cleared table. One was of a recumbent nude and was in fairly good shape. Then something struck me about it. My hands went to my glasses, and that's a nervous trick of mine when I come suddenly up against the unusual.

"Extraordinary!" I said, and gave that unframed picture to Bintwood. "But isn't this Viola Vetch?"

"Good God, yes!" He was staring at it. So was Wharton.

"But it's fantastic," he said. "You don't tell me she ever sat to a bloke like Sindle?"

"He couldn't have done it from memory?"

"Memory?" he said, and gave a little contemptuous snort. "He couldn't have seen her long enough for that. Besides, the whole thing's crazy."

"Does she ever pose commercially?" I said. "If so, he might have got the head from some advertisement or other."

"She doesn't," he said. "The whole thing looks to me like a genuine pose, and I still say that's crazy. And he painted it."

"Why are you so sure?" Wharton wanted to know.

"Because it's my job," Bintwood told him, and not in the least aggressively. "He was left-handed, for one thing. Have a look here. Have a look at those pictures downstairs. See how these brush-strokes generally run from left to right. Awkward for the right hand but natural to the left."

Then he was looking at Wharton.

"Why not ask her herself? She's almost sure to be in."

"No, no," Wharton said quickly. "It doesn't matter all that much. For the present I'd rather keep it to ourselves." The tone changed to the official. "I can absolutely rely on you for that?"

Bintwood shrugged his shoulders.

"As you say. After all, it's no business of mine."

"Just one little question," I said, "and don't be offended at it. Was there the possibility of her posing for Sindle without anyone else in the building knowing it?"

"A possibility—yes," he said. "She hasn't regular hours. Works for one or two schools of art, but mostly private. She'd be in at scores of times when everyone else might be out. But I still hold the whole thing's crazy."

"A lot of things in this life are," Wharton said, with his tone of the man-of-the-world. "All the same, we'll keep it under our hats. Then nobody'll be embarrassed."

There were steps on the stairs. Wharton hastily looked out.

"Downstairs, Matthews. I'll be there in a second."

That was principally for Bintwood's benefit, and the three of us moved off.

"You won't come in for a quick drink?" Bintwood asked just outside his door.

Wharton said we were probably just going. And a drink wouldn't be too good on stomachs as empty as ours. That was when I began to feel hungry. It was almost ten o'clock and the last snippet of food I'd had was a pretence at tea.

CHAPTER IV
THE LONG, LONG ARM

WE DIDN'T go straight to Ferndale's studio. Gulver happened to be in the hall.

"Something I forgot to ask you," Wharton said.

Gulver drew himself up to attention, and I shouldn't have been surprised if he'd saluted.

"Those belongings of Mr. Sindle's," Wharton said. "Who brought them here?"

"Ah, you've got me beaten, sir. They came when I was out."

"Didn't anyone see the van or anything?"

"Well, sir, Mr. Crotch did tell me it was what they call a plain van."

"And who's Mr. Crotch?"

"The artists' colour shop, as they call it, sir. Just a little way along. Miss Maine looked out too, sir, and saw a couple of men taking things up. In the afternoon, it was."

"I get you," Wharton said. "And one other thing. You couldn't make a big pot of tea? For three? And rustle up some bread and cheese?"

"Delighted to, sir." His face beamed.

"A useful chap, that," Wharton told me as we went into the studio. "A pity about the plain van, though. Better put that fire on again, Matthews. It's not too warm in here."

Matthews hadn't done so badly at the Tabby Cat. That business about Sindle's being objectionable had been confirmed, and he hadn't been in since that evening. It wasn't that he was a good customer. All he ever ordered was soup, and he used to break his bread in it and so make a cheap and reasonably filling meal.

"Maybe he was genuinely hard up," I said. "The murderer mayn't have taken any wallet. I mean that small change was all he really had."

"He'd plenty of money to spend on booze," Wharton told me with a snort.

Gulver came in with the tea and bread and cheese. He said he'd take a cup to the man upstairs.

"A nice old boy," Matthews told us. "Snug little place he's got here. I don't know if you know it, sir, but his is the only telephone. It's in a sort of cubby-hole at the far end. Door's always open in case anyone wants to use it."

"Yes, I saw it," Wharton said. "But about tomorrow."

I didn't quite see what was going to happen to myself in the next day or two, but from what Wharton was saying I could visualise him seated at the end of massed telephones like some business tycoon. A wide net would be thrown out for Sindle. Every conceivable contact that he ought to have made would be hunted for and checked, and, though London would be unaware of it, beneath it a kind of secondary anthill would be noiselessly at work. As a last resort there might be a broadcast appeal, but there'd certainly be advertisements.

"The police are anxious to get in touch with . . ." That would be the kind of thing, to catch the eye of the men who'd moved Sindle's few pieces of furniture, and anyone who might have noticed him in town, or the dealers on whom he'd called, or where he'd bought his drinks and his material, or someone who'd posed for him, or seen him at some spot he'd sketched.

"That reminds me," Wharton said. "Wonder if Ferndale's home yet?"

He gulped down his second cup of tea, wiped his huge moustache with vast sweeps of as vast a handkerchief, and went out.

"Tramp, tramp, tramp, the boys are marching," Matthews told me. "Looks like being a dog's life the next few days. Nice girl, that Nancy at the Tabby Cat. Might drop in for a meal myself some time."

I told him about that nude of Viola Vetch. He raised lascivious eyebrows.

"Painted up there, was it?"

"Can't say," I said. "There wasn't any background to indicate where it was painted. Just a rough suggestion of anything. No couch or chair or chesterfield. Lying full length on a sort of drapery thrown over something."

Matthews didn't see why she shouldn't have posed for it. She looked the sort, he said, who could take care of herself. And why shouldn't she earn an honest penny if she had time on her hands. I echoed a why not, and then Wharton came back.

"He was in," he said, and I gathered he meant Ferndale. "Just got in, and he'll do his best to do a drawing of Sindle. He's doing it at once. You can call for it in the morning." It was to me he was talking. "After that I want you to call on the owner of this place. We've got to know how Sindle obtained possession."

There seemed to be nothing else, so I thought I'd get back home. Then I remembered something. That woman I'd seen peering in at the window.

"Good God!" he told me, and I might have been Smith Minimus in the headmaster's room. "Why the devil didn't you mention it at once!"

"Too many things to take it off my mind," I said. "Besides, I thought she might be a passing neighbour."

He looked as if there was something wrong with his ears.

"Passing!" he said. "How the devil can anybody pass? It's a private garden."

He let out a snort, grabbed a torch from his bag, and was nodding back at us. We went out at the front, along a few yards, and then down that passageway where I'd caught a glimpse of a uniformed constable. He had long since gone off duty and that back space was deserted. We moved left and along the studio window. Wharton was keeping us behind him and flashing the torch. He suddenly stopped. I peered over his stooped shoulders, and there was the deep imprint of the heel of a woman's shoe.

He grunted.

"Here's where she came up. . . . This is where she stood."

He was muttering to himself. He moved round carefully for a minute or so, then straightened himself.

"No good," he said. "That's all there are. Too dam' hard for anything else. But she must have come in the same way we did."

"And she must have known the lie of the land," Matthews said. I was keeping my mouth shut. When you're guilty as I was, it's the best way.

"Yes," Wharton said. "And it couldn't have been any of those women in the house. They were all in there. Better get another torch, Matthews, and make some casts."

We went quietly—very quietly—through the passage to Borden Walk.

"Anything else for me, George?" I said humbly.

He gave a grunt and went right on towards the door. I took it as read and made for Howe Street and the chance of a late bus.

You don't want to know about my sleep and my dreams. The next morning saw me awake at seven and ready for action an hour later. I'd rang Norris to remind him about the Chale interview, and there was nothing on my mind except that gaffe of the previous night.

And that was quite enough to have on any mind. If only I'd nipped round quickly, I might have caught that woman as she came out by the passageway. That she was some woman friend of Sindle's I had no doubts, and under our hands had been someone it might now take days to find. And though I could justify myself a dozen ways, I was a long way from happy or even resigned. Unless something turned up to take his mind from it, Wharton would be throwing that slip in my teeth for a very long time. Not that I'm unable to handle George. He can't have the coat off me as he could off a uniformed constable. I may work for the Yard and even deteriorate sometimes into something of a stooge, but I work my own way. It's Ludovic Travers, plus cussedness, or no Ludovic Travers at all. And he knows it. And it's always worked pretty well, so far.

Just as I was leaving for Ferndale's flat the Yard rang up. Wharton had left a message that I was to see that sitter who had been with Ferndale at the time of the fire—Mrs. Solness of Gorham Place, Knightsbridge. It looked as if I'd be steering a somewhat erratic course, with Sloane Square first, then back to Knightsbridge, and then more or less back again to Millbank, so I saved the taxpayers' pockets, abandoned the idea of a taxi and got out my car.

I timed the call on Ferndale for nine o'clock, and as I came to the block of flats I was wondering what sort of a hand he'd made of that memory sketch of Sindle. As for the flats, they looked good class and not too pretentious. Ferndale's was on the ground floor, and the only room I saw was the lounge. It was comfortably furnished with quality stuff. Some nice china was in a cabinet and there were plenty of books in a reproduction Chippendale case. A rack held several pipes, and the room had a faintly aromatic scent as of good tobacco and pot-pourri.

Ferndale had breakfasted, and I refused his offer of coffee. He saw me looking at a remarkably nice portrait that hung above the mantelpiece.

"My mother," he said. "A very handsome woman when she was young. Been dead some years now. But this sketch of Sindle. You can't judge what it's like, of course, never having seen him. I suggest you people hand it round at No. 7 and hear what the others say."

I had a look at it. I said truthfully that it was a fine job, whether it closely resembled Sindle or not. It was a charcoal sketch on board, with touches of coloured chalks. Then I must have been peering at it.

"Something wrong?"

"Not at all," I said. "It suddenly struck me that I'd seen that mouth somewhere. Isn't it rather like the late Arnold Bennett's?"

"God forbid!" he told me, and had another look himself. Then he chuckled. "I don't know that you aren't right. Quite a lot of Mr. Prohack in it. You people are having reproductions made?"

"That's the idea," I said. "Something to show people when making enquiries. You don't mind if we keep it a day or two?"

"Keep it?" he said. "Keep the dam' thing for ever as far as I'm concerned. Put it in your Rogues' Gallery if you have one."

"If you've no objections I think it may end up in my own gallery," I said, and that made him stare.

"You married?"

"Why?"

"Surely grounds for divorce to make a woman live with that?"

"It's a fine bit of work and I like it," I said. "Besides, I might induce her to think it's really Bennett. And by the way, I'm just off to Knightsbridge. Just a formal call on Mrs. Solness in case she happened to see anything yesterday."

"Good," he said. "If you haven't done so already, I'll give her a ring to say you're coming."

He walked with me along the corridor and waved a cheery hand as I went through the hall door. I drove back to the Yard and left that sketch for Wharton. I hoped the photographers wouldn't smear the charcoal and chalk. Sindle mightn't look the most attractive of people but the sketch itself struck me as something uncommonly fine.

Gorham Place was a much more ornate and expensive range of flats. I'd put Ferndale's in the £300 class. Hers was more like £500. And she had money enough to keep her own maid—a rather desiccated woman of about forty who asked me to wait for a minute or two in the far too furnished lounge. It reminded me of the drawing-rooms of my youth with its knick-knacks and photographs and its walls covered with faded watercolours and plates. On a low table were a collection of periodicals and magazines, and two were the journals of a spiritualist society. A couple of theosophical journals were there too, and one that looked as if it had to do with palmistry. With an ear cocked for a sound I peered round at the books in the long case, most of them modern and still in their jackets, and I thought that Mrs. Solness must be either mad about things esoteric or highly gullible, or both. Then she came fluttering in.

"So sorry you've been kept waiting. And please sit down. That chair is comfortable, or isn't it? Take this one. What a lovely morning it is."

"But a bit cold," I said.

"Yes, it is," she told me promptly. "Mr. Solness, my late husband, felt the cold dreadfully. Personally I don't mind the cold. I mean, one needn't feel cold. Don't you think so?"

Maud Solness was a ditherer. She was tallish for a woman, on the plump side, and in the forties. Everything about her was expensive: the clothes, the musk-like scent, the three-stoned diamond ring and the jade pendant on the platinum chain. I suppose it was a good five minutes before I managed to bring her fluttering mind to the previous afternoon. But we weren't there more than a few seconds. I had to hear about the portrait. In her time she had been much mixed up, apparently, with amateur theatricals, and was still the president of one of the minor societies, and she had always intended, though somehow she had never quite got round to it, to have a portrait of herself in one of her own earlier roles. And out of all that there emerged the fact that Ferndale was doing her as Lady Macbeth. I think I gaped a bit when I heard it. I winced when I thought of Sargent's Ellen Terry in the Tate.

"I'm sure it will be very nice," I said. "Mr. Ferndale's a very accomplished painter."

"Yes," she said, and I should have seen a girlish blush. "We're engaged, you know. Only our friends know at the moment. Next Thursday week the wedding is. A purely private affair."

I must have uttered congratulations, though I can't remember what I said. I do know what I thought: that she and Ferndale would be a highly incongruous couple, and that he wouldn't be doing himself too bad a financial turn. I think I added a mental and apologetic rider to the effect that it took all sorts to make a world.

"But about yesterday afternoon, Mrs. Solness," I said. "Would you mind telling me what happened when you first became aware of the fire?"

"But I didn't," she said. "I mean, it was Gordon—Mr. Ferndale. No. That's wrong. It was that woman calling, 'Fire!' A Mrs. . . . now what was her name?"

"Maine."

"Yes. The poor woman who used to be an actress. I do think we treat our old professional servants quite abominably sometimes—if you could call her a professional servant. And after all . . ."

We got back to the fire. What I managed to gather was that Ferndale had paused in his painting at the sound of the voice, and then he'd laid down palette and brush and had gone to the door. Mrs. Solness had heard voices and no more, and then Ferndale had called back, "Just a moment or two, Maud. Something I've got to see to. I shan't be long." She thought he must have been away for about ten minutes in all, and when he did appear he was the most extraordinary sight. There'd been a fire somewhere in an upstair room and he'd been trying to put it out, and then the fire brigade had come. It had been most thoughtful of him, she said, not to mention the fire which might have given her quite an alarm: if, that is, she had known it was on the actual premises. After the sitting it had been arranged they should go on to the R.B.A. in Suffolk Street, but Mr. Ferndale had had to go to his flat to change.

I hope all that is right, for we went off at so many tangents that I couldn't be sure.

"At what time was the actual sitting?" I asked her.

"Actually at three-thirty," she said, "but of course I had to be there at three-fifteen. It was the first sitting and we had to arrange pose and the dress and so on. I do think that mediaeval dress is so . . ."

I managed to get her back to the minutes when Ferndale was out of the studio. Had she seen anything or heard anything which might be called unusual? She had heard nothing except Ferndale returning from the fire alarm, which was just in Howe Street, but he dashed straight up the stairs. She didn't like to move because she was naturally expecting the sitting to go on for a few minutes after his return.

I was glad enough to leave it at that, and when I did contrive to get away my brain was as fuddled as if I'd had a morning's chess. Not that I play chess. My relaxations are crosswords, and preferably the harder sort, though why I drag that in I can hardly say, unless it is that the memory of that harassing half-hour brings even to myself a certain and inevitable garrulity.

It was well after eleven o'clock and I treated myself to coffee, and then drove towards Victoria and along the river to Mill-bank. There were plenty of blocks of flats, and I was wondering which one was Capron Court when I thought I saw ahead of me a someone who was oddly familiar. I drew up alongside him and it was Gulver. I got out.

He flicked his hand to his hat by way of salute. He'd been reporting to Mrs. Oddfort, he said: giving first-hand informa-tion about the fire. In any case he always called two or three times a week in case there might happen to be odd jobs.

"One curious thing has struck me," I said. "However did she come to allow a black sheep like Sindle to have that studio?"

"She never told me," he said. "I rather reckon she was obliging someone."

I must have stared. I didn't gather quite what he meant.

"Some friend or other," he said. "You never know. Someone who Sindle had pitched some yarn to. She's too soft-hearted, that's what's wrong with madame. Now the old Colonel . . ."

A new kind of garrulity, but I had all the time in the world. Then I got the chance to ask if he'd reported what Sindle was like—after he'd settled himself in, that is, and after everyone at No. 7 had had time to find him objectionable.

"I'd thought about it, sir, and then I never did," he said. "After all, it wasn't as if we had to associate with him. If he wanted to keep himself to himself—well, let him. And she's too kind-hearted herself, as I said. I remember once—in Lahore, it was—there was a . . ."

I listened, intelligently I hope, to all that, and then got him to tell me the whereabouts of Capron Court. It appeared I'd passed it a hundred yards back.

"Mrs. Oddfort's easy to deal with?"

"A very nice lady, sir. One of the best in the world."

I could see his lips shaping another 'I remember', so I hastily nipped in the car again, said I might be seeing him, and began slowly backing towards a side road.

Capron Court was very solid and most unpretentious. Mrs. Oddfort herself opened the door of the flat. She looked well over seventy, petite but all alertness. She had delightfully old-fashioned manners and the most bewitching of smiles. I had to sit in a spindly armchair, and she insisted on a cushion, and then gave a robin-like peep to see how I looked.

"I've just seen Gulver," I said, and with an idea of slipping smoothly into what I really wanted to know.

"A nice old man," she said. "My late husband thought the world of him. He supplemented his pension and I let him have part of the lower floor at Borden Walk. Everyone likes him there."

"I'm from Scotland Yard, as you may have been told," I said, and got up to give her my warrant card. She waved it away. The Yard had rung her, she said. She added, with a smile of apology, that I didn't look like a policeman or a detective—or had she made a mistake?

"No mistake," I said. "I'm really a bit of everything. But what I've come for is this. There seems to be very much of a mystery attached to this unfortunate man Sindle who died in the fire, and at present we know nothing much about him. His relatives ought to be communicated with, if he has any. All sorts of things to arrange, as you can imagine. And he was a very queer, uncommunicative sort of person."

"Yes," she said, and her look was curiously direct. "Between ourselves, Pamela Maine wrote me a confidential letter about that. I've still got it somewhere."

"Please don't bother," I said. "I gather she told you he wasn't the nicest person to have in that top studio."

"Yes, she did. But she's rather—what shall I say?—rather hazy at times, poor dear. I did answer the letter, but she's probably forgotten all about it. A tragic case, hers. You know she lost her daughter?"

I said I'd heard about it.

"An embittered woman in some ways," she said. "Perhaps one can't blame her. She simply idolised her daughter, and someone always has to be blamed. That's one of her lamp-shades, by the by."

I got up to look at it. It was an old parchment deed—Tudor by the lettering—that had been deftly adapted. I thought the effect was extraordinarily good.

"She's very clever," she said. "That Mr. Bintwood helps her a lot. Manages to get old deeds and things for her. She paints quite well too—the shades, I mean."

"I shall have to buy one for my wife," I said, and that was unfortunate because I had to tell her about Bernice. Then at last we got back to Sindle.

"You handle the property yourself?" I said.

"Oh, no," she told me quickly. "Far too involved for me. And nowadays there're far too many Rent Restriction Acts and things. I suppose, being a man, you're inclined to laugh at me."

"Heaven forbid!" I said fervently. "I'm the biggest fool in the world when it comes to Restriction Acts and Orders in Council and forms in triplicate and the rest of the mumbo-jumbo."

She laughed.

"I must remember that for Percival Lenny."

She caught my enquiring look.

"Of Lenny and Mistral, the agents. They're at Brice Road, Chelsea."

"And it was they who gave Sindle the tenancy?"

"Well, no," she said, and frowned. "I was asked personally to let him have the studio just before it fell vacant. A Mr. Wood who was going away, you know. I told the agents he was to have it."

"That's the very thing I've come here to find out," I said, and I must have sounded a bit excited. "Whose was the recommen-dation, Mrs. Oddfort?"

"A nephew by marriage," she said. "My niece died some years ago, but we've always kept slightly in touch. As a matter of fact he's living in another property of mine."

"And his name?"

"Chale," she said. "Dr. Chale. He's living at Meriton Gardens."

Chapter V
THE CHALE PUZZLE

I must have given a startled look. I know my fingers were suddenly fumbling at my glasses.

"A Dr. Chale," I said. "Where exactly in Meriton Gardens, Mrs. Oddfort?"

"At No. 15. It's not such a long walk from here."

"Yes," I said, and it sounded pretty lamely. "A general practitioner, is he?"

"He used to be," she said, "but now he's a psychiatrist. Very clever, I believe. I've never had reason to consult him myself."

She gave a little laugh at that. I said, and gallantly I hoped, that I could well believe it.

"In fact I haven't actually seen him for quite a time," she said. "My husband and I were in India till just after the war broke out, and then we managed to get to South Africa. That was where he died. I came home in 1946."

"But about Sindle," I said. "What did Dr. Chale tell you about him when he asked you to let him have the studio?"

"I almost forget," she said. "I'm certain, though, that he said he was a former patient of his and deserving of help."

"Nothing derogatory?"

"I don't think so," she said. "Now I come to remember, he did say he was a bit nervy and—what was it now? Taciturn, or something like that. Yes," she said, and smiled. "That was it. I remember thinking about it when I received Pamela Maine's letter. After all, you know, if one is suffering from nerves it does excuse a whole lot of things."

"How very true," I said, and got to my feet. "I'm most grateful to you, Mrs. Oddfort. You've helped us enormously."

"May I offer you a glass of sherry?"

"I'd love it," I said, "but I have to be getting back to Scotland Yard."

"You'll be seeing Dr. Chale?"

"Yes," I said. "I'll have to hear what he knows about Sindle. Get him to supplement what you've been good enough to tell me."

"You'd like me to ring him and say you're coming?"

"Please don't bother," I told her hastily. "As a matter of fact, I think I'll see him now. I have my car. I'll be with him almost as quickly as one could telephone."

That was one white lie. As I sat in the car, drawn up again beyond the flats, I was thinking about lies in general, and what I was to say—if anything—to Wharton. It was a quarter-past twelve and Chale would be with Norris, so what it all amounted to was this: that what I'd tell Wharton would depend on what Chale had told Norris, and the extent to which Norris believed the story to be true.

But it wasn't quite so easy as that. Wharton had an unreasonable prejudice against detective agencies. I don't say he considers them lice upon the body politic: his might be more the attitude of the owner of a West End store who sees the spivs on his pavement, disposing of surreptitious nylons; or of a director of the National Portrait Gallery who knows his own pavements to be the favourite pitch of the chalk artists. In fact I would have liked to present Chale to Wharton as wholly unconnected with the Broad Street Detective Agency; and while I'm always prepared to lie in the cause of justice, I have far too many hampering reservations when it comes to my personal and private affairs. And there's always the question of the privacy of a client.

Finally I moved the car on along the Embankment, and ten minutes later I was at Broad Street. No taxi or car was there, so Chale must have gone. Somehow I couldn't see him coming by bus.

"Dr. Chale gone yet?" I did ask Bertha as I went through.

"Him!" she said. "He hasn't even turned up or telephoned or anything."

I felt a sudden uneasiness. My watch said half-past twelve.

"Only half an hour late," I said. "He may have been kept."

I went through to Norris, who was phlegmatically reading a newspaper.

"Chale hasn't turned up, Bertha tells me."

"No," he said, and glanced round at the clock. "Thought I'd give him till half-past."

"Give him a bit longer," I said, "and I'll wait here with you. There's a whole lot you ought to hear."

I gave him the main facts, and I suppose it took me nearly ten minutes. His only comment was that there seemed to be some truth in the doctor's story to me the previous afternoon.

"He said he was scared of somebody, and this Sindle used to be a patient of his, so why wasn't it him he was scared of?"

"Why not?" I said. "But it hasn't worked out that way. It's Sindle who's dead—murdered, to put it bluntly. Mind you, Chale must have had hundreds of patients. His connection with Sindle may be only what it seems on the face of it—just a recommendation for the studio, and no more."

We did a bit more arguing. It was ten minutes to one. I made a sudden decision and asked Bertha to get me Chale's number. Nothing happened for a moment or two after I was through. Then I heard a woman's voice. A clear, hard sort of voice.

"May I speak to Dr. Chale?" I said.

"Who's speaking, please?"

"The name's Travers. I'm one of the principals of the Broad Street Detective Agency and I'd like to speak to the doctor."

There was quite a pause before she said she was sorry, but the doctor had been called away.

"Who's speaking?" I asked.

"Miss Wolde. I'm the doctor's secretary."

"Then listen, Miss Wolde. The doctor had an urgent appointment here at twelve o'clock this morning. He hasn't arrived and he didn't telephone to cancel it."

"An appointment!"

"Yes," I said patiently. "An appointment. He made it with myself on the telephone at two o'clock yesterday afternoon."

"But that's—"

She broke off. I thought for a moment or two the line was dead.

"But that's what?" I said.

She was still there. She gave a nervous little laugh.

"Well, that's . . . I mean I can't believe it! What on earth should the doctor want with a detective agency?"

"Look, Miss Wolde, be patient with me," I said. "This may be a mighty serious business. Dr. Chale did make that appointment, and from 15 Meriton Gardens, at two o'clock yesterday afternoon. So why are you sceptical? Am I right in supposing the doctor never makes any appointment without your knowing it?"

"In a business way, yes," she said.

"But this was purely private business. He added that he couldn't see me yesterday evening because he had an appointment in North London for six o'clock and might be back late. Have you got that on your appointments page?"

There was a longer pause, and I guessed she was checking up. There was a briskness when she spoke.

"I think I can explain everything. Dr. Chale did have that appointment. He telephoned me from a call-box just after seven last night and said he had to go to another sudden appointment, and would I have a bag ready for him when he got home, as he'd have to hurry to catch his train."

"A bag? You mean a medical bag?"

"Oh no. A personal bag. For three or four days, he said."

"And what happened when he got home?"

"Well, he hadn't a minute. The taxi was waiting and he dashed in, collected his bag, gave me instructions, and then left."

"Pardon me, but what sort of instructions?"

"Well, about rearranging the appointments for the rest of the week. I'd have to telephone or write at once."

"I see. And not a word to you about the appointment with me at Broad Street?"

"Not a word. But I do assure you he was in a very great hurry. He couldn't have been here more than two or three minutes."

"Well, that's explained that," I said. "And now would you mind giving me the address where I'll be likely to find him."

"I'm sorry, but I can't."

"A professional secret?"

"No, no. He just didn't tell me. He simply dashed in, talked, and dashed out. I hadn't time to say a word. He did all the talking."

"But he *will* be sending you an address?"

"Yes. I think he's sure to."

"And I can absolutely rely on you to let me have it as soon as you know it? I do assure you it's most important."

"You shall certainly have it," she said. "Would you mind giving me the address again?"

I gave her my name and address, spelling everything out. Then I thought of something else.

"I suppose you didn't by any chance happen to notice the number of the taxi?"

I suppose it was a preposterous question. After all, who does notice the numbers of taxis? It seemed a bit of a surprise, for there was quite a pause.

"Well," she said, "there was something rather funny about that. I'd expected it to be a taxi, but when I went to the door with him it wasn't a taxi at all. It looked like a private car. A long, low sort of car. And the driver wasn't a taxi-man. He was a youngish sort of man in ordinary clothes. I just saw him as he got in again."

"Listen," I said. "I think I can find an answer to all that. It must have been the car belonging to that person he visited in North London. So will you do something for me? I don't want to pry into any professional secrets, but will you ring up that person in North London and ask if he used his or her car? And if so, if it's known where Dr. Chale was going?"

"Yes," she said slowly. "I think I could do that."

"I'll be waiting here," I said. "Perhaps you'll be so good as to ring me back when you've had an answer."

That was that. Bertha buzzed through to ask if I wanted a typescript. I said I'd like it as soon as she could type it out. And a couple of carbons.

Norris had had his ear close to my receiver, but I filled in a thing or two he'd missed.

"Curiouser and curiouser," I said. "I didn't think psychiatrists dashed off to sudden cases. Doctors certainly, but surely not psychiatrists."

"I don't know," he said. "A patient of his might have suddenly gone loopy or something. And all this psychiatry business is very hush-hush."

I said I'd slip across to the pub and have a sandwich and a beer. Heaven knew when I'd get a meal once I was at the Yard. When I stepped inside the saloon bar it was even more jammed than usual, and it was twenty minutes before I was back in the office. Nothing had happened, Norris said, and then, almost before I could sit down, Bertha was buzzing through and I was listening to Miss Wolde again.

"Mr. Travers?"

"Speaking."

"Well, I have some rather strange news for you. Dr. Chale had told me he was going to North London, but he didn't go there at all. I don't know where he went. If you'll promise to keep it strictly confidential, I'll tell you where he was supposed to have gone."

"Most certainly it shall be confidential."

"Well, it was to a Mrs. O'Hara, of Heathlands, Chumleigh Road, Cockfosters."

I wrote that down. I asked if I could be told what Mrs. O'Hara had said.

"She said the doctor must have made a mistake when he wrote that appointment down. She hadn't made any appointment."

"I see. And so he couldn't have used her car."

"She hasn't a car. She always hires."

I must have given a Whartonian grunt. Then I thanked her, said I was still relying on her for the doctor's address when it came, and rang off.

"That's the very devil," I told Norris. "Chale must have gone somewhere last night."

"He made a slip when he wrote the appointment down," Norris suggested, "but he had the real appointment in his mind."

"Maybe," I said, "but why does it have to happen at about this time? But just a minute."

Once more I got Bertha to ring Meriton Gardens. A few moments and Miss Wolde was on the line.

"Travers troubling you again. Miss Wolde. I wonder if it would help us if you told me whether or not the doctor used his own car to go to that North London appointment, or wherever he went."

"I don't know how or where he went," she said. "He left here at about three o'clock. There wasn't any appointment and he was spending the afternoon in town. He must have gone on from there."

I thanked her again and rang off. Norris and I had done all we could—we were of one mind about that. And we agreed that Wharton ought to be told what we knew about Chale. It was something that had to be done, and something that neither of us liked, even if Chale had never been an actual client. So I collected Bertha's typescripts and scurried off to the Yard.

Wharton was in his room, and he seemed to be bearing no malice. He didn't even ask what had kept me so long, and maybe because I threw my story at him before he could as much as strike an attitude. He did make a wry face when I mentioned the agency, which shows the kind of casuistry in which he loves to indulge. For Wharton, if the Yard hadn't begged him to stay on, would have been occupying Norris's chair in the Broad Street office.

When I'd finished he read the typescripts—to make sure, presumably, that I hadn't pulled on him anything as fast as he'd have pulled on myself. The moustache shot out to the horizontal as he pursed his lips.

"There's probably a good reason for everything," he told me. "Better wait, hadn't we, for a day or so? He's almost bound to send an address. Meanwhile something might turn up."

"As a mild suggestion," I said, "couldn't we save time and make sure by putting out a broadcast?"

"Might come to that," he said. "Plenty of time, though. We've only just got things going."

I suppose I was shaking my head, for he asked me what I'd still got on my mind.

"Things I can't get away from," I said. "Why Chale had to go away at just this time, for instance."

He gave me a sudden, sideways look.

"You don't think he's bolted?"

I said I didn't know what to think. Take one other peculiar thing, and assume that Norris's suggestion had been right: that in an absent-minded moment Chale had written the wrong name in the appointments book but had nevertheless made the right appointment somewhere outside Meriton Gardens.

"You're with me so far, George?"

"Carry on," he told me curtly.

"Then at that place, which we'll call Somewhere, he's rung up and is told of a very urgent job to be done: a job that means the rest of the week away from home and an immediate trip by train. It's so urgent that he rings his secretary and he borrows the car of the Somewhere patient. Out of that arises the first question. Miss Wolde said he'd rung her from a call-box. Why didn't he save time and ring from the Somewhere patient's house?"

"Don't know," Wharton said. "But there ought to be an answer."

"I don't see one to the second question," I said, "and that's this. How did this new patient know where to get in touch with Chale? Why did that patient ring Somewhere instead of Meriton Gardens?"

"Yes," he said slowly, and pursed his lips again. "That wants a bit of answering."

There was a heavy silence for a good minute. He glanced at his watch.

"Look. I've got to get to Borden Walk. Nothing special arose out of this morning besides this Chale business?"

"Nothing."

"Well, write your reports," he said, "then go along to Meriton Gardens yourself. The personal touch with that Miss Wolde might tell you something more. I ought to be back myself at round about five.”

I settled down with the stenographer, and when I was almost through the buzzer went. It was Cave, wanting Wharton. I told them to put him through to me.

“Is that you, Travers?” Cave said.

“Travers it is. Wharton’s at Borden Walk if you want him.”

“Right,” he said. “I may go round there.”

“Anything new?” I cut in hastily.

“Don’t know,” he said. “All sorts of things I’d like to go into.”

“Such as what?”

“You’re a pertinacious sort of devil,” he told me, “but here’s just one thing. Why did this chap Sindle choose to have the one bath of his life probably the same day he was killed?”

“Because he was expecting a visitor. The one who killed him.”

“Fine,” he said. “Nothing like ringing up someone who knows all the answers.”

“Wait a minute,” I said. “Just what—”

The line was dead. I shrugged my shoulders and went on with my dictating. When I’d finished I didn’t bother about tea. It was exactly four o’clock when I drew my car up outside No. 15 Meriton Gardens.

A short, middle-aged woman came to the door. She had a round, homely, friendly face, and in her black dress and white apron looked like one of those advertisements for someone’s starch or baking-powder.

“Is Miss Wolde in?”

“Sorry,” she said, and she looked as if she really meant it. “She’s gone out for the afternoon.”

“You don’t know when she’ll be in?”

“Well, I’m staying on till five, and if she wasn’t in then I was to go.”

“May I just come in?” I said. “I’m from Scotland Yard, as you see.”

She took the warrant card, gave me a look and shook her head.

"I can't read it. Haven't got my glasses. They're in the kitchen."

"Then let's go to the kitchen," I said, and gave her my best smile. I've often thought there must be something deceptively honest or naïve about my face. She gave me just another quick look and was drawing back.

"Straight along the passage," she told me, and came padding after. The kitchen door was open, and I went through.

"Absolutely spotless!" I said. "Everything shining and polished like a picture. Nice and warm too."

I hoped that would please, not that it wasn't true. She was smiling as she took off the glasses and gave me back the card.

"Dirt's one thing I can't stand," she said, "and being in a muddle is another." Then her face straightened. That warrant card was having a meaning. "Scotland Yard? You don't mean you want anybody for anything?"

"Not this time," I said, and the smile seemed reassuring. "It's just that we want some information about one of the doctor's former patients. Miss Wolde was telling me over the telephone that the doctor was away, so I thought I'd call and see if she could give me the information I wanted. You weren't making a cup of tea, by the way?"

In three minutes we were having a cup of tea together and a biscuit with it. She'd told me she knew nothing about the patients and couldn't be a help. Her name was Nippen, and she was a widow with one son in the Navy and a married daughter at Plymouth. Her late husband had been a petty officer. She herself was a kind of superior daily help. She was living at Hammersmith and arrived each morning at half-past eight and stayed till half-past six, with a holiday on Saturday afternoons and Sundays.

"And this afternoon you're going early?"

"Having a bit of a holiday, now the doctor's away," she said. "Someone has to answer the door and the telephone. I don't mind the door, but I can't stand that telephone. Never know what to say to people."

"The doctor's kept pretty busy?"

"I think so," she said. "Always seems to be someone here during his hours. He's not what I call a real doctor, you know. He's a psy . . . psychi . . ."

I came to the rescue with *psychiatrist*.

"That's it," she said, and laughed. "I never can get my tongue round that word."

"And you like working here?"

"It's not bad," she said, and the private appreciative nod said it was a long way from it. "The doctor's nice. Never makes no trouble."

I waited a moment, but she didn't mention Miss Wolde.

"And Miss Wolde. She's easy to get on with too?"

A moment's hesitation, and she was telling me that Miss Wolde was all right. Something rang not too true about even that modest praise.

"You don't happen to know her address?"

"She lives here," she said, and looked surprised. "Has a sort of flat on the second floor."

It wasn't what she said but how she looked after she'd said it.

"Elderly, is she?"

"Her!" She sniffed. "Same age, I'd say, as my daughter, and she'll be thirty-two this month."

"She been here long?"

"About three years. Only been living in about six months now."

I left it at that. The important thing was that she'd been so ready to talk about that secretary, and I was thinking of that afternoon when I'd seen her come down the steps to the car.

"The doctor gone away in his car?"

"No," she said. "He's gone by train. Somewhere a long way away, so Miss Wolde thinks."

"He goes away pretty frequently?"

"Not to *be* away. I've been here four years now, and this is the first time I've known him away, except for his holidays."

"Let me see," I said. "Isn't the doctor's a big blue car? Bright blue?"

"No, his is a black car. I've been out in it more than once with Emmett. The doctor's had him drive me home when it's been a bad night."

"Emmett's the chauffeur?"

"He likes to call himself that," she told me, and laughed. "I suppose he is really, but he has to help in the house and do the garden. This is his afternoon off."

There was nothing else that I thought she could tell me, so I said reluctantly that I'd have to go.

"If Miss Wolde should be in before you leave, ask her to give me a ring. She knows the number."

"She won't be in," she said. "Once they get to town you never know when to expect them back."

She went with me to the front door, and the leave-taking was so friendly that I expected her to ask me to drop in again if I happened to be passing. As for what I'd learned, it seemed little more than chit-chat or scandal. Miss Wolde wasn't too popular. Maybe she didn't always sleep in her own bed. Mrs. Nippen hadn't liked her, and neither, probably, had Emmett, which was why he hadn't even put out a hand to open the car door.

All of which didn't amount to much so far as finding Sindle's murderer was concerned, but it did lend a kind of anticipatory pleasure to the idea of a personal chat with Miss Wolde—who, as Mrs. Nippen had let fall, had the quite romantic name of Hermione.

CHAPTER VI
COASTS OF BOHEMIA

WHARTON wasn't in, so I wrote a formal report on my call at 15 Meriton Gardens, with a note on what I'd learned or surmised about its occupants. It was then about half-past five, so I had Chale's number rung and with no result. Mrs. Nippen was right. Hermione Wolde was making the most of an afternoon in town.

The two evening papers I glanced through had nothing about Borden Walk. The morning papers had had a paragraph, and no more, so Wharton was still, and for reasons of his own, keeping murder well up his sleeve. And it was not mine, as the poet said, to reason why.

When we're working together on a murder case, ours is a peculiar, haphazard, spasmodic kind of association. I'm not concerned with routine. George, as Grand Inquisitor, rides the whirlwind and directs the storm. He may do a hundred things of which I'm unaware: routine things that reach me only as negative results; the things I was to be told in the next day or two, for instance—that no prints had been found in the studio, and no friend or acquaintance of Sindle's had been run to earth.

I'm a kind of Gulver or Emmett: a handyman who never knows what he'll be doing next. George's routine work may produce some positive result which I'm thought competent to investigate. Also I'm supposed to have the right kind of manners to interview the right kind of people, and I'm credited with specialised knowledge on certain matters—far too many at times for my peace of mind. I'm even permitted, though generally with George's contemptuous comments, to theorise and suggest. If I'm wrong, the theory was *mine*. If it looks promising, it's *ours*. If it happens to be a winner, I ultimately discover that it was *his*. Which doesn't worry me in the least. I'm the one disproof of the supposed or the perfect proof of the theorem that to travel hopefully is better than to arrive.

I began reading those newspapers in earnest, and just when I was thinking of leaving George a message and going home he came in. There was about him never a trace of that pose of forlornness, and his manner had that ill-concealed alertness that always announces the unusual. He didn't tell me what it was, so I told him quickly about my visit to Meriton Gardens. Then I asked him why Cave had thought it necessary to see him at Borden Walk.

"Something queer's turned up," he said. "I've just been with him and a dental specialist. Something's wrong about Sindle's teeth."

"The rabbit teeth?"

"They're rabbit all right," he said. "The trouble is there're too many of them!"

I stared. I reminded him that there hadn't been enough teeth. Cave had said three were missing, and I'd gathered he'd found them. So how could there be too many!

"Let me explain," George said. "Draw up a chair."

He reached for a sheet of paper.

"You have dental plates, haven't you?"

I said I hoped they weren't all that obvious.

"Never mind that," he said. "Are they part plates or whole?"

"Part plates. Each in the middle. Pinned to the back teeth with the usual little hooks that slip round."

"Right," he said. "That's what Sindle's mouth was like. A tooth or two each side top and bottom for the false teeth to be attached to. The fire melted and burnt the plastic of the plates, but it couldn't do any real harm to the natural teeth in his jaws. You got that?"

I said I couldn't miss it.

"But about the teeth after the plastic had gone," he said. "Cave said he had some missing because he was trying to reconstruct the plates and the teeth had to make a certain pattern. That's a dentist's job, but you see what I mean. But when he got the teeth in place and tried to fit them in Sindle's mouth they were too wide. The top set were two teeth too wide and the bottom four teeth too wide."

"Then the plates weren't Sindle's at all!"

"Apparently not. In fact they definitely weren't. The specialist chap hasn't any doubts."

"Yet you say they were rabbit teeth?"

"Protruding teeth," he said. "The fact that they were just a little bit larger and longer proves that. Mind you, even the specialist couldn't be dead sure."

I clicked my tongue. Everything seemed either uncertain or contradictory.

"It's simple," he said, and just as though he'd known it all the time. "Where you go wrong is this rabbit teeth business. It isn't the teeth at all; it's the way the gums lie in the mouth. If the gums stand out at an abnormal angle, like this, then the teeth have to stand out. That pushes back the upper lip a bit and makes the front teeth visible. That's what people call rabbit teeth. And when a dental mechanic makes plates, the plates have to fit the gums, not the other way about. Now do you see it?"

I said I did. But I also still thought that rabbit teeth meant big teeth in the front of the upper set, false or real.

"Quite right," he said. "But a person may have big teeth in the top front and still not have rabbit teeth. He wouldn't have unless his gums protruded. If his gums were set at the normal angle, so would his teeth be."

"I get you. But where does it get us?"

"Isn't it obvious?" he told me with a touch of impatience. "Why was Sindle put face downwards in that fire? To burn the plastic of his dental plates and destroy his features. To come back to what we're talking about now, to make sure his identity couldn't be discovered from his teeth. Whoever did it tried to make doubly sure. He took out Sindle's plates and put another pair—probably an old set of his own—inside his mouth. They wouldn't fit, but that didn't matter. All that would be left was a handful of blackened and maybe cracked artificial teeth. He didn't reckon on a possible reconstruction."

"I see all that," I said, "but there's one other question. Sindle had large, protruding front teeth. Isn't it a tremendous coincidence that his murderer—the one who stuck in his mouth a set of his own—should also have had large front teeth? Notice I don't say large protruding front teeth. I only say large front teeth. Even so, isn't it very much of a coincidence?"

"I was coming to that," he told me blandly. "The odds are very much against it. Unless . . ."

"Well: go on."

"Unless the two were related. Teeth run in families, like a lot of other things."

A moment or two later he was accusing me of not being very enthusiastic. But how could I be? We still had to find someone who really *knew* Sindle and whom Sindle knew, let alone finding one of his relatives.

"No use worrying about that," he said. "This is what's being done. The whole of Sindle's mouth was burnt. That fire was damnably hot and fierce and that plastic was burning as well. Not that we weren't lucky. If it hadn't been for that Miss Maine and Ferndale, the whole top storey might have gone. But about Sindle. There's going to be an exact reconstruction of his jaws and his own teeth, and every dentist in town'll be questioned. Every dentist in England if it has to come to it. If nothing comes of that, then my name's Robinson. Add what we hope to get from Chale and anything else we pick up, and we ought to get a line on someone with large front teeth. Any relatives we happen to find will be suspect from the start."

That sounded more promising. My small touch of enthusiasm made him more pleased with himself than ever. It was he who asked for Chale's number again, and he didn't seem too disappointed when once more there was no reply.

"Anything for me to do?" I said.

"Yes," he said. "I've had a good look through those reports of yours, and it mightn't be a bad idea if you called on that Miss Maine. You did mention buying a lampshade?"

I mentioned virtuously that my reports were always meticulously complete. I'd mentioned lampshades to show that Mrs. Oddfort did know Miss Maine personally, and my buying one as a possible excuse for a call.

"Well, you call," George said. "She was the only one in the house except Ferndale and his sitter, and she might have heard or seen something she hasn't let on about. She has fits of absent-mindedness, so you say. And then, after that, you might make an opportunity to drop in on those two girls upstairs. Run a particular eye over the Vetch girl. Last thing of all, you might slip round to Meriton Gardens. That Miss Wolde is bound to be home by then. It's almost certain she may even have known Sindle. He was one of her boss's patients."

"A night in Bohemia," I said, and my lip must have drooped with the gentlest of ironies. There I was in that room, with its fine desk, its filing cabinets, its safe, its everything that made the room of a Chief Superintendent at the Yard. Reach out a hand and you were in touch with the world. And I'd been thinking there was still a Bohemia.

"Do you good," George said. "By the way, do you know Sindle's first name? Vandyke. Got it through the house agents. He called on them personally before he took the place. Not that it helped except to confirm the description. He paid three months' rent in advance, by the way. Hundred pounds a year. Put down twenty-five quid in notes."

"Vandyke Sindle," I said. I was trying to get the feel of the name.

"Real or fake?" George asked me. "Funny for a painter to have a name all ready, so to speak?"

"One of those things that run in families," I told him and put on my coat. He didn't see the irony. Maybe it wasn't there.

"A pretty long assignment tonight," I said from the door. "I'm wondering if I'll get time to eat. And where."

"The Tabby Cat," he said. "Take those two girls along. Didn't you gather that was the idea?"

It was just after seven o'clock when I got to Borden Walk. Those two girls would need a meal early. Wharton hadn't thought of that, but I went past Pamela Maine's door and up the last stairs. A faint smell of charred wood was still there, but the landing was clean and the door of the studio had been roughly repaired and put back on its hinges.

Viola Vetch opened the door. She stared when she saw me. I gave a smile. A voice from inside was asking who it was.

"That Mr. Tracy," Viola called back to her.

"Travers," I said: "not Tracy. You're getting mixed up with the movies. Might I come in?"

"It's in a proper muddle."

She drew back to let me through, and I stepped straight into the living-room. There didn't seem any muddle to me: the room was just full enough for comfort. Someone had been doing some mending, and she snatched up some feminine fal-lals and whipped them into a workbag. She looked neat and workman-like herself in the green jumper and brown skirt.

I gave a sniff.

"Someone doing some cooking?"

"Helena," she said. "The milk boiled over."

"A pudding?"

"Only coffee." She laughed. "Helps down something out of a tin."

Helena Grace was taking a peep round the door. I called to her before she could dodge back.

"No need to worry about appearances," I told her. "I happen to be a married man."

There had been something too formal about her when I'd seen her last, and I liked her better in the long housecoat with her hair less immaculate and little make-up. But the straining for poise was still there and that touch of the refined.

"I've really come to see you both," I said. "You remember Superintendent Wharton, the one who gives me orders? He thought I ought to have a look round the Tabby Cat because Sindle used to go there. I wondered if you two people would show me the ropes."

They looked at each other. Viola looked at me. She seemed amused.

"All fair and square," I said. "I pay, but you've got to earn your keep. Tell me who's who and so on. There may be someone who knew Sindle."

"Sindle," Helena sniffed. "I don't think there's anyone who'd have known Sindle. All the same, we'd like to go. Or wouldn't we, Vi?"

"You bet we would. Give us five minutes to powder our noses."

"Look," I said. "I want to drop in on Miss Maine. I saw a lamp-shade of hers at Mrs. Oddfort's this morning and I'd like one for my wife. What about you two calling for me on your way down?"

I went down the stairs, and as I reached the landing Bint-wood came out of his door.

"Hallo, young fellow: where're you off to?"

"Hallo, Mr. Travers," he said in that quiet way of his. "Matter of fact I was just going round to the King Harry in Howe Street. You get quite a good meal there."

"Why not make one at the Tabby Cat?" I said, and explained.

"Glad to," he said. "Mind if I look in on Miss Maine too? I ought to have seen her today."

He tapped at the door and went straight in.

"No ceremony here," he said back at me. "Everybody's room is everybody else's. Hallo, Miss Maine. How're things with you?"

She was coming in from the bedroom. She smiled at Bintwood. I had a peering look, and it almost seemed as if she didn't remember me.

"This is Mr. Travers," Bintwood said. "He was asking us last night about the fire."

"The fire?" She shook her head. Then suddenly she was smiling at me and giving me a little bow. "Of course I remember Mr. Travers. You were at the party. Who was it you came with?"

"Just string her along," Bintwood was whispering.

"Does it matter?" I told her. "But I've really come about a lampshade. I saw one of yours at Mrs. Oddfort's and liked it so much that I want to buy one for my wife."

"Of course," she said. "I'd love your wife to have one."

She was looking round the room, hands clasped in front of her, and I was thinking what a handsome woman she must have been in her younger days.

"This is my workroom," she was telling me, "but I keep it very tidy. I only work in the daytime because of the strain to the eyes."

It certainly was tidy. It was the room of a woman of taste, and there's no need to say more. A shade too crowded, perhaps, but a room to live in. I liked the pastel above the small table, but I didn't let my eyes dwell on it. Something told me it was her daughter. But she wasn't watching me in any case. She was making her way towards a cupboard that occupied all the corner by the bedroom door. I was surprised at how well she walked. There was a limp and what I'd call a dip of the shoulder, and no more.

I went across. On one shelf of the cupboard were her working materials, and on another were three or four shades. I said I wanted a large shade for a tall standing lamp.

"Something like this?" she said.

I'd have liked one like Mrs. Oddfort's—till I saw the one she was handing me. It was of off-white parchment and painted all round with a rural scene that had an amazing early-Victorian feeling, from the landscape itself to the figures of the lover and his sweetheart.

"Something like a Baxter print," I said back to Bintwood.

"It is," he said. "When I get hold of reproductions I let her have them. If you want that one, give her six pounds."

Somehow I didn't like to mention money.

"Look at it with the light behind it," she was telling me.

I did, and the colours were suddenly and entrancingly alive.

"Perfectly lovely!" I said. "May I have it?"

"Of course," she said. "I don't know what you think it's worth."

"At least six pounds."

"That's very generous of you," she told me. I got out my wallet and put the notes into her hand. She seemed very happy about it.

"You'll take it with you now?"

"I'll take it," Bintwood told her. "Mr. Travers can call for it on his way back. He's going out."

He was making for the door, and I followed him. We turned and there was a ceremonious shaking of hands.

"Very nice of you to call, Mr. Travers," she told me. "Perhaps you'll come again when my daughter happens to be here."

"I'd love to," I said, and then Bintwood was nudging me to get out.

He went straight across to his door, unlocked it, and put that shade of mine somewhere inside. He locked the door again.

"Have to lock up," he said. "Gulver isn't always here. This was one of her bad nights, by the way. That fire disturbed her a bit."

"But a charming old lady."

"Yes," he said, "and absolutely harmless even when she's at her worst. You were looking at that pastel."

"The daughter, was it?"

"Yes," he said. "Ferndale did it for her from a photograph. He's very good to her."

"And so are you."

"I wouldn't call it that," he said quietly. "We're all sort of one family here. You couldn't exactly call us Bohemian, but that's no reason why we shouldn't look after each other."

Then he was looking up and cocking an ear. A moment, and the two girls were coming down the stairs.

At the lower end of Borden Walk we turned sharp left from Howe Street. Viola was asking Bintwood about Pamela Maine.

"She doesn't seem too inactive for her age," I said to Helena Grace.

"She varies," she said. "Sometimes the knee troubles her quite a lot and then it'll be almost all right. You wouldn't think it, but she often takes a walk at night before she goes to bed."

"Alone?"

"Oh, yes. She won't let anyone go with her. Only on dry moonlight nights in the winter, of course, and when her knee isn't too bad."

"Well, here we are," Bintwood was telling me, and pointing just ahead. "That's the Tabby Cat, if you don't know it."

"Didn't think it was so close."

"Two or three hundred yards," he said. "A bit early. We ought to get a table. Mind if I fix things up?"

"Go ahead," I said, and drew back to let the girls inside.

There was one long, narrowish room, with about twenty tables and just room to walk between. There was just a slight fug and an appetising smell of food, and there seemed quite a lot of vacant tables. Round the top of the distempered walls ran a frieze of tabby cats in every kind of attitude, and below it were the usual oils and the watercolours ready for an eye and a hopeful sale. Just inside, where we stood, was a door through to the kitchen. A pleasant-looking woman in the late thirties came through with a loaded tray. She smiled at Bintwood and the girls. Bintwood followed her and we came behind.

The tray was unloaded and she took us to a table at the far end of the room. She said she could manage a bottle of wine, and a good Bordeaux would be fifteen shillings. While she was gone we had a look at the menu. I had my back to the wall and was having a look at the room.

About half the tables were occupied, and it looked to me like any of the quiet little restaurants you'd see in Soho. No men waiters, of course, and the linen a bit more spotless and everything clean as new pins. I could see only two diners that looked like artists, one with longish hair and the other bald as a coot. There were a couple of arty women, well into the forties, but the rest were as commonplace as myself.

Helena passed me the menu: nothing *à la carte*, but just the dinner—three-and-nine including coffee. Something was wrong about that. Sindle, I'd been told, had ordered just soup and bread.

"That's only till seven o'clock," Helena told me. "You can get soup and snacks till then."

She was having curried halibut. I chose the steak pie. Then I saw my bottle coming.

"Is that one Nancy?" I said.

"That's Laura," she told me. "Nancy's the thin one. They're cousins."

We settled down to the vegetable soup. It was hot and tasty, like all the food: plain, nicely served and distinctly good. The wine was much better than I'd feared.

"Pity the menu wasn't in French," Viola said. "Mr. Bintwood's terrific on French. Remember him talking to that waiter that dinner we had in Soho?"

Bintwood laughed deprecatingly.

"Doesn't take much to do that. I had five years over there between the wars," he told me. "The firm I was with had a branch in St. Sulpice."

Helena was sitting next to me and facing Bintwood. She'd thawed out quite a lot by the time we were into the second course. The room was filling up and she was telling us the names of people she spotted. Viola kept craning round, and she gave an ecstatic wave to a short, very fat middle-aged man. His own wave was very pontifical.

"That's Langer. He's at the Whistler Memorial," Helena told me. "Vi does a lot of work round there."

By the time we were on our coffee the room was practically full. Most people were drinking beer, though I did see one wine bottle. A cheerful party were making whoopee just along from us. One was Makin, the sculptor, and the thin woman with him was a miniaturist whose name I didn't catch. There was quite a lot of waving from our table. I could only sit there like an exhibition piece and feel not quite a part of things.

I caught sight of Nancy and waved for my bill.

"Nancy, tell my friend Mr. Travers about that scene with Sindle over the soup," Bintwood said.

"Oh, let him rest," she told him. "I can't bear to think of anyone ending up like that—even if he was a bit cracked."

Bintwood said there was no need to hurry, and we sat on smoking and yarning. Bintwood insisted on paying for a couple of ports for the girls, and he and I had whisky.

"We must do this again some other time," I said. "I haven't had so cheery an evening since Aunt Maria died."

"We certainly must," Bintwood said. "Only next time I'm going to be in the chair."

It was after half-past nine when we got outside. Bintwood and Helena had somehow moved ahead and Viola grabbed my arm. All sheer friendliness and *joie de vivre*, I hoped, in spite of the moonlight and the way she snuggled close to my ribs. She kept asking me about my work.

"Let's talk about you," I said. "Tell me about your work."

It sounded prosaic enough, the way she put it. Then already we were at the bottom of Howe Street.

"What would you do if your wife suddenly came round the corner?" she asked me, and squeezed my arm more tightly.

"Put on false whiskers," I said. "And that reminds me of something. What would you have done if Sindle had asked you to sit to him?"

"I'd have spat on him," she said. "But what about you? Don't you paint or model or something?"

I told her hastily that where art was concerned I was a moron, and then we were at No. 7. They wanted me to come up for more coffee, and I had reluctantly to refuse. My mother had made me promise I'd always be in bed by ten. The girls thought that very amusing, which shows what a quarter bottle and a port—or was it two?—will do. We shook hands all round, and I was calling more good-nights from twenty yards on.

Then everything was suddenly very quiet, with just the noise of traffic by the river. It was quite warm and the moonlight so clear that the pavement looked white as paper. I walked on in what I judged the general direction of Meriton Gardens, and I was wondering what I could put on my report. That Helena Grace had let her hair somewhat down? That Viola Vetch would have spat on Sindle? That Pamela Maine had had one of her vacuous nights? That Bintwood spoke very good French? That Nancy Grew had thought that Sindle was cracked? Not much, that, to set against the expenses account, even if I added that the Bright Boy of St. Martins—as Wharton had once roguishly called me—had unexpectedly become persona grata at No. 7.

I asked a passer-by for the whereabouts of Meriton Gardens and found I was at the north end of it. As I went up the steps I remember the moonlight threw my shadow across the iron railings to the next house, and everywhere was curiously quiet. I pushed the bell and heard it sound inside. I waited and then rang again. I waited and rang, waited and rang, and there was never a sound from the house.

Five minutes had gone. The sound of a neighbouring clock came clearly and struck ten. I crossed the road to the shadows and looked across at the house in case there should be a belated someone at the door. That was when I saw the woman, and as she came slowly near I knew her at once, in spite of the hat and coat and the stick. It was Pamela Maine. She stopped at the gate of the house and stood there looking at its door. She was so motionless that but for her shadow she might have been some trick of the moonlight. For two or three minutes she stood like that, and then she moved slowly on.

At the end of the road I was just behind her: she on one side in the moonlight and I in the opposite shadows, and it seemed to me that every now and again she was talking to herself. Then we came to Borden Walk, and there I waited. The last I saw of her was as she neared the door of No. 7, moving through the faint light that came from Gulver's window.

CHAPTER VII
THE ELUSIVE HERMIONE

THAT night I began my report, and I was up early in the morning to finish it. I had a word with Norris, and half-past eight found me at the Yard. Wharton and Matthews were there, and I gave them an abstract of the previous night.

While we were waiting till it should be time for me to go to Meriton Gardens I heard more of how things had gone. Plenty of contacts had been made with Sindle. Crotch, of the colour and frame shop in Borden Walk, had sold him materials shortly after his arrival, and he furnished a description which was precisely that of everyone else. The off-licence had been found where Sindle had twice ordered his drink: a dozen beers each time and a bottle of whisky. In each case they had been delivered near a specified time in the afternoon, and Sindle had been there to take them in. The man in the office, who had taken the orders, and the delivery man had each given a description. Once seen, Sindle was something never forgotten. Then there'd been a grocer—a small shop in Cranley Road, near Hammersmith— from whom he'd bought his groceries and bread, and they'd always been left in a carton—rarely more than once a week— outside the studio door. But not one of those contacts had ever seen Sindle other than alone.

"Isn't there something wrong about that beer and stuff?" I said.

"Lucky to get the whisky," Matthews said.

"Maybe. But if he was a heavy drinker, a couple of dozen beers wouldn't be much for a month, even with the whisky."

"We may find he dealt somewhere else," Wharton said.

"My idea is the drinking was incidental. I think he was taking dope. That'd account for the bloodshot eyes and his nerves."

"Then there was that sissy that Ferndale saw him with," Matthews said. "Hundreds of 'em in the West End. You couldn't rope the whole lot in for an identification parade."

"It's that fire-escape that was so damned handy," Wharton said. "Any surreptitious pal of his could nip up there and never be seen. Not a house in that opposite road saw a thing the afternoon he was killed. But what about that Vetch girl? You think she might have posed for that nude?"

I said frankly that I couldn't be sure. But I was almost sure there wasn't any vice in her. I put her down as temperamentally gay and good-natured, but, as Matthews had said, quite capable of looking after herself. I wouldn't call her oversexed. With a good model, and she seemed one, sex could be put into strictly watertight compartments.

"Any dope found in Sindle?"

"There wasn't," Wharton said reluctantly. "But there wouldn't be with certain kinds."

"What about the knife or whatever it was that killed him?"

"There again it's difficult," he said. "The back was soaked in paraffin. Every hair was burnt off the head and the back was all charred. Take a look at the photos."

I said quickly that it didn't matter. Wharton can look at such things as if they were out of the family album. My stomach isn't quite so constant.

"There were two wounds," he said, "and one—the second obviously—got him right in the heart. The first glanced off a rib, but it may have knocked him out. But you can't see where the blade entered. Cave puts it down as any sharp-pointed knife. About an inch across the base."

It was after nine o'clock and I said I'd be going. I oughtn't to be long and ten o'clock should see me back. Wharton said he'd be there. But it turned out I was to be back far sooner.

It was Mrs. Nippen who opened the door of No. 15. She didn't give me time to speak.

"Here you are again," she said. "But Miss Wolde isn't here. She's spending the day with a sister at Clacton. She left me a note. You can see it if you like. I've got it in the kitchen."

We went through. She was wearing a print dress with a snood arrangement round her hair.

"This is what she left," she said. "Propped up against the tea-caddy, it was. I generally make myself a cup soon as I've looked round."

Dear Mrs. Nippen,

As there's nothing much for me to do, I'm having the day off with my sister at Clacton. I mightn't be back till some time in the morning, but you know what to get on with and you can leave at five the same as yesterday.

If that Mr. Travers calls, tell him the postman's been and there was nothing from the doctor.

H. WOLDE.

A nice quality sheet of paper with embossed address. Firm if slightly angular writing, and a neat signature.

"What time does the postman come?"

"About eight," she said. "She must have left soon after. I was here at nine on the dot."

"Ever hear her mention this sister at Clacton?"

"Can't say as I did," she said. "But she and me never talked—gossiped, as you might say. What you might call very superior, she was."

Her lip had drooped slightly. No love lost there, as my old nurse would have said.

"What was her actual position here?"

"Supposed to be secretary and what they call receptionist. Showed people in and sort of made herself useful."

"She and the doctor were friendly?"

"Yes," she said slowly, and frowned.

"A bit too friendly?"

She gave me a look. I didn't change a muscle.

"Some people might think so," she said, and sniffed as she looked away. "But there: people don't think nothing of that nowadays. A lot of fast hussies, most of them, though it's more than your place is worth to say so."

I left it at that.

"Don't you ever say a word about that," she was suddenly telling me, and she even held my arm.

"You needn't worry," I told her. "In my job you have to hear all and say nothing. As far as you and I are concerned, Mrs. Nippen, we haven't done more than pass the time of day."

She saw me off at the door, and I gave her a reassuring wave from the car. In five minutes I was drawing in at the Yard.

"Yes," Wharton said. "I'm beginning to think there's something extraordinarily fishy. That Wolde woman's dodging you. I wonder why?"

I said I'd had the same idea. But we both might be wrong. Why should the Wolde woman bother about me? I was merely a someone making enquiries. Mightn't her absence be just a case of the mouse playing while the cat was away?

"She was on good terms with that doctor," he said. "On very good terms indeed."

He gave a leer that was like a dirty story.

"Secretary, receptionist, bed-warmer. She could have had a day off to go to Clacton whenever she liked. If she had some free time now, what'd she do with it? Have her hair permed and go round the stores and stand herself a lunch."

I said, and I hope without irony, that his knowledge of women went deeper than mine. He took all that for granted.

"As for that doctor," he said, "I'm giving him no more rope. I'll get out an S.O.S right away. Get them to broadcast it at one o'clock. And again at six."

That meant a conference with Commander 'Crime', and he was getting to his feet. He gave a wry shake of the head.

"I still can't help thinking we might have got somewhere already if you'd caught that woman. Why you didn't nip out of that studio'll always be a mystery to me."

"I don't admit it was a mistake," I told him. "Even if it was, you took me on for better or worse. Forget and forgive, George. And what do you want me to do now?"

"Don't know that there's anything at the moment," he said, still a bit pained. "You had a pretty longish day yesterday. Let me know where I can get hold of you, that's all."

I said he could get me via the flat. Then I rang Bernice and said I'd be in for lunch. I dictated a quick account of the morning's call on Mrs. Nippen, and then I had things to do. Wharton couldn't possibly want me before lunch, and I had my lampshade to collect from Bintwood's room. But I thought I'd better see him about it first.

As I drove to Sloane Square, I was thinking about Pamela Maine and that fit of abstractedness when she'd stood for a minute or two in the moonlight, eyes intent on Chale's house. Maybe something had caught her eye at one of the windows, and all at once it struck me that Hermione Wolde might have been in the house after all, and peering at me from behind the curtains. Maybe it was that that had attracted the attention of Pamela Maine: attracted it for a moment, that is, and then a quick absentmindedness had kept her there. And if all that was right, then Wharton also had been right, and Hermione Wolde had been deliberately avoiding a meeting with myself. And just why I couldn't for the life of me imagine.

I drew the car up outside Henry Markov's shop. Not all the big dealers live down West, as I knew, and at the club I'd been told that Markov was in quite a big way of business. In the one large window was a Barker of Bath, flanked by two small interiors by some artist unknown. Inside, the shop itself was that of a hundred other dealers—more of an office with a few handy canvases. The showrooms and the main stock would probably be upstairs. A thin, elderly man with a stoop approached me. He said Bintwood was with a client, and perhaps I wouldn't mind waiting.

I waited about ten minutes. Bintwood's client must have gone out by some other exit, for I was conducted upstairs. Bintwood was in one of the showrooms.

"Hallo, Mr. Travers," he said, and gave me his quiet smile. "Sorry I had to keep you waiting. Quite a nice time we had last night. I hope you were in bed by ten."

I laughed. I admitted I'd had such a good time that I'd completely forgotten my lampshade.

"I saw it this morning," he said. "I guessed you'd be calling round for it. But Gulver's got a master-key. He's bound to be in."

"I'll call round then," I said.

"The girls enjoyed last night," he said. "Does them good to get out. Me too. I like my pleasures simple."

He was asking me if I'd seen that Barker of Bath. The firm had bought it privately with a small collection that was largely junk.

"It's catalogued?"

"Yes," he said. "And it's right. We traced it through the collection of a Dr. Rose of Bath."

"How'd you get into this game?" I said. "Grow up in it?"

"I suppose I did," he said. "My father was an antique dealer. I always did like pictures. Started off in life in a picture-framer's shop. But you don't want to hear about me. Got time for a look round?"

I had an enjoyable half-hour. He was more than knowledgeable, and what frankly amused me was that he told me I was very knowledgeable too.

"I put all my knowledge in the shop window," I told him. "I own I'm fond of pictures. Always was. If I'd had any sense as a young man I'd have been a collector."

"You'll have to pop in and see one or two things I've got," he said. "I'm saving them up for my old age. I've got one set of Gauguin drawings that I picked up in Paris that I wouldn't take quite a lot of money for."

It was almost eleven o'clock when I left him, and I was thinking what a likeable, genuine, unaffected chap he was. I was thinking nostalgically, too, of my young manhood and the chan-

ces I'd had and the things I might have owned if I'd had the
sense to specialise. And I couldn't do other than admit ruefully
that the Travers of then was the Travers of now: the same
scatterbrain, the same fluttering from interest to interest. And
yet perhaps I'd had a lot of fun.

I left the car just short of Borden Walk and walked the few
yards to No. 7. The front door was open, and the first thing I saw
was that Ferndale's door was open too. I peeped in. The partition curtain was drawn back, and in the studio Gulver was busy
with a duster. I coughed to attract his attention.

"It's you, sir," he said. "Hear you were out last night with the
young ladies and Mr. Bintwood. Come along in."

News travelled quickly in No. 7, I was thinking.

"How are you, Gulver?"

"Very fit, sir. Hard at it as usual. Mr. Ferndale's coming at
half-past, so I had to see everything was just right for him. Been
cleaning those top lights."

I told him about Bintwood and the lampshade.

"Just a couple of minutes, sir, and I'll be with you. You knew
about Mr. Ferndale's marriage, sir?"

I said I had heard something.

"A very nice lady, that Mrs. Solness, sir. Very well-to-do, so
they tell me."

"You know her?"

"Bless my soul, sir, I know everybody." He actually paused in
his dusting. "I do little jobs for Mrs. Solness and for everybody.
I often wonder, and I don't say it boastful like, what they'd all do
if I weren't here. Not that they aren't all very good to me. Like
one big family here, sir. That's what we are."

He'd been smiling away, as near excitement as he'd ever get.
He sobered down as he waved a hand at the easel.

"That's Mrs. Solness he's doing there, sir. Out of one o' them
Shakespeare plays, so he told me."

I had a look, and if Gulver hadn't been watching me I think I'd
have frowned. It was a portrait and not a portrait. That Sargent
canvas, as I tried to remember it, was seven foot, perhaps, by
three: a portrait of Ellen Terry as Lady Macbeth trying on the

ill-gotten crown. Ferndale's canvas was about four by two and a half, and he'd chosen the sleep-walking scene. It is true that Lady Macbeth in the person of Mrs. Solness dominated the picture. She was shown at the foot of the stairs, groping out with one hand, and a candlestick with rush light in the other. In the right background were roughly blocked the figures of, maybe, the physician and two others of the watching household.

But even Mrs. Solness was very incomplete, and it was on her that Ferndale was probably going to work that morning. And he would need some work. Two enlarged photographs, made maybe from press flashes of years before, showed the Lady Macbeth of those earlier acting days, and Ferndale would have to reconcile them with the Maud Solness whom the years had considerably plumped. What the whole thing would amount to, or so it seemed to me, was a kind of composite: a flattering portrait of the lady with just a reminder of a not too intrusive past.

"It's going to be very nice," I told Gulver.

"It is, if Mr. Ferndale's doing it," he said. "A very clever gentleman at his work—so they tell me. And now I'm ready for you, sir. He should be here now in about ten minutes."

He led the way upstairs and unlocked Bintwood's door.

"Step inside a minute, sir. I'd better wrap this up for you if I can find any paper."

"Don't bother," I said. "I've got my car and I'm going straight home."

But I'd had a quick look round all the same. It was a man's room, but with a tidy, ordered comfort. There was a nice quality bookcase, and the walls were crowded with pictures, mostly smallish oils. There was one head of a man that looked as good as a Franz Hals, but I didn't want to step farther into the room after what I'd said. And there'd be another day.

We went down again, and Gulver peered along Borden Walk to see, perhaps, if Ferndale was coming. I slipped half a crown into his hand.

"No, sir, no!"

I made him keep it.

"You've done quite a lot for me," I said. "Even if you still think you haven't, let's call it something in advance."

Bernice loved the lampshade. She said it would have cost at least ten guineas in any West End shop. That gave me a chance to ask her if she remembered Pamela Maine. When I prodded her memory she just recalled her as on the London stage, and no more. But she did remember the daughter, Barbara, though nothing much beyond the final tragedy.

She was going out that afternoon, and I didn't blame her. When I'm on a case my hours are worse than erratic. And I didn't want to stay indoors alone—the day was too fine, for one thing— so I had the telephone switched to the hall-porter's cubby-hole with word that if wanted urgently I'd be at my club.

I'd been thinking first of a stroll through the Park, and then as I walked through Leicester Square I changed my mind, or my mind changed things for me. Somewhere I've read—I believe it was in a book of Marquand's—that the writing of a novel is in one way a harassing business—for the people who have to live with the novelist. If that book of his is to be real and alive, it has for the time of its duration to be the whole of his life. He lives, in fact, in two worlds, of which the ordinary world about him is the one that's suddenly unreal. And that's very much how it is with me when I'm on a case. I live it, I eat it, and I sleep it. My world is mainly peopled with its actors, and life has little inter- est beyond their personal selves, their actions, their possible motives, and even their imagined thoughts.

That afternoon the case was just enough of an obsession to gnaw at me without exactly becoming an irritant. I wanted to know a whole lot more about several people. I would have liked to have a half-hour's chat with all or any one of the tenants at Borden Walk, but not one was available. Except, perhaps, Pamela Maine, and, if I remembered rightly, she always rested in the afternoons. But there was still a way of finding out a lot more about her. That's why I went down the subway to Piccadilly and rang Tom Holberg. He said he'd be free in about ten minutes.

Tom's is the best-known theatrical agency in town. I've known him for donkey's years, and I've never ceased to be surprised at the vastness of his knowledge on matters theatrical. From time to time I consult him, and he never charges a penny for the use of his time, so I try to make it up by an occasional dinner. According to him, I once did him a favour, and he still chooses to think it much bigger than it was.

His office is in Shaftesbury Avenue—a mere three minutes from where I was—so I took a walk round to pass the time. He was ready for me when I arrived. A word or two's chat and I was asking him about Pamela Maine.

"No, I didn't handle her," he said. "I think Mandleheim did, but he was bombed out. Killed, if you remember, in almost the last blitz."

"Pretty good, wasn't she?"

"Very reliable. Always in work. Irene Vanbrugh sort of parts. Married to a chap called Clamp. Rather a bad egg, I believe."

"What about her daughter, Barbara? You remember the details of the tragedy?"

"Something of it," he said. "She was with Drew & Callister of Charing Cross Road. A better actress in some ways than her mother. Took a long while getting up, but she'd have stayed there."

"And the tragedy?"

The chubby fingers caressed the chubbier face.

"I think it began with a car accident. Don't remember who her husband actually was, but he was killed in a car accident when he was taking the boy to prep school. Or may have been public school—I forget. The boy died shortly afterwards, and she had a nervous breakdown. I think she was actually dead before I heard even that much of it. Jumped out of a hotel window."

I told him about Pamela Maine and Borden Walk. I mentioned I'd heard she was an embittered woman. I said he'd gather from what I'd told him that her own mental health had been badly upset by what had happened to the daughter and grandson.

"Let me think a moment," he said, and was rubbing his chin again. "Something about legal action."

He nodded to himself.

"That's it," he said. "I think the whole thing got Pamela unhinged straight away. I believe she wanted to bring an action against the doctor who'd treated the daughter, and then she was dissuaded out of it. I do know she left the stage just before the daughter died. Sorry I can't think of anything else."

I said he'd answered all my questions, so what more could I want. We had another word or two, and I said I'd take up no more of his time. As he was seeing me out he added a something.

"I don't think the old lady's financially embarrassed; but if she should happen to be, let me know. I might be able to do something."

A good chap, Tom Holberg, I was thinking as I made my way back towards the Park. And he'd made everything clear about Pamela Maine. Not that that helped in the slightest degree towards solving the Sindle case. If it did anything at all, it clarified the feeling that pervaded and the background that lay behind Gulver's one big family at Borden Walk. It even explained such trivialities as that moment when Pamela Maine had left Ferndale's studio, that first evening when Wharton and I had done some preliminary questioning: the way, for instance, that Helena Grace had taken the old lady's arm to help her through the door, and that close, protective kind of look she had given me as she went through herself.

I suppose the short time I'd spent with Tom Holberg had eased my mind momentarily from the case. I know I kept it fairly distant from my thoughts while I had tea and read this and that. It was not till well on the way to seven o'clock that I went back to the flat, and there'd been no message for me from the Yard. I asked the hall-porter about that S.O.S. for Chale, and he thought there'd been one. Then I waited for Bernice and we had a service dinner.

Next morning I woke with something on my mind, and I knew what it was before I'd plugged in the electric kettle. Hermione Wolde had said in that message to Mrs. Nippen that she'd at least be in some time during the morning. Very well then, I was telling myself; that morning, if Wharton was of the same mind, I'd go to Meriton Gardens and camp there till Hermione Wolde appeared. As soon as she opened the door, the first person she'd see would be myself.

"Darling, whatever are you muttering to yourself about?"

I smiled sheepishly. I hadn't known that Bernice was awake.

"Just work," I said. "And women."

She smiled tolerantly at that last. I wondered what she'd have thought about both if by any chance she had suddenly appeared that previous night around the corner by Howe Street.

Chapter VIII
SEEING MISS WOLDE

I didn't have any talk with Hermione Wolde that morning, and there wasn't any need to wait. But I was at Meriton Gardens. I was very much there and a long way from alone. Wharton was there and Matthews and Cave and all the rest of the travelling circus. The same flashlights from photographers, the same fingerprint men, the same everything that follows hard on a murder.

I'd been in Wharton's room listening to a few more negative results, and it had been agreed that I should go round to Meriton Gardens soon after nine o'clock. Nothing had come in from the absent Chale, and Wharton was a bit short-tempered. As he said, nobody these days could put himself beyond the range of the wireless. Matthews suggested that the doctor might be incognito, and had his head almost bitten off for his pains.

Then the buzzer went. Wharton picked up the receiver and grunted as usual. Then his eyes began to pop.

"Of course it does!" he told somebody. "How long ago? . . . Right. I'll be along right away."

He slapped the receiver back, looked hard at Matthews, then gave me a glare.

"Didn't I tell you there was something fishy about that Wolde woman?"

"What's happened then?"

"Dead," he said. "Someone did her in. Last night, they think."

"Where? At Clacton?"

He looked at me with an infinite pity.

"So you fell for that yarn, did you?"

He grabbed his coat and hat, and there began the exodus to Meriton Gardens. Which brings us back to where we started.

Mrs. Nippen, interviewed in the kitchen, said she'd heard the clock of St. Andrew's strike the hour as she let herself in at the back door. The curtains were down and there were some dirty plates and things in the sink and that told her at once that Miss Wolde was back. She listened and there wasn't a sound of her, and no note had been left to say she was out.

"I thought she might have come in late and was having a lie-in, so I told myself I'd have a look upstairs; and when I looked in her room, there she was. I didn't know if I ought to disturb her or not, and then there looked something funny about her."

Another minute and she was making a shaky way down the stairs to the telephone and dialling 999.

"What made you do that?" Wharton asked her. "Why didn't you call a doctor?"

"It was the marks on her throat," she said. "And this gentleman here"—it was I she meant—"had said he was from Scotland Yard, and something told me—"

"That's all right," Wharton said. "You did the right thing. Stay on here, Mrs. Nippen, will you, and I'll be seeing you again. Make yourself a cup of tea."

We went upstairs to where Cave and the local inspector were waiting. We had a quick look in what was obviously Chale's bedroom and went on up to the second floor.

Hermione Wolde was lying on her back at full length in the three-foot bed, a handsome divan that was doubly sprung. The mouth was agape, and even from the door one could see the bruises on the throat.

"What was it?" Wharton said. "Manual strangulation?"

"That's it," Cave said. "Usual crack on the back of the skull and then the strangulation. Getting a bit too frequent, if you ask me. They'll have to pass a law against it."

"What time?"

"Can't say yet. Ten o'clock last night won't be so far wrong."

Wharton whipped round on me.

"You didn't happen to come round this way last night?" I said I didn't. The previous night—yes.

"Better get a move on," he told the inspector. "Have enquiries made right through the road. Ask if anyone saw her come in, and if she was alone. And if anyone else was seen coming in."

We looked round the room. Her clothes were neatly placed on the chair by the bed, and the shoes she had worn stood beneath it. On the bedside table with its reading-lamp was her handbag. There was also a clean ashtray.

"Just cover her lightly up," he said. "Matthews, you bring that Mrs. Nippen up here."

We had a look in the large walnut wardrobe. That mink coat—second or third grade—was on a hanger. Plenty of frocks and dresses and a couple of costumes. At least a dozen pairs of shoes stood on the bottom, all carefully treed. Wharton opened the drawers of the walnut chest, chock-a-block with lingerie and oddments.

"Someone's been through these drawers," he said. "A woman wouldn't leave things all rucked up like this."

He pushed the drawers to again. Mrs. Nippen was coming in.

"Shan't keep you a minute," Wharton told her. "About the curtains. They were drawn like this when you came in?"

"That's right, sir."

"The light was on?"

"No, sir. I'd have known if it was. I switched it on myself."

"What about downstairs?"

"The kitchen curtains were drawn," she said. "I spotted that as soon as I opened the door. Then I saw the things in the sink. 'Hallo,' I says. 'So my lady's home after all.'"

"What about the other rooms?"

She hadn't been in any other rooms. She had telephoned from the hall and had been told to stay where she was and touch nothing. But she'd been scared of staying in the hall and had shut herself in the kitchen till the police came.

That was all for the moment. Matthews was told to take her down and report on the other rooms. I reminded him that the curtains in the doctor's room had been drawn.

"I saw it," he said. "Let's have a look at her bag."

We tipped the contents on the bed. There were the usual make-up knick-knacks but never a scrap of paper: no letters, no bills, not even a bus ticket. But there was a bunch of keys. In an inner compartment was a used handkerchief and a spare, a notecase with seven pounds in it and some silver and coppers. Wharton put everything back and replaced the bag. Matthews came in again.

"The waiting-room and consulting-room both had the curtains drawn," he said, "so did the doctor's bedroom and the office. Mrs. Nippen says her Ideal boiler is all choked up with burnt paper."

"Right," Wharton said. "Get everything photographed and then she can go away. Fingerprint right through the house and start up here."

Cave drew the sheet back. There must have been some trick of the light, for suddenly there was something peculiar about the dead face. Something remembered, maybe, from that last Monday afternoon when I had caught a near glimpse of her in the car. A good-looking brunette: I'd had just the time to docket her as that, and to run as quick an eye over the fur coat.

I moved a bit nearer to the bed. I shifted to change the play of light on the face, and then suddenly my fingers were fumbling at my glasses.

"I've remembered something, George. I'm practically sure she's the woman who was peering into that studio window on Monday night."

He stared. I shifted ground again. I got on my knees and looked at the full face.

"She was the one," I said.

"But why?" he said. "What the devil was she doing round at Borden Walk?"

"Can't say," I told him. "But as soon as you heard this morning about all this, you knew it tied up with the Sindle case." I could have added, 'Or so you said', but I didn't.

"Of course it ties up," he said.

He stood there for a good minute, looking down at the face with its slightly gaping lips.

"About that crack on the skull that stunned her," he said to Cave. "She couldn't have got it while she was in the bed?"

Cave shrugged his shoulders.

"Isn't that obvious? The bed-head's against the wall. No one could have stood behind it."

"What if she was looking sideways?"

"At a blank wall?" Cave shrugged his shoulders again.

"All right," Wharton said. "Since you know all the answers, what's your own idea about her?"

"I'd say she mightn't have been killed here at all. If she were, he could have used the pillow to smother her instead of using his hands. She might have been killed anywhere in the house and then brought up here and undressed. She wouldn't be all that much to carry. Well under nine stone."

"Sure about a he?"

"More like a man's job than a woman's."

Wharton grunted.

"Well, get her away when they've finished. I'll have a look downstairs. We'll test the heels of her shoes with those casts of yours, Matthews, that you took at Borden Walk." He thought of something else. "There's a gardener about here somewhere—"

"Emmett," I said. "Chauffeur and handyman."

"Probably he cleaned the shoes," Wharton said. "Bring him up here and see if he can pick out the pair she wore last Monday night."

We went into the kitchen. Wharton wanted to hear from Mrs. Nippen about the Ideal boiler.

"Emmett saw to it," she said, and was taking us through to a scullery. "I just asked him why it didn't burn, and he said it was all choked up with burnt paper. Rare mess he's made. You can see for yourself."

Small fragments of charred paper were everywhere, like soot. Wharton wanted to know where the doctor kept his records, and she thought it must be in the upstairs office. On the ground floor was a little dining-room with a serving-hatch from the kitchen, the consulting-room and a small waiting-room.

"What about this morning's letters?"

She said they were on the hall table by the telephone. Wharton nodded to me, and we went out to the hall. There was a begging letter and a couple of circulars, but never a word from Chale.

"Looks more and more fishy to me," Wharton said. "Let's have a look through the rooms."

There was nothing noteworthy in the little dining-room, unless it was that none of the usual letters and circulars were parked behind the bronze ornaments that flanked the marble clock. We went through the sideboard drawers and there was never a scrap of paper.

The consulting-room would have looked a cosy place if the fire had been on. We were interested in the flat-topped desk and the cupboard. Both were locked. I slipped upstairs and fetched the keys from the dead woman's handbag, but those two small ones didn't fit. Matthews was sent for. He did some manipulating with a bit of wire and the skeleton keys from Wharton's bag.

Five minutes later we still hadn't found a scrap of paper.

"He must have kept some records here," Wharton said. "Besides, there isn't even a circular or anything. Someone must have made the devil of a clean sweep."

There was nothing in the waiting-room plus cloakroom, so we went up to the first floor. It had three rooms: a lounge at the nearest point to the landing, then the office, and across the landing the doctor's bedroom. We took the bedroom first. It was a long room with bath and lavatory at its end.

As soon as we began opening drawers we could see that they'd all been searched. We went through the pockets of every article of clothing in the wardrobe: we went through that room, in fact, with a small-toothed comb, and we didn't find a scrap of paper. A walnut desk that should have held at least his cheque-book had no papers of any sort. That left the office.

In that room there'd been a second fire, for the hearth was covered with charred paper and the grate was choked with it. Filing cabinet, filing trays, desk drawers—every record had gone.

"Someone must have been here most of the night," Wharton said. "Who could it have been but Chale."

I wasn't looking too enthusiastic.

"Who else had the keys?" he asked me. "Not a single lock anywhere was forced. And the keys weren't in her bag." He tried the smallish safe that stood by the far wall, then I had to go down and telephone the Yard to send a man to open it.

"Not that there'll be anything in it," Wharton said. "I'll lay a fiver on that. Half the morning gone and nothing done. Let's see what's going on upstairs."

Cave and the body had gone and the bedroom was clear. Wolde's prints had been everywhere with a few of Mrs. Nippen's, and a couple—checked against others in the consulting-room— were almost certainly Chale's. Matthews came in.

"These were the shoes she wore that night," he told us. "Emmett cleaned them the next morning. They had mud on them and he wondered where she'd got it from. Also the pattern of these little rubber heels checks with the casts."

"Put everything together and get his statement," Wharton said. "Learn anything else from him?"

"Only that he hated the sight of her. Far too uppish, according to him. Bossed him about more than the doctor."

"Find out from him where he took her in the car last Monday afternoon," I said. "It might give us a line on her friends." When Matthews had gone Wharton stood there shaking his head.

"It can't be a mistake," he said. "She must have been there. But what the devil was she there for? If it'd been Chale, I could have understood. If Sindle was the patient he was scared of."

I could have put forward a theory, but I didn't. Perhaps it was as well, for it would have been very wide of the truth. And

Wharton was letting out a deep breath and making for the dressing-table. The two small keys from her bag opened everything, and we went through the drawers, but once more there wasn't a scrap of paper. We tried the chest of drawers and had no luck. We went through the pockets of costumes and coats: we almost ran that room through a vacuum cleaner, and there was never a letter or personal note. And there was nothing in her bathroom.

The room across the landing was apparently her sitting-room, but it had a chilly, haphazard, uncomfortable look as if it hadn't been used for a very long time. The desk in it was open, and it, too, had been thoroughly emptied—if, that is, it had ever contained any personal correspondence. So we tried the third room, but that was only a boxroom. Wharton switched the light on, nevertheless, and we grubbed about among the dust of trunks and boxes and miscellaneous junk. Even there someone had been before us.

The expert had come from the Yard, and in a couple of minutes he had the office safe open. We might have saved his trouble. But there were marks in the slight film of dust on bottom and shelf.

"Cleaned out like everything else," Wharton said. "Someone had a pretty long night."

We went down the stairs together. Wharton turned off to the waiting-room.

"Get hold of Matthews," he told me. "Can't do anything till we see how we stand."

It was nearly one o'clock, and we were in that waiting-room with the fire on, busy with a pot of tea that Mrs. Nippen had made us. Matthews had had a stroke of luck. Emmett had driven Hermione Wolde to Acacia Road, Finchley. Now and again he would drive her there, to No. 18, and his instructions always were to park the car and call back with it at a quarter-past five. That was what had happened on the Monday afternoon. Whom she saw at Acacia Road and what went on there he didn't know. Miss Wolde, one gathered, was far too superior to discuss her affairs with a man like Emmett.

"You might slip along there this afternoon and find out," Wharton told me. "The sooner we get a line on her, the better."

As to finding out how we stood, all we knew was that we were on precious little solid ground. Cave had been rung and he'd narrowed the time of death to between ten and half-past the previous night. No one so far had seen her enter the house. That wasn't too much of a disappointment if she had entered not long before she was killed. It is true that it'd been moonlight, but at ten o'clock the tenants of Meriton Gardens would be snugly indoors.

Wharton's idea was that the murderer had been waiting in the house. He had struck her down as soon as she entered, strangled her and carried the body up to the bedroom. He'd undressed her, put on her nightgown, and then set about the night's business of destroying every record in the house. So vital did he consider it that he took no chances on what was revealing and what was not. Every piece of paper had been burnt.

"But doesn't that point the other way from Chale?" Matthews said. "If he was burning everything that might give some game or other away, wouldn't he have known what to burn and what not?"

"It was a question of time," Wharton said. "It was quicker and safer to burn the whole lot than go through everything."

"What was the particular game you had in mind?" I asked Matthews.

"Anything crooked," he told me vaguely. "Blackmail, for instance. And if we couldn't trace who his patients were, then we couldn't get a line on that."

"Might be an idea," Wharton said hopefully. "Especially after that affair at Brumford. Ask Mrs. Nippen to fetch this tray. One or two things I'd like to ask her."

What he wanted to know was if Hermione Wolde had ever mentioned any relatives, apart from that supposed sister at Clacton.

"A pity," he said, when she said there were none. "But did she ever drop any hint at all about her life before she came here?"

"No," she said. "But I did have the idea that she and the doctor had known each other before she came here."

Wharton pricked his ears.

"What made you think that?"

"I can't exactly say," she said. "Not now. I know that was the idea I had at the time. I reckon it was something he said. About my finding her easy to get on with. Or something like that."

"They were friendly from the very start? More friendly, shall we say, than a doctor and his secretary usually are?"

"I don't know," she said. "Not at the start, they weren't, or else I didn't notice anything."

"But they were later?"

"Too friendly, if you ask me," she told him with a virtuous sniff. "Not that it was my business, in a way of speaking. Only when she was all superior-like, I used to think to myself, 'All right, my lady. A pretty fool you'd look if I was to open my mouth.'"

Wharton left it at that. I had a question ready.

"Mrs. Nippen, I wonder if you'd mind thinking back to last Monday afternoon. It seems now as if everyone—except you, perhaps—was having a free afternoon. Miss Wolde was going out in the car. The doctor was going out and then on to North London—"

"I didn't know that," she said. "I knew he went out, but I was expecting him in for tea."

"He told you he'd be in for tea?"

"No," she said, "but he didn't say he wouldn't. I had it all ready for him, and he didn't come, so I went home at my usual time."

And so to the important question. When I'd told Hermione Wolde over the telephone that the doctor had rung me at two o'clock that afternoon she had sounded a bit surprised. Could Mrs. Nippen throw any light on that?

"Why, yes," she said. "It was the next day, I think, and Miss Wolde came into the kitchen all excited like. 'Maud,' she says, 'a gentleman just told me the doctor rang him with a message at two o'clock yesterday afternoon, and he keeps on saying he did.' 'That he certainly didn't, Miss,' I said. 'He was having his nap same as usual.'"

I got her to go into that. The doctor, it appeared, had his lunch at a quarter-past one: not at the hour because a patient might linger on after the official closing down at one o'clock. The meal usually lasted half an hour, and just before two o'clock he would settle down to his nap. As soon, in fact, as Mrs. Nippen had cleared the table. And though he snored, he was a light sleeper. That was why she didn't wash up till he'd woke at his usual twenty past two. What she did was make herself a cup of tea and read her paper. And that afternoon she was prepared to swear on her dying oath, as she put it, that the doctor hadn't used the telephone at two o'clock. She couldn't have failed to hear him if he had.

"What sort of a voice had he?"

"Well," she said, "a sort of a man's voice. Sort of a bass voice."

That was all I wanted to know.

"What was the idea?" Wharton was firing at me before the door had hardly closed. "Think it wasn't him who did the telephoning?"

"That's what I think now," I said. "What else can I think after what we heard?"

Wharton raised hands to heaven. More complications. If Chale himself hadn't telephoned to me, then who had? And how could we now believe the rest of what the supposed-Chale had told me: about the North London call and so on.

"But he didn't come in to tea and he did go somewhere," I said. "Wolde herself told me all about that. He probably went to some patient or other and came back here in a private car and dashed off again to catch a train."

Wharton snorted. He got to his feet.

"I'm going to get this case right in the open. I'll spread every newspaper with the real truth about Sindle, and have that Ferndale sketch. I'll open this wide too. Have her picture on the front pages. And put out another special S.O.S. for Chale."

"He's our man, sir?" ventured Matthews.

Wharton glared, then threw up his hands again.

"How do I know? If Sindle was trying to kill him, he might have got in first. Wolde might have known too much about that. She was poking about round at Borden Walk, wasn't she?"

He stamped off out of the room, but only as far as the hall.

"Look," he said to me. "You get yourself a quick meal and then get on to Finchley. If you run across anything promising, ring me here. I'll be back from the Yard by then. Take one of the cars outside."

I said I'd hop a bus and take my own car. We didn't know what might be at the other end, and a police car was rather too obvious. Wharton wasn't listening. He was already halfway up the stairs. All I got was a quick, cheerful wink from Matthews.

CHAPTER IX
CONCERNING MISS WOLDE

I WANTED a snack and a drink and no more, so I hopped a bus a street or two away and went into a little pub I sometimes visit at Leicester Square. Over my plebeian pint and plate of sandwiches I tried to do some thinking. Wharton, I told myself, would be thinking too. It wouldn't have taken him long to realise the full implications of Mrs. Nippen's insistence that Chale had been sleeping, not telephoning, at two o'clock on that Monday afternoon.

This, as I saw it, was the change that that insistence had brought to the case, and while I had my frugal meal I wrote my conclusions down. The logic of them seemed clear and inescapable. Summarised, they amounted to this: that if Chale hadn't telephoned, then all I had heard over that telephone was untrue. The props had been kicked from under the case and the whole structure of thought had collapsed into nonsense.

Did I think that Mrs. Nippen's evidence was reliable? The more I tested it, the more I did. Someone else had rung the Broad Street Detective Agency using Chale's name. That explained why he had not turned up at Broad Street for an appointment he had never made.

That brought me to the person who had used Chale's name. A man or a woman? Certainly not Wolde, or Mrs. Nippen would have heard her talking. But whoever it was, he had known that Chale *was* going out that evening, or else he had made an uncommonly good guess. And if it were he who had killed Hermione Wolde, then he must have had some knowledge at least of the house. And that rather pointed to a patient.

And what of the props that had been kicked out from under? We'd assumed that Chale had considered himself in danger, and almost certainly from a patient or ex-patient. That was a fabrication. *Or was it?* Was it true after all, and was X, the murderer of Wolde, aware of it? And a rider that had to be added was that the records had been burnt because they contained something that would incriminate X, the former patient. And Wolde had been murdered because she could have given the police the information, even though the documents were destroyed.

But when I faced up to Wharton's hint that Chale himself was our man, there ceased to be any logic. If Chale hadn't telephoned, then why had it been done by someone else? And how did it tie up with the Sindle case? Only because Sindle had been a patient of Chale. And, as I remembered, because Hermione Wolde had been snooping at Borden Walk on the night of the fire. But Chale hadn't been killed. It was Sindle who'd been killed.

And there was something to add to that snooping by Hermione Wolde: something that must have occurred to yourself. As near as I could remember, it was between half-past seven and eight o'clock when I had caught sight of her. But that night, if you remember, Chale had come dashing into his house at about half-past seven and had dashed out again after collecting his bag and giving Wolde certain instructions. So as soon as he'd gone off in that private car she had made her way to Borden Walk. She couldn't have been anxious about Chale. Was it about Sindle that she was anxious?

I didn't know. The answer should have been yes, but by the time I'd got that far my notes were a mass of contradictions and my wits were beginning to wobble. Thoughts were the squirrel in the cage. It was like being on a mental merry-go-round and circling and circling and never catching up with the horse in front. I gave it up. I'd finished my sandwiches, and I emptied the tankard and made my way out. I walked round to the garage and got into my car, and it was like a happy release. You can't do any thinking when you're driving through London traffic.

It was just short of three o'clock when I drew into Acacia Road with its plane trees and semi-detached Edwardian houses. I caught sight of an approaching postman.

"Could you tell me who's living at No. 18 now?"

"No. 18?" he said. "The name's Arnell."

"Arnold?" I hadn't caught it clearly.

"No," he said, and spelt the name for me.

I thanked him and moved the car on. I stopped just short of the house. It had an air of bourgeois well-being: its paintwork good, its curtains neatly hung, its crazy paving well cemented, and its formal, rather finicky beds of wallflowers and tulips. I walked up the front path between the standard roses and pushed the bell. I had to ring twice before I heard a sound, and then a woman opened the door. She looked as if she'd been tidying herself for the afternoon, and I caught a whiff of scented soap. She was a synthetic blonde, quite tall, slim almost to leanness, and in the early thirties. Two showy bangles trailed down the arm that held the door.

"Mrs. Arnell?"

"Yes," she said, and waited.

"You're a friend of Miss Hermione Wolde?"

"Yes," she said, and the eyes were opening a bit wider.

"I'm sorry to say she died very suddenly this morning."

Her mouth gaped.

"Died!" she said, and stared. "Not Hermy!"

"Afraid it's true," I said. "I'm from Scotland Yard. Perhaps you'd like to see this warrant card."

She took it, but I don't think she saw it. Her head was shaking and she was moistening her lips.

"Mind if I come in?" I said. "We think you could give us some help."

She merely turned away from the door, and I followed her into a tiny hall. She opened another door and drew back for me to enter. Her lip was puckering. She grabbed her bag from the sideboard and was dabbing at her eyes with a handkerchief.

"It must have been a shock to you," I said. "You saw her only on last Monday afternoon."

That was enough. All at once she was leaving the room. I heard a quick sob or two in the hall and her feet on the stairs. I sat on. It was a stodgy kind of dining-room furnished in fumed oak. The prints were meretricious and the mantelpiece garish. The usual marble clock was in its centre and two hideous vases flanked it. The room had a curious smell, and I tried to separate its ingredients. One seemed to be furniture polish and another was rather like boiled cabbage.

It must have been five minutes before she came back.

"It was silly of me," she said, "but I just couldn't help it. I've known Hermy all my life and it was such a shock. Will you have a cup of tea?"

"I expect you'd like one yourself," I said. "But just a question first. And perhaps I'd better explain why I'm here."

I made no bones about saying Hermione Wolde had been killed: possibly, I said, by a burglar. Mrs. Arnell must have read about such cases. I had to go carefully, mind you, to steer her gently from another flood of tears. I made quite a good hand of it. I had her so busy talking that she forgot all about the tea.

Alice Field was a farmer's daughter of Stedgham, a village about fifteen miles from Brumford. Hermione Wolde was an orphan who lived there with an aunt, and the two girls went to the village school together, then on to the local grammar school, and their minds were made up to go in, as Mrs. Arnell put it, for nursing. I gathered that during their training they put their heads together again and decided to specialise in obstetrics. That part was just a bit sketchy, but I didn't want to interrupt the even flow of talk.

Their first post was together at a maternity hospital near Leicester, and they were there till 1938. Then Hermione's aunt died and she'd come in for a nice sum of money. She'd been none too happy in her work—'Matron didn't understand her'—and the upshot was that she answered an advertisement and secured a post with Drs. Chale and Morse in Brumford.

"Pardon my interrupting you," I said, "but just what sort of a post?"

She thought it was what she called all sorts. She was secretary and receptionist and was qualified as a nurse. I was beginning to gather that Alice Field had had a girlish crush on Hermione Wolde: that Hermione—a year older—had dominated her, and that the passion of the younger woman for the older had lasted through their lives.

Alice Field knew very little about the Chale-Morse affair, other, I gathered, than what she had learned from Hermione. Hermione herself had stayed on with Chale till he left Brumford. Then she saw Alice and told her she was taking a job with an ambulance unit. Some months later Alice had a letter from Italy, where she was working at a base hospital. Alice answered the letter but had no reply. She thought that Hermione must have been killed.

Then suddenly she appeared again, and her specious story—that's what I thought it—was that she'd been sent home sick and had been given her discharge. Alice was then at Hollindale Maternity Hospital, on the outskirts of Brumford. There was a famine of nurses and Hermione got a job there too. That was in 1944. She had had what Alice called 'ever such a nice testimonial from that Dr. Chale'.

In 1945 she left, and in what seemed something of a hurry.

"It was the matron," Alice told me. "An old beast she was. Tried to make out Hermione was doing something she shouldn't. No one ever knew. A trumped-up affair, that's what I thought it, and Hermy knew it. But what could she do? It was her word against Matron's."

The next thing Alice heard was that Hermione was actually back with Dr. Chale, and in London. She herself had left Hollindale at about that time to get married—her husband, I gathered, was now something to do with radio-therapy—and to come to Acacia Road. She got into touch with Hermione and the old association was resumed. Hermione often came to see her, and they'd have tea together and a long chat or go shopping locally. Occasionally they'd have a day in town together. Once, when Chale was away, Alice Arnell had had an afternoon at Meriton Gardens.

That was the main story. There were a few probing questions it seemed necessary to put.

"Miss Wolde liked it at Meriton Gardens?"

"Oh, yes," she said. "She was well paid and she always did like that Dr. Chale. She was ever so comfortable. Treated her like a daughter, he did. She had a lovely mink coat he gave her this last Christmas. Said he couldn't get on without her."

"Ever hear her mention anyone called Sindle?"

"Never," she said. "Why, was it someone she knew?"

"She might have done," I said.

"I think she'd have told me," she said, and frowned. "We never had any secrets from each other, if you know what I mean."

I thought she was putting that a bit wrongly. The truth probably was that Hermione knew all about Alice, and had contrived to impart only just so much about herself. Credulous and besotted: that was how I was summing up Alice Arnell.

"What happened when she came here last Monday, Mrs. Arnell?"

"Nothing really," she said. "We had tea and talked, and then just as she was going my hubby came in, and that made her a bit late. Usually she went soon after five."

"She had nothing on her mind? No troubles or worries?"

"Not Hermy," she said. "Hermy had nothing to worry about."

"Curious she didn't marry," I said.

She flushed at that, and I didn't quite know why.

"I expect she could have done," she said. "We aren't all the marrying sort, you know."

She had almost bridled up. I slid gently away from the dead Hermione, and she remembered the cup of tea. I said I had to get back to Scotland Yard and she'd been more than helpful, and we were most grateful.

"Will it be in the papers?" she said.

I said it might be in that evening's papers.

"You haven't a photograph of her by any chance?"

She said she had several. She went up to fetch them from her bedroom and came down with quite a bundle. It looked to me as if she'd kept every possible photograph from her girlhood days. There were grammar-school groups; hospital groups; singles, in uniform and out, of herself and Hermione; and there was even one of Hermione that had been taken only that last Christmas. I asked if I might borrow it.

"You'll take great care of it?" she was telling me dubiously. "I wouldn't lose it for anything, especially not now. It's ever so good of her."

At the door she was saying she hoped we'd get whoever it was that had done it. I said that that was where she could be a help, and maybe I'd have to see her again.

I thought of telephoning Wharton, then changed my mind and drove straight back to Meriton Gardens. Nothing of consequence had happened since I'd seen him, and he was pricking his ears at what I had to tell.

"Been a bit of a flyer in her time," was how he summarised Hermione Wolde. "A first-class liar too, or my name's Robinson. That Arnell woman seems a bit of a fool."

"I'm wondering if she ever was in Italy," I said. "Also I'd like to know why she got the sack from places."

"Yes," he said, and pursed his lips. "That last place she was at. What'd you say it was called?"

"Hollindale Maternity Hospital. In the outer suburbs of Brumford."

"Look," he said. "Drop in at the Yard and have them take a copy of that photograph. Then go on to this Hollindale place and see what you can find out. I'll let them know you're coming."

That's what I did. While I was waiting for the photograph I got a room booked for myself at the Regal Hotel. I also had a look at a large-scale map of Brumford and made a note of the bus route. Then I went on to the flat, packed a small bag, and caught the six-five. I had dinner on the train—that kept me from too much thinking—and I'd nicely finished my coffee as the train drew in. I took a taxi to the hotel, decided I might as well keep it waiting, and it got me to the hospital at about nine o'clock.

It was a biggish place. The secretary was waiting for me, and we went into his office. His name was Sparling: a kindly, benevolent-looking man: tall, rather bald, and aged about sixty.

"I've had quite a long talk with your Chief Superintendent," he told me, "and I think I'm fairly conversant with what you want to know. I've been looking up our records, such as we have."

"What we want," I said, "is everything whatsoever that has in any way to do with this Hermione Wolde. Nothing's too insignificant."

"I gathered that," he said, and was smiling as he passed me his cigarette-case. "I've jotted down some facts in chronological order, as far as I've been able. But one thing I haven't put down. It's highly confidential. It's to do with the reasons for her dismissal."

I said it might help straighten things out if I first told him about my afternoon at Acacia Road. I even told him my views on the relationships between Hermione and Alice.

"That's what we have so far," I said. "Now then; you tell me what's wrong with it."

"Well," he said, and almost apologetically, "I'm afraid that everything's wrong with it. The Wolde woman must, as you say, have had the other woman completely under her thumb. As you put it, she was credulous and besotted. The actual facts are these."

That story about the matron was a gross fabrication. The relationships between her and the staff were uniformly good. Individual people might have grievances at various times—that was inevitable—but to allude to her as the Arnell woman had done was malicious libel.

"But about Wolde," he said, and was giving me a quizzical sort of look. "A hospital like this is for the just and the unjust. There's no discrimination against the unmarried mother."

"Why should there be?"

"Exactly. And it was an unmarried mother who was behind this Wolde affair. The baby was born dead and the mother had a bad time. Some months later the mother married, and she didn't tell her husband that she'd borne a child to another man. Wolde happened to know about this marriage and attempted to blackmail the wife. The wife came to me. She was terrified of publicity, which is why she didn't go to the police. You may not believe it, but I'm the recipient of quite a lot of confidences."

"On the other hand, I most certainly believe it," I told him.

"Well, there it was," he said. "There was a confrontation and Wolde was dismissed on the spot and warned that if she made the least trouble the police would be given the facts. I'm not sure now that that was the wisest action. And that's almost the last I heard of her till this evening."

"What was Wolde's attitude at the confrontation?"

"Most indignant. Brazen about the whole thing. Said it was her word against the other woman's. Which it was, really, except that we had no doubts. Especially after a second and similar case came to fight after she'd gone."

"She'd begun making it a racket?"

"That's what it looked like," he said. "I regarded her as a very dangerous woman."

"I'm most grateful," I told him. "What I've learned is just the kind of thing we wanted."

"You're not going into things any farther?"

I assured him there'd be no need, and that there'd be no publicity. Then I was asking him if Wharton had mentioned the name of her last employer. Wharton hadn't.

"Chale," I said.

He stared.

"Not Arthur Chale!"

"Arthur Chale," I said. "He used to be in Brumford. You knew him?"

"Did I not," he said. "And his cousin, Colin Morse."

"Then do you remember that when Wolde applied for an appointment here she put in an excellent reference from Chale?"

He said that was news to him. But the war years had been a hectic time, with innumerable comings and goings, and he'd been far from handling everything himself.

"To be perfectly frank," he said, "we were often so short of staff that only the most elementary enquiry would be made into credentials. But Wolde was well qualified, mind you."

"Getting back to Chale," I said, "and everything in the strictest confidence. That celebrated blackmail case, for instance."

"Chale got off," he said reflectively. "I don't see anything else that could have been done. It was a mistaken direction ever to have proceeded against him. He was merely Morse's partner."

"A queer sort of partnership, surely? A general practitioner and a psychiatrist?"

"Not necessarily," he said. "Chale was more than a general practitioner: a physician and surgeon in fact. He and Morse had a big house and worked under the same roof. Probably had some arrangement about profits, and that's all there'd be to it. Occasionally, of course, there'd be overlapping. Chale might think one of his own cases might be better handled by Morse."

"And what did you think of Chale?"

"Chale?" he said. "Well, he was just a bit colourless. A quiet, rather pontifical sort of manner. Quite a good surgeon."

I said I'd heard applied to him the phrase about still waters running deep. In fact it had been hinted to me that he'd had a narrow escape.

"I wouldn't like to say," he told me. "He was the sort of chap you could never get thoroughly into, if you know what I mean."

"He ticked, but you never knew how."

"Exactly. But Morse—he was very different. A man of tremendous charm. Most attractive sort of chap. And yet, you know—and don't accuse me of being wise after the event—I never really cottoned to him. I didn't exactly trust him."

"You knew he was dead?"

"Yes," he said. "Double-crossed even the Germans, if I remember rightly, and they shot him."

"What one might call rough justice," I said. "But about Chale. You didn't know that he's in practice in London, as a psychiatrist? Isn't that rather a curious switch-over?"

"I don't know," he said. "Both he and Morse were highly qualified. Chale would be bound to have a pretty good knowledge. I imagine that, except in actual surgery, either could have acted for the other. Hence, you might say, the partnership."

"Were they spenders?"

"I don't remember that Chale was. Morse certainly must have got through quite a lot of money. He was a heavy subscriber to various things and entertained a good deal."

"A good amateur painter too, I'm told."

"I'm no judge, but I believe he was. A many-sided man. A pity that one with his gifts should have made such a sorry mess of life."

That was practically where our talk ended, and it was in some ways how it had begun. Sparling wanted me to walk the few yards to his place for coffee or a drink, but I said I'd have my report to write, and the first train in the morning would be seeing me away. But when he learned that I was going back to the city by bus he insisted on getting out his car. A fine character, Sparling. And yet he'd been rather puzzled why people should come to him with their troubles.

I began that report that night and finished it in the morning's train, and one thing that struck me was that Sparling had either been charitably minded or had totally lacked my kind of curiosity, for except in the case of Wolde—and there it had been only a suggestion—blackmail had never been mentioned. And yet I was now seeing it as the very warp and woof that patterned the case.

I even ventured for once to set down such ideas as had occurred to me, and keeping to those which Wharton would find it hard to refute. There was the fact that Wolde had worked with Chale before that blackmail case and had stayed on with him till he left Brumford. And after the picture I'd been given of Wolde it wasn't unreasonable to wonder if she'd known far more about things than Chale had thought, and that she'd even applied a certain amount of pressure. And there was the undoubted fact that after she'd been dismissed for attempted blackmail she'd made straight as a homing pigeon for Meriton Gardens and Chale. And in due course she'd taken up her quarters in the same house.

Then was Matthews right? Had Chale been in the blackmail racket in his Brumford days, and was he still in it? Had he—as Wharton had begun to think—killed Wolde because she had become an incubus, and destroyed the records because they might lead to the truth? I was inclined to think that both were right. In any case, it was something I should want to talk over with Wharton.

CHAPTER X
CLIMAX

I WASN'T to see Wharton that morning. As soon as I got to Euston I rang the Yard and was told he wasn't there, but he'd left word for me that he ought to be back by the end of the morning. Matthews, I was told, was at Meriton Gardens, so I took a taxi and went straight there.

Meriton Gardens was still cordoned off and traffic diverted, and that was just as well considering the revelations in the morning's papers. Wharton had certainly carried out his threats. The popular papers had had their banner headlines and the columns were splashed with pictures. Both cases were there. About Sindle there was as much as I knew myself, with a reproduction of Ferndale's sketch. There was a photograph of the studio as the firemen had left it, and in the text a subtle query as to whether or not Sindle had been known to any dealers.

In the other case the studio portrait of Hermione Wolde had been reproduced, with a front view of No. 15, Meriton Gardens. There was also, and again very subtly, a picture of

Chale—unearthed, it subsequently transpired, from the morgue of the Brumford paper. And the two cases were connected by a question in heavy type: a question doubtless insisted on by Wharton—

WHY WAS HERMIONE WOLDE AT BORDEN WALK ON THE EVENING OF SINDLE'S MURDER?

I walked from the end of the road to the house. A man was on the door and another at the telephone, and one or two others were still working in the house. Matthews was in the kitchen having a cup of coffee with Mrs. Nippen. He and I adjourned with my cup to the waiting-room. I wanted to know where Wharton was.

"Don't know," he said. "A call came through from Cave and his eyes shot out of his head. I heard him say 'It can't be right!' just as if the devil had kicked him endways."

"Anything new here?"

"If so, I haven't heard it," he told me. "Plenty of Wolde's prints, and Chale's. No record of either of 'em at the Yard. Nothing in the mail. Not a damn' thing, except that Sindle was a vegetarian."

I took a quick look at him. I never know when Matthews is trying to pull my leg.

"That's okay," he said. "He told his grocer so. Used to buy a lot of stuff out of tins: baked beans and vegetables and all that. I reckon that's why he had nothing but soup at the Tabby Cat."

It was still only eleven o'clock, and I seemed to have time on my hands. A couple of things had occurred to me as I'd been reading those newspapers, so I asked Matthews if he'd send my bag round to the Yard, as I was thinking of making a couple of calls. But I took the precaution of having the Markov number rung. Bintwood was there. I said I'd be along in about ten minutes.

He was on the look-out for me. It was he who suggested we should have a cup of coffee in a nearby café. I hoped it would taste more like the real thing than the one I'd just had from Mrs. Nippen.

"Borden Walk's right in the news," he told me as soon as we'd sat down. "Can't say as I like it a lot myself. Bit of a startler too, to hear that Sindle was murdered. I suppose you've known it all along."

I said he knew how it was. There were things about murder cases that you couldn't even breathe to your wife.

"Funny about this other murder case," he said, "and that woman being seen at No. 7 after Sindle was killed. And about that doctor she was working for. They tell me there's twice been an S.O.S. out for him."

Our coffee came. He didn't take sugar, so there was the more for me.

"About this Wolde murder," I said, and stirred the coffee reflectively. "I've been wondering a couple of things. For instance, did she ever go to the Tabby Cat?"

He frowned.

"Can't say that I ever saw her there myself—unless that picture in the paper was a bad one."

"You can take it from me that it was uncommonly good," I said. "But there's something I'd like you to do, if you can spare the time and you think there's anything in it. We could drop in at the Tabby Cat on our way."

I explained that we'd been interested in Meriton Gardens— for reasons I wasn't free to state—even before Wolde was murdered. I'd gone there when I'd left him and the girls that night after our dinner at the Tabby Cat, hoping Wolde would be in. Nobody was in, and yet I suspected that she had been in the house and had deliberately refused to open the door: again for reasons which I wasn't at liberty to state. But that night Pamela Maine had taken a walk that way, and I told him what I'd seen.

"I know that Wolde wasn't murdered that night," I said, "but what kept Miss Maine staring at that house? Did she see Wolde watching me from behind the curtains? And could she be asked? And there's a more important question. Did she go that way again on the night of the murder? If so, she might have seen something we'd be uncommonly grateful to know."

"A tricky business," he said. "Mind you, she's very clear-headed of a morning. I might try if I can get anything out of her. Can't say I like it, but there we are. Better let me do the talking."

I said I'd be only too glad not to talk myself.

"Might as well get going," he said, and finished his coffee. It had been good coffee and I wouldn't have minded another cup. He paid at the desk, slipped across to the shop for a minute, and then we were on our way. We skirted Meriton Gardens and in three or four minutes were at the Tabby Cat. He waited outside while I did the questioning.

I saw both Laura and Nancy. We looked at the picture in their paper and at the photograph I still had in my breast pocket. Hermione Wolde had never set foot inside the Tabby Cat.

"If she had, I'd have been sure to remember her," Nancy said. "I can't even remember anyone like her."

That seemed conclusive. Bintwood and I walked on to Borden Walk. A constable was doing sentry-go outside No. 7, ready to handle the overcurious.

"I live here," Bintwood told him. I flashed my warrant card and in we went. I could hear Gulver about somewhere in his rooms, but it was quiet enough on the landing. Bintwood made a gesture for silence and listened at Pamela Maine's door. Then he was tiptoeing across and opening his own door.

"Someone in there with her. I think it's a Mrs. Thorne. One or two friends from the old days look her up regularly."

He left the door just ajar, and when we talked it was with an ear for the opening of that other door across the landing.

"I'll show you that Gauguin sketch," he said, and went into the next room, which I could see was his bedroom. What he showed me was a sheet of brown cardboard. That brown had been left untouched for the flesh tints of two native girls whose figures had been roughly blocked in. The faces were almost finished and swift lines of red and green indicated a background of sand and palms.

"You don't like it?" he said.

"As a bit of Gauguin—yes," I said. "But I don't like Gauguin. I've queer tastes like that. For instance, I hate the sight of majolica, and ivories, and French clocks. I don't even care a lot for glass. That doesn't say I don't know this is something pretty valuable."

"Picked it up in a dirty little shop in the Rue Costanges," he said. "It was framed and glazed, and it and some more junk cost me sixty francs."

"How long ago was that?"

"As far back as '29. I happened to be over there for a few days."

"And what's it worth?"

"Depends on how badly someone wants it. A couple of hundred pounds? Three? I don't know."

There was a sound from outside and then the women's voices. Bintwood opened a handy drawer and put the Gauguin away. We stepped out to the landing. Pamela Maine was giving a last wave and a goodbye to the visitor. She turned at the sound of us.

"Hallo, young lady? You're very gay this morning?" Bintwood said jokingly.

"I feel gay," she said, and just a bit archly. "It's Mr. Travers, isn't it?"

"It is," I said. "How are you, Miss Maine?"

"I'm very well indeed," she said. And she looked it. The cheeks had a slight flush and the eyes were almost mischievously alert. She had taken it apparently for granted that we should follow her through the open door.

"I want to tell you how very much my wife admired that lampshade," I said. "She thought it was simply beautiful."

"That was very sweet of her," she said, and she was putting on the linen smock again. Beneath the window stood a small trestle table, and on it were her painting materials and some parchment that had been temporarily wired.

"You're making another?" Bintwood said.

"This is for Muriel," she said. "Muriel Thorne," she explained to me. "She used to be in musical comedy, you know. A dear, kind soul."

She showed us a coloured print: a panoramic view of the Strand with the Gaiety dominating the left foreground; horse vehicles everywhere, and women in trailing skirts and all the rest of the early Edwardiana.

"It's a kind of souvenir," she said. "Quite nice, don't you think?"

We said it was charming.

"I'm going to enjoy painting it," she said. "Almost my only enjoyment nowadays, and perhaps it's as well."

"Come, come now," Bintwood told her amusedly. "You mustn't talk like that. What about those little evening walks of yours. Don't you enjoy them?"

He didn't wait for an answer. He was striking, as it were, while the iron was hot.

"Which reminds me. Mr. Travers caught sight of you out for a walk last Tuesday night. You got as far as Meriton Gardens."

"Meriton Gardens?" Her head turned slowly and she was looking at me, and all at once there was something different about her eyes. "At Meriton Gardens?"

"I saw you distinctly," I said, and forced a smile. "You were just coming home from your walk. Then you stopped and had a good look at one of the houses. Don't you remember? Just as if you'd seen something unusual."

Her eyes were on me, and yet I was sure that she didn't really see me. There was something uncanny about it and the sudden heavy silence in the room.

"Yes," she said. "But I didn't see him. I *have* seen him. I see all sorts of things. It's no use him trying to hide."

"Whom have you seen?" I asked her gently.

"You know," she said. "Everyone knows. And he knows. That's why he's trying to hide."

There was something almost frightening about the curl of her lip. Bintwood was pulling at my sleeve. Even he couldn't find quite the right words.

"We have to be going now," he told her, and put out his hand. I was already at the door, and I heard him telling her that I'd be coming again some other time. I wondered if she'd heard him, and then Bintwood was closing the door.

"That was dreadful," I said. "Did you see that look in her eyes?"

"My fault," he said, and made a gesture of exasperation as he turned to the stairs. "Something I ought to have known, and I only thought of it when she began running on about Meriton Gardens. I ought to have spotted it in the paper this morning when I saw the name and the photograph."

"What photograph?"

"The one of that psychiatrist—Chale."

"What about him?"

"Well, he's the one she was talking about. The one she reckoned killed her daughter. He lives at that No. 15 where you saw her."

I couldn't speak for a moment.

"All the same, I wouldn't have had it happen for worlds," he said. "Right up to the time of the fire and that Sindle business she was practically as right as rain. Remember when you and the superintendent had us in Ferndale's place? Just as sensible, she was, as you and me. Everyone was thinking she'd forgotten about that delusion, and now you and I have to go and start it all over again."

"We couldn't have told," I said. "And it was something that had to be done."

"She'll get over it," he told me more cheerfully. "I did tell you about the daughter, didn't I? After that breakdown of hers someone recommended her to go to that psychiatrist, Chale. He was still treating her, if that's what you call it, when she did that jump out of the window. Poor old Pamela was always against her going to Chale, and that's how she got the bee in her bonnet."

"A bad business," I said. "Let's hope she begins forgetting it again."

We'd been walking back towards Sloane Square, which was really out of my way, so we had a last word, and then he went on and I turned back. I'd intended going through Howe Street, but as I came to the corner I saw Gulver having a word with the constable at the door of No. 7. Just as I got there the two separated. The constable resumed his beat, and I followed Gulver in.

"Hallo, sir?" he said, and tipped a finger to his forehead. "Rare nice weather we're having. Reckon we shall have to pay for it later, though."

I said perhaps we should. I asked if I could have a quick, private word with him, and he opened the door of his sitting-room, as he called it.

"You're pretty snug here?" I said. "Nice little spot for a cold winter night. Do you hear a lot of Miss Maine up there above you?"

"Very little, sir. I hear her wireless sometimes of an evening. And that's a funny thing, sir. You'd think she'd like plays. But does she? Not a bit of it. Music is the only thing she likes. Can't stand them wireless plays at any price."

"No great men since Agamemnon," I said, "which is Greek for the fact that there were no times like the old times."

"And isn't that true, sir?"

"Maybe," I said, "but we mustn't let anyone hear us say so. Those are the times Miss Maine lives in. And that reminds me."

It didn't take a lot of catechising to learn that he knew all about Barbara Maine and the delusions of her mother, but it was news to him that Chale was the mem. Things worked up to quite a climax as he gradually realised that much, and that he'd Chale's photograph to hand in his newspaper, and that there'd been a murder at Chale's very house.

"His secretary, wasn't it, sir?"

I said it was.

"I suppose you didn't know her, sir?"

I said I'd talked to her over the telephone before she was murdered. That seemed to give me in his eyes a vast respect, or should I say notoriety?

"I'm going to trust you, Gulver," I said. "You're not being exactly put on the payroll at Scotland Yard, but there's something we'd like you to do."

I asked him if Miss Maine ever confided in him: talked freely, if he liked, about herself. He said she did. He did all sorts of odd jobs for her and was glad to. And she seemed to regard him as of her generation, though he didn't put it quite like that. So I told him precisely what we wanted him to do: to bring talk round to her nightly walks. Not to stress things, but to get her, if possible, to do the talking. We were convinced, I said, that she must have seen something at Meriton Gardens on the Tuesday night. If she also saw something on the night of the murder, there was no need to stress the importance of that.

Tact and more tact, and the need for yet more tact—that's what I kept driving in.

"For instance, suppose you're on the look-out tonight and she goes for one of her walks. That gives you the chance to mention her walks. You might even walk a few yards with her. You might even pretend you're going her way. You might watch her start off and then overtake her. All sorts of choices, but you see what I mean."

He said he saw it.

"And another thing," I said. "Make an excuse to see the girls and mention the Meriton Gardens murder. Bring in, sort of casually, that Miss Maine often walks that way of a night. Then you look surprised. 'Why!' you say. 'She might have been past there right at the time of the murder! Wonder if she saw anything?' If you play your cards right, that ought to make the girls pretty inquisitive, and you bet your life they'll try and find out anything they can from Miss Maine in their own way; and if they do hear anything, you'll be told about it."

"I reckon I can manage that, sir," he said. "And what about Mr. Bintwood?"

"He knows all about it," I said. "All the same, you're on no account to let him have the faintest idea that I've had this little talk with you."

"I get you, sir. And what about Mr. Ferndale?"

"He's different," I said. "He doesn't actually five here."

"But she has a very great liking for him," he said. "He can do more with her than anyone—even Mr. Bintwood."

"Well, you'll have to use your own judgment," I told him. "But never a hint, of course, that you've been talking with me. He'll be here today?"

"Never on Fridays, sir—not if he can help it. Tomorrow morning he'll be here. He's doing some alterations to a Lady Someone-or-the-other. Real faddy some of 'em are—so he was telling me."

That was all, but I went over it again. I made him understand that on no account was her peace of mind to be disturbed. It was she who was somehow to do the talking. Then when I'd finally left him I was having queer twinges of conscience. I actually stopped in my tracks, and I was trying to reconcile the urgent needs of justice with the mental needs of Pamela Maine.

And all at once I was hating it all. I knew with a quick alarm that Gulver would never play rightly that role of which I'd so casually assumed him capable. I almost turned back with the sudden determination to see him again and cancel the whole thing; and then I realised that I'd put ideas into his mind, and that, whatever I now said, he'd have his own methods and urge to find things out. He couldn't do otherwise. It was part of the make-up of his social class: the morbid interest in murder and the joy in it as a topic for conversation.

I walked on, and I was telling myself that everything would be purely private, and that even if Pamela Maine had seen something vital we would never dream of putting her into a witness-box. We wouldn't even let her know that it was of importance. And it might be of importance. There was, in fact, no telling what she might have seen on that murder night. She might have seen Chale entering his house. 'I *have* seen him.' That's what she'd said. 'I see all sorts of things.'

It's funny how that thing we call conscience will never let us rest. That's one of my liabilities as a sleuth. I'm not ruthless enough: I even have too sloppily sentimental a heart. As I walked on towards my bus I was still unable to get Pamela Maine entirely from my mind. I distracted myself with the old tag that the world was a very small place, and how curious it had nevertheless been that Borden Walk should have had yet another connection with Meriton Gardens. I looked about me as I walked and tried to keep the whole thing from my mind, but all the time a face would keep coming between me and the things I only partly saw: the face of Pamela Maine, the set look of it, the unseeing eyes, and the queer smile that had drooped her lip when she had told herself aloud—not us, mind you, but herself— that Chale had hidden himself because he knew.

Knew what? That was what I asked myself. Knew some secret truth about the death of Barbara Maine? A truth that Pamela herself had discerned? I didn't know. And then I saw my bus approaching and I lengthened my stride to catch it. And taking my seat made a kind of finality and the end of an episode, and I could tell myself that what had happened that morning at Borden Walk was a purely private affair of my own, and that never a word of it should be mentioned to George Wharton.

Who should be in Wharton's room but Matthews. He had had a telephone message from Wharton to get back to the Yard.

"Don't know what it is," he said, "but something's cooking. You can't mistake that tone in his voice."

It was getting on for half-past twelve. I'd breakfasted soon after seven, and I lighted my pipe to stay a gnawing stomach. Matthews lighted a cigarette and we naturally began talking about the Meriton Gardens case. He'd had the job that morning of going through all Chale's medical books leaf by leaf in case there might be some loose sheet inside with any sort of clue.

"Didn't come across a thing," he said. "Just a few notes in the margins which I was noting down when I got that telephone call."

"The books were all on what you'd call psychiatry?"

"All sorts," he said. "Medical books. Don't know if the Super told you, but we steamed off a book-plate from two or three of them and found someone else's name underneath. A cousin of his, who used to be in practice with him."

"A Colin Morse?"

"That's it," he said. "And a Brumford address."

A familiar step was on the landing. The door opened and Wharton came in. He peered at us as if we'd hardly a right to be there, then hung up hat and coat.

"Find out anything special?" he asked me.

"Quite a lot about Wolde," I said. "For instance, she was summarily dismissed from that hospital for attempted blackmail."

He raised his eyebrows.

"Thought it might be something of the sort," he said, and began stoking his pipe. Something was in the wind, for he did even that with too great an air of nonchalance.

"You didn't happen to find anything about Chale while you were that way?"

"A few things, opinions mostly. You'll find everything in the report."

"It may be useful and it may not," he said, and I knew that something was coming. "I've been learning things this morning about Chale myself. And I'll lay you a fiver you'll never guess what."

"Take that as read," I said. "What was it you learned?"

"That he's dead."

I gaped. I heard a kind of grunt from Matthews.

"Yes," said George, enjoying his moment. "He's deader than mutton. It was his body in Sindle's studio. It wasn't Sindle."

Chapter XI

A FRESH START

WHARTON explained. According to him there wasn't a shadow of doubt about who'd been killed in Sindle's studio. Chale's own teeth had been recognised by Chale's own dentist, a Mr. H. of Russell Street. Only some twelve months previously Chale had had three extractions, followed by the necessary alterations to both plates. One of the extractions had been difficult, and intricate X-ray photographs had been taken before and after. Those later ones were in every way identical with the jaw and teeth that had been supposed to be Sindle's. The specialist agreed and so did Cave.

But there was more in it than even that. Cave hadn't been happy from his first examination of the corpse. Certain things were out of keeping with what he'd been told about Sindle. For one thing the body was far too clean. Sindle had been described as slovenly and dirty. And there'd been no trace of drugs or alcoholism.

But as soon as those teeth revelations now pointed to Chale there had been a further cross-checking through the stomach content. Chale's lunch had been at one-fifteen as usual, and Mrs. Nippen had remembered the menu. That alone furnished unquestionable proof that the dead man was Chale, and it placed the time of death at between half-past three and four o'clock.

The whole thing was beyond argument, Wharton said, and, as if to prove it, he began asking me about the Brumford visit. After I'd given him a quick synopsis I thought I'd better tell him that I'd just learned from Bintwood that it was Chale who'd been treating the late Barbara Maine. He seemed interested.

"Anything about him is important now," he said. "Looks as if we've got to make a fresh start."

"We can really start off with the certainty that it was Chale's body in the studio?"

"Take it from me that you can," he said. "And there's another confirmation those dentists don't know about. We've been worrying why Wolde went to Borden Walk. Now we know. She was looking for Chale, not Sindle."

We settled down to a conference. I'm not going to bore you with everything that was said—that would take several chapters—but I'll give you a few highlights: just the kind of questions you may be asking yourself. Maybe you'll find different answers.

I believe I set the ball rolling with the rueful remark that everything that Wolde had told me about Chale's movements on that Monday evening had been sheer invention and carefully calculated lies. Chale must have gone straight from Meriton Gardens to Borden Walk that afternoon, and that was the end of him. That statement about his ringing her up and coming home in a private car and dashing out of the house again was nothing but bunkum and lies.

"That's pretty plain now," Wharton told me piously. There's always something in the follies of our friends which is not wholly displeasing to us. "Ingenious, that about the private car. She didn't want us to prove the story wrong by a check-up on taxis. About Borden Walk. As I see it, she expected to find him at home when she got back from Finchley, but he wasn't. But she'd known he was going to see Sindle, and she got more and more anxious, and finally she went round there herself to spy out the land. We don't know how long she was in the neighbourhood before, you saw her. She must have learned about the fire, though, and Sindle having died in it: after all, the firemen didn't make any secret of it. And what would she think? I say that Chale had killed him. Why she thought that doesn't matter for the moment; but if she didn't think it, why did she start covering up for Chale and inventing things about his movements? And that's why she kept dodging an interview with you, Travers. She thought she might make a slip if she was closely questioned."

"When I think about those broadcasts for Chale!" Matthews told us exasperatedly. "Flogging a dead horse, that's all we were."

"I wouldn't say that," Wharton told him. "It got his name into people's minds. It may pay some dividends yet. And it isn't as if we've lost a lot of time."

"Time enough for Sindle to get clean away," Matthews said.

"If he killed Wolde as well," Wharton pointed out, "then he hasn't had all that time."

I asked if we might make a start by getting various things unquestionably clear. For instance, why did Chale go to Sindle's studio?

"Sindle was an ex-patient," Wharton said. "That's one of the few absolute certainties. Chale got him that studio because he wanted to help him. We know that from Mrs. Oddfort."

"Then let's start building on that," I said. "I suggest that if Chale went to Sindle, then it wasn't anything to do with treatment. Any treatment would surely have been at Meriton Gardens. Therefore Sindle asked Chale most urgently to come and see him for a purely personal reason: for financial help, shall we say, or to get him out of some scrape."

Wharton didn't agree. He didn't see Chale going to see an almost down-and-out like Sindle unless he were absolutely forced.

"I'm going to suggest in a minute or two," he said, "that Sindle had some hold over Chale. Just note it down with a question mark and leave it, and let's approach it from another angle. I'd like to know, for instance, who it was that rang you, Travers, at the Broad Street Detective Agency last Monday afternoon. Mrs. Nippen was positive that Chale himself didn't."

"And I'm just as sure that Wolde didn't," I said. "When I told her I'd been talking to Chale at two o'clock she showed an immediate and genuine surprise. It was so genuine that at once she tried to cover it up. So the only one who could have been talking to me, trying to use Chale's voice, must have been Sindle."

Wharton pursed his lips. That Sindle should have rung was fantastic. He must have known that he was going to try to kill Chale an hour or so later, and yet he'd warned the Broad Street Detective Agency that Chale was in danger of his life!

"Everyone says Sindle was a bit cracked," Matthews said. "If so, there's no accounting for his actions."

"Cracked?" Wharton said. "If he was cracked, then he had more brains still left than a good many people I won't name. He planned that murder and carried it out. He put his own clothes on Chale and probably put Chale's clothes on himself. He put a spare set of his own teeth in Chale's mouth and got that fire going so that we shouldn't recognise Chale's features or get his prints. He'd concealed his own tracks and he had somewhere to dodge afterwards. If all that's the work of a lunatic, then I wouldn't mind being mad myself."

He gave himself a smile as a kind of pat on the back.

"There's no denying much of that, George," I said. "But it still doesn't answer your own question as to why Sindle should inform me that Chale was in danger."

"Wait a minute," he said. "I wouldn't be so sure. Just let's try to work up to something. You agree that Sindle and Wolde must have been well acquainted with each other?"

"They must have," I said. "One gathers that Sindle had a fairly protracted treatment from Chale, so Wolde must have seen him often enough at Meriton Gardens."

"And Wolde knew Chale was going to see him that afternoon?"

"She did. That's why she knew where to go looking for him."

"And therefore she regarded Sindle as a dangerous customer?"

"Presumably, yes."

"Right," he said. "Let's see if we can assess why he was dangerous. In a physical or bodily way? I'd say no. If he had been, then Chale wouldn't have gone to his studio alone. So that brings us to this. I say that Sindle was a menace in another way. He might even have been blackmailing Chale and Wolde. He might have been threatening to bring some sort of action for wrong diagnosis or treatment. After that business of Barbara Maine, Chale wouldn't want that kind of publicity."

I said I was with him practically all the way. But we still had no answer as to why Sindle should ring me about Chale being in danger of his life. Wharton smiled. It was that Colosseum smile, as I've often called it: the one made by a lion who's chosen for himself a particularly plump Christian.

"I'm just about to give you the answer. But let's clear something up first. You'll agree that Chale wouldn't want any scandal and neither would Wolde. That's got to be true: otherwise why did she tell you all those lies and why didn't she go to the police? So Sindle must have had some real hold over the pair of them. And now about that question that's worrying you. I say the answer's perfectly simple. Sindle didn't telephone. *Wolde did.*"

"Wait a minute," I said. "That makes Mrs. Nippen's evidence all wrong."

"Oh, no," he told me blandly. "She was prepared to swear that Chale himself didn't do the telephoning. She didn't say anything about Wolde. She didn't even mention where Wolde was. I say that Wolde slipped out of the house and telephoned. And because she was privately a bit scared about Chale going to see Sindle."

"What about her voice?" ventured Matthews.

"Got a short memory, haven't you?" Wharton told him brusquely. "What about that Epsom case and Mrs. Horlet? Why shouldn't a woman be able to imitate a man's deep voice? And I think we have a confirmation. Mr. Travers said the voice was pompous, and that's another word for stilted. He also said there was a lot of throat-clearing, and that suggests someone not too sure of his or her voice."

He waved a hand of dismissal.

"In any case there's a test we can apply. We can find out if Wolde *couldn't* have telephoned."

He asked for the Meriton Gardens number. A couple of minutes and he was speaking to Mrs. Nippen. Two more minutes and he was thanking her and ringing off.

"There we are," he said. "She thought Wolde might be upstairs. She didn't know. She just thought."

What could I say? I hadn't a better theory myself, and Wharton's was at least a basis on which to build. And we had to begin somewhere.

"Would you mind just spending a minute or two more on it?" I said. "Let's assume that Wolde did the telephoning and because she was anxious about Chale's safety. Then why didn't she want a bodyguard for him *at once*! Surely that afternoon was when someone ought to have been keeping him in sight?"

"Don't know," Wharton said, and suddenly he was far less happy. "It certainly does look as if she didn't think there was any immediate danger. I think, by the way, that when Chale got home that evening—which he didn't—she'd have told him what she'd done. She'd have induced him to keep that appointment she'd made for the following morning."

"Maybe," I said, "but still everything isn't clear. Let's listen to her doing that telephoning. She says Chale may need a body-guard and she makes an appointment for noon the next day. Then why obscure it all by telling me about North London, and going into reasons why Chale couldn't have me see him at once, and pretending to think of something that would make Chale come to me and not I to him?"

"That was nothing," Wharton told us. "She was just sparring for time. Wanted to bolster the yarn up a bit. Besides, she couldn't really do anything till she'd talked later to Chale."

"Very well," I said, "but answer me this. We've agreed that Wolde was anxious about Chale last Monday afternoon?"

"Most certainly we have."

"If she hadn't been," Matthews said, "she wouldn't have gone snooping round at Borden Walk."

"Then what about this?" I said. "When I was at Finchley I questioned Mrs. Arnell most carefully as to whether or not Wolde had shown any anxiety or been anything but her normal self that afternoon, and she assured me there'd been nothing the least abnormal about her. And not only that. Wolde didn't hurry back. She even stayed on after her usual time chatting to Mr. Arnell."

There wasn't an answer. We were trying to build something firm and solid, and you can't get very high when the base itself is tottery. A minute or two and Wharton was suggesting exasperatedly that we should shift ground to the actual Wolde murder.

"Sindle killed her? That's agreed?"

It was agreed. We settled down to the question of why. And the only answer had to be that Wolde knew something dangerous about Sindle.

"But just a minute," he said. "We don't want to obscure the question, but we haven't yet thought about why Sindle killed Chale. I'd say that Chale knew too much about Sindle, and Sindle was afraid he'd blow the gaff. But getting back to Wolde. I don't think there's any doubt as to why Sindle did her in. Not only did she know whatever it was that Chale knew, but after Chale's murder she knew something else. She knew that nobody but Sindle could have killed him."

Matthews said he still didn't get it why she didn't go to the police.

"She couldn't," Wharton said. "Or, rather, she daren't. She couldn't give Sindle away without convicting herself."

Then he was suddenly frowning.

"I wonder if she had the brazen effrontery to try and black-mail Sindle about Chale's death? It seems in character. That might be why Sindle did her in. He'd have taken Chale's keys from him, and he could have let himself into the house whenever Mrs. Nippen wasn't there."

I doubted if she'd have blackmailed him for money. It looked to me more like an attempt by Wolde to strike some kind of bargain.

"About what?" Matthews said.

"Well, she knew he'd killed Chale. On the other hand, we're assuming he knew a good deal about her. And in that context, we're not sure that it was Sindle who burnt the records. She might have done it. Everything was stone cold that morning when we got there."

After that we came to a brick wall. We hunted for openings and found none. We went over everything again, hoping that something new would emerge, but it didn't. It was only the same old merry-go-round and chasing each others' tails. And it was nearer three o'clock than two, the room had a fug of tobacco smoke, the three of us were pretty hungry, and brains were none too bright. Wharton said we'd adjourn and he'd try the routine approaches: get hold of Chale's solicitors and bank, possibly through Emmett, and the names of some of his patients through Mrs. Nippen. He might get hold of Wolde's bank too, and see if Chale had been seen in the neighbourhood of Borden Walk that Monday afternoon. And, of course, the hue and cry would have to be out for Sindle.

"Plenty to do," he said, and then all at once he was adding a something else.

"I don't want to start all over again, but I can't help wondering if all this ties up with that Brumford blackmail business of just before the war. Undoubtedly Wolde had some kind of hold over Chale. And I'm not talking about sex. After all, she wasn't living at Meriton Gardens till six months ago."

"I think there *has* to be a connection," I said. "In any case there'd be no harm in doing a bit of research. Would you like me to go back there and see if there's anything I can unearth?"

That was why I was on the late afternoon train. I put up again at the Regal. I was in time for a meal, and then I didn't stir from the hotel, for Wharton had rung Baker of the *Brumford Gazette* and I found waiting for me the paper's files on the blackmail case. It took me till bedtime to work my way meticulously through. Just one single word in that verbose reportage might have some kind of a clue.

I ended up, and I woke the next morning not much wiser than when I'd begun. The new facts I'd learned were of no special consequence: that, for instance, bail had been put up by a leading local political light and by one of Morse's former woman patients—a thousand pounds each—and that he'd skipped his bail during the week-end adjournment. That had brought the case to its virtual end. I made a note to ask Baker if he knew whether or not Chale had repaid the two thousand pounds.

Wolde's name hadn't been mentioned in the case: there was no reason why it should have been. As for the partnership, things had been apparently just as that kindly old Sparling at Hollindale Hospital had told me: that Chale and Morse hadn't acted as a team, even if at times it had been convenient for Morse to treat one of Chale's patients.

One other thing I learned was that too much stress hadn't been laid on that matter of extracting information by means of hypnotism. The plaintiff had been shrewdly handled by Morse's counsel, and it looked to me as if there would have been a shifting of ground and a conviction sought for criminally using information extracted in the ordinary course of psychopathic treatment. But one damning fact had been introduced just before the adjournment; that Morse had paid into his bank the very sum in cash that the plaintiff had specially drawn out. Even I, at so many years' distance, could see things shaping ominously for Morse. It was no wonder that he had bolted. The wonder was that he had been allowed bail, even though, reading between the lines, one gathered that he had had plenty of influential friends.

I had been thinking about all that up in my bedroom. When I came down and saw the morning papers there was the new sensation spread across the front pages. Brumford, I thought, ought to be particularly interested, what with Chale having once practised there, and Wolde, his secretary, with her own local connections, and now the dramatic murder of the pair of them. So it seemed to me that if ever I was going to get more information, now was my time. But how? And from whom? I didn't know, but as soon as I'd finished my breakfast I tried to get Baker at his office. He wasn't there, but I got his private address, and a taxi had me there soon after nine o'clock.

I gave him back his files and we had a more or less confidential chat about things.

"You've already been to Hollindale," he said, "so I don't see where you can get any more information about Wolde. I dare say I could find you some people who remember Chale well enough, but I don't see how it would help. You want to know if he was involved in that blackmail business even though he got off."

"What about your own views again?"

"Well," he said, "I still think he was involved. He was an unctuous sort of chap: much more likely to have had his tracks covered than Morse was. Take that business of indemnifying the two who went bail. Two thousand quid out of his pocket, you'd say. Or was it a good investment?"

"I see your point," I said. "It sort of confirmed his acquittal. Showed that he'd washed his hands of Morse."

"Personal guesses don't help much," he said, and then seemed to have an idea. "I'll tell you a really knowledgeable chap you might see. Frank Timson: used to be secretary of the Arts Club. He lives quite near. If you like, I'll give him a ring."

Timson would see me. Baker gave me directions, and I said I'd drop in at the office before I left. Five minutes' walking brought me to Timson's house.

He was a man of over seventy, hearty enough except for a bit of rheumatism. Baker had primed him with what I wanted, and he'd obviously read his morning paper.

"I knew both Chale and Morse," he said. "Naturally I knew Morse better. I was secretary then—as a matter of fact I've only just retired—and he was president. That business came as a great shock to us all."

I asked if he'd ever met Wolde.

"Oh yes," he said. "I only saw her once or twice. A very smart, good-looking girl. Very competent, and confident, if I may say so. But I was at the house on club business, of course."

"What about Chale?"

"A reserved sort of man," he said. "Not so much on the surface as Morse. A very good doctor, so I've heard. Used to do quite a lot of surgical work too."

"And what were your own ideas at the time about his possible guilt? I know he was acquitted, but I'd like your own private views."

"I didn't know then, and I don't know now," he said.

"Which means you had doubts."

"Well, yes." He smiled. "I suppose I did. Perhaps because he was the sort of fellow you could never really get to know."

We chatted on, but there was nothing new that he could tell me. I thanked him at last and said I'd be going.

"Something you might like to see," he said. "It's in the drawing-room."

We went into a room on the opposite side of the hall, and he was pointing to a fairly large oil that hung above the mantelpiece. I polished my glasses and had a look at it.

"It isn't you?" I said. "Or is it?"

"Not too good a likeness, even then," he said. "But I'd completed my twenty-one years as secretary, and the committee thought it would be a nice gesture to present me with my portrait painted by the president. He didn't paint a lot, mind you—far too busy a man—and then it was usually landscapes, but he said he'd like to do the job, and there it is."

"A very nice souvenir," I said. "You may not think it the best of likenesses, but it's a picture you can live with. By the way, where'd he learn his painting?"

"His father was Patrick Morse," he said. "Quite a well-known Irish painter, and I think with considerable private means. Morse himself, so he once told me, was originally intended for a painter. He actually did a certain amount of studying in France, then he switched to psychiatry and medicine. No money in painting, as I've heard him say more than once, unless it was house-painting."

"Harking back to Chale. You knew his wife?"

"She was an invalid," he said. "Bedridden for quite a long time before she died."

There was one other question just before I left him. Had he been surprised to learn that Chale had switched from general medical work to psychiatry?

"In a way I was, and yet I wasn't," he said. "I remember Morse once telling me that both he and Chale had originally intended to go in for it. I may be wrong, but I have the impression that Chale actually studied it before he changed over to surgery. I'm pretty sure that was in Paris. Besides, if Chale thought any stigma was attached to his name over that blackmail business, he'd feel happier doing different work. I know he was in London and the world's a small place, but people wouldn't connect him with the Brumford Chale if they happened to run across the name."

I thanked him again, and he told me where to catch a bus for the city. It was a good thing for me that it was a longish ride, for it gave me more time to think.

Chapter XII

BRAINWAVE

I DON'T say blatantly that by the time I'd got back to the city I'd acquired that extraordinary idea. All I'd done up to then was to review what I'd learned that morning and jot down a few notes for a subsequent report. It must have been that reviewing of the facts that somehow made my mind so susceptible to what the subconscious was later to suggest. And, of course, what I was to hear from Wharton.

I rang him because there was obviously quite a lot of research still to be done. I'd touched only on the fringes of things. He seemed disappointed that I had nothing sensational. But there was no need for hurry, he said, and the best thing I could do was carry on.

"What about your end?" I said.

"Got a lot of what I wanted," he said. "Not much at the solicitors except that he didn't leave a will. Mighty interesting thing at his bank, though. That Monday morning he drew out two hundred and fifty pounds in cash."

"The devil he did!" I said. "So Sindle was blackmailing him or else Chale was genuinely trying to help."

"Help?" he said, and I heard him snort. "To the tune of two hundred and fifty pounds!"

"Maybe I was right the first time," I said. "And what about the lady?"

"Dealt at the same bank," he said. "Total assets, far as we've been able to work it out, of over three thousand pounds."

"Anything unusual about Chale's payments to bank?"

"Yes, and no," he said. "Cheques for professional services fewer than I'd thought. One or two very useful cash payments."

"Not unlike blackmail," I said. "Be seeing you later. Might be tonight or it mightn't be till tomorrow."

He said he'd ring Bernice and save me the trouble, and that was that. I didn't know when I'd have time for a lunch, so I found a place for coffee and a bun. I began thinking about what I'd just heard from Wharton, and then it was as if everything all at once coalesced and that idea suddenly hit me like the kick of a mule.

Ten minutes later I was at the *Gazette* office. I had to tell Baker what I'd learned from Timson, and I had to put my question with all the casualness in the world.

"I don't suppose it will tell us very much, but is there a chance of seeing that man of yours who was in Paris at the time of Morse's death?"

"I expect he's about," he said. "I'll try and get him for you."

The name was Stanning—Bernard Stanning. Baker was due for the morning conference and we talked in his room. I told Stanning frankly that I was after information about that trio with whom he'd once been journalistically acquainted, and that I'd be most interested to hear at first hand about that strange coincidence in Paris.

"You mean about Morse," he said. "It *was* rather queer, when you come to think of it. I mean, there was I who'd done quite a lot of work on that blackmail case, happening to be in Paris just at the right time."

That had been hard on the heels of the departing Germans and at the very beginning of the hunting out of collaborationists.

"Everything in our gang was at sixes and sevens," he said, "and that's why I was shoved temporarily into military police. I wasn't going to sweat blood over it, though. I'd had a pretty grim time in Normandy, so the chap I was working with and me, we got ourselves a nice cushy billet and took it easy. It was on the second day and we'd just reported at headquarters and were almost back at the billet when we saw the fire. In a little back street, it was—the Rue Martine, just back of the Avenue de l'Opera. Not a bad street and those tall apartment houses— you know them." He and his colleague had gone to have a look. Members of the resistance movement were carrying out a private vendetta or act of justice, but the man they'd been after had escaped their clutches, and he was a Frenchman named Auguste Noisan. But they'd put out the fire and they were lugging out what was left of his partner, a supposed Belgian named Jules Delorme who'd been shot at close quarters through the head.

"I wasn't too bad at the lingo and those resistance chaps were a pretty good lot, so George—my colleague—George and I hung on there and helped them have a good look round. That's how we found the original passport belonging to Colin Morse. You could have knocked me down with a feather!"

"He *was* Morse, this supposed Belgian?"

"He must have been," he said. "I'd seen Morse, but this chap was too badly charred by the fire. But who else could he be? Height and everything else was right according to how I worked it out at the time. Those resistance chaps reckoned the Germans had shot him."

"Why?"

He said he'd smelt a good story for his paper, and he'd had plenty of time, so he'd gone into things very thoroughly. Noisan and Delorme had been partners in an art dealers' business in the Rue de Rivoli. Noisan was the virtual owner: Delorme had joined him only just before the war.

"That fitted in with the time when Morse might have got there after he slipped his bail," Stanning said. "And he probably spoke French like a Frenchman, or near enough to pass as a Belgian. And those two apparently became collaborationists straight away. What I gathered was that they were a kind of clearing-house and consulting agency for loot: the sort of pictures and stuff that found their way to Goering and other top Nazis. At any rate they were well enough protected and had plenty of money to burn."

"Then why was Delorme shot?"

"I was coining to that," he said. "Of course I couldn't have any private ideas of my own, but according to these resistance chaps the two had been double-crossing the Germans. Either that or the Germans saw which way things were bound to go, so they shot Delorme because he knew too much. They'd have had the other one, too, if he hadn't bolted."

"This apartment house was where they both lived?"

"That's right," he said. "Quite a swagger place inside and full of the right stuff."

"And was Noisan ever caught?"

"Not to my knowledge," he said. "When I got back to the paper I made some enquiries, but that was three years later. None of his papers, by the way, were found in that apartment. Delorme's papers were in his pocket where you'd expect them to be. Pretty well burnt, but enough to prove who he was."

I gave a Whartonian grunt. So that, I said, was the end of Colin Morse. A queer story, as Stanning had said.

"I don't know if you've ever thought of writing a novel," I said, "but there's almost a novel in it. Suppose, for instance, you gave it another twist: made it Noisan who was dead and not Delorme; that Delorme had shot Noisan and left that passport where it could have been found, and burnt the body to conceal the identity."

He laughed.

"Pretty ingenious, that. Might make a good thriller."

"You write it," I said. "And don't forget to send me a copy."

"I wouldn't count on it," he told me. "There's just so much the public can swallow."

"You ought to know," I said, and almost gave him a Whartonian dig in the ribs. "But I'm very grateful to you for a highly interesting yarn. And something you might do for us. Put that story in type and make it as detailed as you possibly can. Charge for your time. I'll see you get paid."

He said he'd do his best to get it off by the next morning's post. I told him to send it to my private address. By then it was nicely time for lunch, so I decided to have it at the hotel. It would be quieter there, and over the meal I could do my thinking. It was no use going back to Wharton with a theory that had more loose ends than facts.

What was the theory? Simply this—*that Sindle was Colin Morse.* I put it less positively, and with something Euclidian: *let it be supposed that Sindle is Colin Morse.* All that remained after that was to begin the proof.

Firstly there was the matter of two fires. In Paris a man had been shot and his body had been deliberately burnt in order to conceal his identity, and so that his killer should escape the consequences of previous crimes. In London precisely the same thing had just happened. Sindle had killed Chale and burnt his body but had juggled with clothes and teeth to give the impression that it was Sindle who had been killed. And, working back again from that, it seemed a certainty that Morse's old passport had been deliberately planted, as had the papers of Delorme that had been found in the dead man's pocket.

Two identical crimes, except for one thing: that one man had been shot and the other stabbed. But that seemed of little moment. Paris, at the time of Noisan's murder, was a place of gun-shots, and one more or less would not have been noticed. But to have shot Chale at Borden Walk would have been highly risky. It was necessary to kill him quickly and silently, so that his killer should be undisturbed while he did that juggling with clothes and teeth and lighted the fire.

With that I went back to the right place and time—Brumford in 1939, and the adjournment of that blackmail case. I had to assume that Morse knew what the verdict must be; that Chale had also been involved, and that it had been agreed that Morse should bolt and so be the scapegoat. Chale must have provided him with temporary funds and financed him later. Most likely it was Chale's money that had bought the partnership with Noisan.

And so to the liberation of Paris. The partners must have seen it happening days before the allied troops arrived. Doubtless both had been making preparations to bolt—down south, perhaps, or into Spain—but Morse saw a better way, for himself. And he was certainly sure that in the confusion of the times the change of identities would be accepted. Who would trouble about the death of a Belgian collaborator when Frenchmen were hunting out Frenchmen?

So Morse ceased to be Delorme. What name and nationality he took one couldn't tell, but he was almost certainly provided with abundant funds. It was impossible, too, to guess when he'd returned to England, and from where. After the war, and from Lisbon, he might have gone anywhere. Had he returned to England within a year or so? I was inclined to think he had. And this is why.

I'd obtained two excellent photographs from the *Brumford Gazette*: one of Chale and one of Morse, both taken at the time of the trial. I looked at Morse under my glass and then I tried to visualise Sindle. What could Chale, *the former surgeon*, have done to Morse to make him into Sindle? I didn't know, but I was pretty certain that these were things any surgeon could have done. The corners of the eyes might have been drawn in, perhaps, and the mouth altered in some way to admit of a different sort of dental plate. The growing of a wispy moustache and the little imperial, and all sorts of things that Morse himself would think of, would help to obscure the original identity.

Very well then: Morse became Sindle, and what did Sindle do? Again I didn't know, though it must have been Chale who continued to finance him, for unless that French money had been shrewdly manipulated it must have depreciated to almost nothing. Nor could I guess where Sindle went. All that seemed certain was that he deteriorated morally—drugs and drink, or both—and became much of a nuisance and a risk. That was why Chale virtually installed him within easy reach at Borden Walk. Cautious enquiries must have told him that even there Sindle was a danger. That was why he had determined to pay him that two hundred and fifty pounds as the price of a firm promise to leave England for good and all.

But Sindle had had other ideas. From his point of view, it was Chale who was the danger. Chale might give him away, and if it came to a showdown with the police it would be Chale's word against his own: the word of a man who'd once been honourably acquitted against that of a man who'd skipped his bail. But Sindle had made one big mistake. Maybe he knew nothing about Wolde. How could he conceive that there could be anybody in whom Chale could have confided?

After Chale's killing, then, what had happened? At the moment no one could do more than make a guess. Sindle had spent very little time in that studio at Borden Walk: he came at odd times and he went. He might sleep off a bout of drugs or drink, or paint for an hour or two, but quite a lot of his time had been spent elsewhere. Did Chale, and therefore Wolde, know where that elsewhere was? Had Wolde found him there and attempted to blackmail him? Or had Sindle laid low for a day or two and then entered Chale's house, where Wolde had surprised him and had been killed? I didn't know. That was where things became too involved. One thing only was certain: that Wolde had known who Sindle really was.

All that had given me a much clearer picture of Wolde herself. She was with Chale in Brumford till he left for London, so it was probably after then that she had done her real thinking. Something must have occurred to her: ideas began to suggest themselves, and when the time came that she wanted a job she obtained an excellent reference from Chale. It was more than likely that when she was at Hollindale she made her own further and surreptitious investigations, and when she was summarily dismissed she went straight to Chale. What she knew, and her physical attractions, made her before long a virtual partner, even if at the first it was thought unwise for her to have rooms in the same house.

Those were the things I thought, and it was long after lunch when I'd finished thinking them. Was the proposition proved? Was Sindle really Morse? I couldn't be sure. But money talks, if you'll allow a slight digression. That's why I'm often highly unpopular at Derby time. Some bore or other will inform me that so-and-so is bound to win. I ask him how much he has on it, and he tells me he isn't a betting man.

"You've got a certainty and you won't even venture a half-crown," I say. "It must be a queer certainty if you haven't got even a half-crown's worth of faith in it."

But I had a half-crown's faith that Sindle and Morse were the same person. I had faith that went far beyond that trifle and stopped short only at the proverbial shirt. And I had faith enough in my presentation of facts to think that I could convince George Wharton.

I just managed to catch the two o'clock. I took a taxi from Euston, and soon after half-past four I was at the Yard. Wharton was in, and he was looking surprised to see me back so soon and without warning. In the train I'd written a detailed report, but that would be for later. What I did was tell him what I'd heard up to that moment I'd left Stanning.

"A funny business," he told me. "Looks to me as if that Morse is still alive."

I wanted to lure him into the same line of thought as myself.

"It is," I said. "And he might have been glad to get rid of Chale."

"Yes," he said, and blew out his moustache. Then he was looking away into space. His mouth gaped slightly while the motionless fingers gripped the pipe.

"There isn't a possibility that Sindle's really Morse?"

"Why not?" I said.

We got down to it. I didn't stress the certainties or slur over the difficulties: I said plainly what I thought and left him with the decisions.

"Just one thing I can't get over," he said when we'd done quite a deal of hammering out. "Sindle killed Chale. But why? You don't kill the goose that lays the golden egg?"

I refused for once to theorise; besides, he'd be reading my ideas when he studied the report. And I was expecting him to find his own answers. And he did what I'd done myself: tried to reconcile Sindle's need for money with Sindle's fear.

"It's the very devil!" he told me exasperatedly. "The worst thing from our point of view was that killing of Wolde. She was the one who could have cleared everything up. What can we really prove now? Just nothing."

Then he thought of another objection.

"Why did Sindle burn Chale's hands?"

"So that we shouldn't get his prints," I said. "Wasn't that always understood?"

"But no one ever had Chale's prints or Morse's either. Prints wouldn't have been taken till after conviction."

"Sindle wanted it believed it was his own body there," I said. "Also he'd want time to get out of the country or arrange a new identity. He was trying to make every complication he possibly could: making us think, for instance, that Sindle had had a record. He never expected us to get on to Chale. Why should he? It was sheer luck seeing Wolde at Borden Walk. That, and what Mrs. Oddfort told me, just happened to connect things up."

"It's all too involved," he said, and made a gesture of impatience. Then he was giving me a look. "Wait a minute. You don't happen to have the telephone number of that Mr. Timson, do you?"

I had it in my report. He rang down for it, and for Timson himself, if possible, to come on the line. He didn't tell me what he so badly wanted. He put a question instead.

"How long do you think Sindle would need for all that job he did in the studio?"

I began working it out: the killing, the clothes, the teeth and the fire, and the getaway.

"Best part of ten minutes," I said.

"We tried a reconstruction," he said. "If the fire materials were handy, and they were, he still couldn't have done it under twelve minutes. That clothes changing was the longest business. And allowing for a final look round."

"Chale must have come in remarkably quietly," I said. "He had to pass Ferndale's door, and neither Ferndale nor Mrs. Solness heard a thing."

"They were back there in his studio," he said. "And of course Chale had to come in quietly. He didn't want to be connected with Sindle. Which reminds me of something you didn't know. That man Crotch at the art shop saw someone pass, and he's pretty sure it was Chale. All he can say is that it was nearer half-past three than four."

I was saying that was a time that fitted, when the bell rang. In a moment or two I knew what Wharton had wanted to know.

"There you are," he said, when he'd thanked Timson and hung up. "Morse was ambidextrous when he was actually painting, and right-handed at other times. And that gets us nowhere. Or else it throws a spanner into the whole thing. Didn't that chap Bintwood assure us that Sindle's pictures had been painted with the left hand?"

"All that may have been a blind," I said. "If Chale was financing Sindle, then Sindle hadn't any real need to paint. Those pictures might have been there to keep things in character: for the benefit of anyone who managed to peep through the door."

"Where that's getting us I don't know," he told me. He gave an exasperated click of the tongue. "First you say one thing and then you say another that contradicts it. Leave that report and let me go through it, then I might have to see the Higher-Ups. If I give you a ring it'll be pretty late."

I went home. Bernice was out somewhere, so I had an early meal and left a note. Then I took a bus to the corner of Howe Street and walked on to Borden Walk.

Gulver didn't happen to be in, so I went up to Bintwood's door. There was no answer to my ring, but from upstairs was coming the sound of a wireless. I went on up and tapped at the door. Viola opened it, and someone behind her switched off the boogie-woogie.

"Well!" she said, and beamed. "We were just talking about you."

I stepped inside. Helena Grace and Walter Bintwood were occupying the settee. On a small table were bottles of gin and lime-juice and vermouth. Bintwood made as if to get up, but a hand of mine pushed him genially down. Helena gave me a smile. She told Viola to fetch the wicker chair from the bedroom.

A couple of minutes and I was part of the general cosiness, and on the way through a gin and lime.

"What's this about talking scandal about me?" I wanted to know.

All three spoke at once, and Bintwood was left with the talking. The girls had got hold of the idea from somewhere that Pamela Maine might have seen something at Meriton Gardens. And while he was talking he was trying to warn me not to mention that he and I had had that distressing scene in the room underneath.

"She *did* see something," Viola said. "I don't know what it was, but she did see that man Chale who was killed when we thought it was Sindle; and then, when I tried to get her to tell me, she had one of her queer fits. Absolutely scared me, she did."

"She's got to be left alone," Bintwood said. "That's how we were mentioning your name. I said you wouldn't like her worried and you'd have talked to her yourself if you'd thought it worth while."

I had to agree. I pointed out that even if there were anything she had seen she would still be quite unreliable as a witness.

"In any case, what apparently *did* she see? According to you, Viola, she thinks she saw Chale. But where? And when? Might have been months ago. And any place."

"Just what I was telling them," Bintwood said. "For heaven's sake let's talk about something else."

He leaned forward and switched the wireless on, but the boogie-woogie had gone and someone was giving a talk. Viola promptly switched it off. I asked if they'd had their meal. Helena said that Bintwood had brought up something and they'd cooked it up there and had just nicely finished when I knocked.

"What about going out to the Harriers?" Viola said. "You play darts, Mr. Travers? Or doesn't your wife let you?"

I said I did, in my own fashion, and she didn't know. So off the four of us went to the Harriers. We didn't play darts, but we watched the experts and had some drinks and chattered and half-listened to the wireless. The others seemed quite upset when at half-past nine I said I'd have to go. Somehow or other we got paired off again, and there was Viola once more hanging on to my arm.

A minute or two and she was trying to pump me about the Chale murder. I managed to slide gently through and round and added a thing or two of sheer invention.

"I think if Pamela did see anything, then you ought to know," she told me. "Walter's an old wet blanket."

Then she was giving my arm a special squeeze.

"If I do find out anything, be all right if I let you know?"

I said that'd be fine. She said she'd have to have my telephone number so that she could let me know.

"I'll find it in the directory," she said. "Then you can take me out somewhere and I can tell you all about it. I'll make up something for Helena."

That was why I had to do a lot of careful explaining to Bernice. Maybe she thinks I'm bullet-proof by now, for she took everything as a matter of course. And then when I'd had my final pipe and was thinking of bed the telephone rang. It was Wharton.

"Got a job for you tomorrow," he said. "Better have a bag ready, just in case, and drop in about nine o'clock for your orders."

"Why the bag?" I said.

"An idea of the Big Bugs," he told me. "You're taking the ten o'clock plane to Paris."

Chapter XIII
SUNDAY IN PARIS

I WAS up pretty early that Sunday morning, and soon after eight o'clock I was ringing No. 7, Borden Walk. What Wharton had learned from Paris I didn't know, but it seemed to me that if I could learn anything from Bintwood it couldn't be other than a help.

Gulver was up, and in a minute or two he had Bintwood at the telephone.

"Sorry to disturb your Sunday morning," I said, "but I'm just off to Paris."

"Lucky man," he said. "Paris in May is a pretty good spot—or used to be. You going on business?"

"In the strictest confidence, I'm making enquiries about Sindle. We believe he spent some time there during the war. But what I was wondering was if you could give me any information about an art dealer of the name of Noisan—Auguste Noisan."

"Not Auguste," he said. "I knew an Albert Noisan. Had a place in the Rue de Rivoli."

"That's the firm," I said. "What was this Albert like?"

"Short, fat, elderly. I ran across him occasionally at auctions. He used to come to our place sometimes, but he was too import-ant for me to handle."

"Our information is that the business was run during the war by an Auguste Noisan. Might that be a son?"

"Wait a minute," he said. "I think you're right. The son was a bit of a painter. Now I remember, his name *was* Auguste. And I think old Albert died just before the war. I seem to remember reading about it somewhere."

"Whom were you with yourself, by the way?"

"Hedleys of Old Bond Street."

"I remember them," I said. "Are they in business now?"

"Bombed out in the war and never started again," he said. "I believe they're still operating in New York. In fact I'm sure they are."

I told him I might have to be near his old haunts in St. Sulpice. But to get back to Auguste Noisan. Did Bintwood ever meet him?

"Not to my knowledge," he said. "I know he had a certain reputation as a painter, though some of that might have been due to being the son of old Albert."

"Albert was in a big way?"

"Good lord, yes," he said. "Certainly one of the three biggest dealers in Paris."

"And what about a dealer named Jules Delorme. Ever hear of him?"

"Never."

"Supposed to be a Belgian."

"I still never heard of him," he said. "Were he and the two Noisans supposed to have been acquainted with Sindle?"

"There's just an idea to that effect," I said. "Hope to tell you more when I get back. Meanwhile, many thanks."

I went to the Yard to get what Wharton had called my orders. There didn't seem to be any. I was to be met at the airport by an Inspector Voiset who spoke excellent English. Apparently he would be guide and mentor, and all I had to do, as Wharton airily told me, was to carry on the investigation into the affair of the Rue Martine from where Stanning of the *Gazette* had left it. I was pretty sure that if there'd been anything more definite he'd have gone to Paris himself. I had, in fact, the idea that the Big Bugs, Higher-Ups, Powers-that-Be—call them, as Wharton does, precisely what you like—were expecting someone to work a miracle, and I was the unfortunate one.

I more or less told Wharton so. Years had gone by since that murder in the Rue Martine, and even then it had been a trivial affair compared with the events that had shaken Paris at the time. I didn't get any sympathy from George. He was at his most unctuous. I like him better when he plainly thinks me a fool.

I could tell you a whole lot about the Paris of that Sunday in May, but it's the case that really matters. Voiset was at the airport. He was in the early forties and his English was distinctly good. I don't say there was a perfection of accent and intonation, but if my French had been as good as his English I wouldn't have minded airing it abroad.

As soon as we left the airport I was asking him if there was a dossier. He said there was one on Noisan. An attempt had been made to compile one on Delorme, but there had been little data on which to work, and the Belgian police had been unable to help.

We drove straight to the Quai des Orfèvres and I saw the dossiers there. That on Auguste Noisan was very complete. His father had died in the autumn of 1938 and he had then inherited the business in the Rue de Rivoli. Delorme had appeared first in the August of 1939. Noisan himself had studied at the *atelier* Ingres from 1922 till 1926.

I worked things out, and it seemed to me that Morse and Noisan must have been of the same age.

"Any chance," I asked Voiset, "of consulting their records and finding out if Morse and Noisan were fellow students?"

His assistant got busy on it at once, though Voiset himself wasn't too hopeful. The Germans had taken or destroyed all sorts of records, even from the Quai des Orfèvres. He did remember that there'd been enquiries from the Brumford police with reference to Morse in 1939, but those records had gone.

I went on reading the Noisan dossier, but it was so bulky that I could do little more than glance through. I did see that almost immediately after the occupation the Noisan firm had been under German protection and had undoubtedly become the clearing-house for looted pictures. That was proved by documents captured in Germany just at the end of the war, and by what the authorities found on the premises in the Rue de Rivoli.

The home of the Noisans had been at Neuilly. Albert Noisan was a widower, and when he died his son continued there; but soon after the occupation the Germans had taken over the house as an administrative office and Auguste had settled down in the apartment in the Rue Martine that had been occupied by his mistress, a woman named Arlette Bandol, who had disappeared just before the Germans entered the city. It was a large apartment with plenty of room for both Noisan and Delorme.

"Any possible chance," I said, "of getting hold of an old servant of the family who was at Neuilly while Auguste was studying painting? What I'm trying to discover is if Morse was a friend of his. If so, Auguste may have taken him to the Neuilly house."

Voiset said it could be tried. Then he was suggesting that I might like to see the actual house in the Rue Martine, and after that we could interview Louis Fourgeon, who had been the actual leader of the party that had discovered the dead Delorme. That would only mean a short drive to Belleville.

We lunched first and then drove out to the Rue Martine. To me it was just a street—more secluded perhaps than I'd thought—and the house itself just another large apartment house. There was not even a trace of the fire. I nodded heavily as if I was interested and then we drove out to Belleville. Fourgeon had been warned to expect us.

He was a chemist: a man of about forty, under medium height and wearing glasses; the one person in Paris you'd never have taken for the leader of a resistance group. He told me in exceedingly bad English that that was one reason why he'd never been suspected. He loved talking that English: Voiset had a job to switch him to French. But he was a nice fellow and quite amusing. I liked him.

He remembered quite well the *affaire* of the Rue Martine. I gathered that all over Paris collaborators had been secretly marked down in readiness, and it had fallen to his group to apprehend the Noisan partners. The smell of the Bosche was still there, he said, when they got to the Rue de Rivoli, and the shop was bolted and barred, but they'd broken in and left men on guard and then made for the Rue Martine.

The fire, obviously deliberate, was in the Noisan apartment, and they'd got it under control before too much harm had been done. The apartment above was empty and in a much worse way. It, too, had been occupied by suspected collaborators. After that the story became what I'd heard from Stanning. I asked him if he remembered the two English military policemen, and he remembered them well. I told him about the English passport that had been found.

He remembered that only vaguely, and what had become of the passport he didn't know. Probably one of his men had pocketed it. He did suggest that probably Delorme had been thinking of trying to pass as an Englishman, and that the passport was a fake.

"You were sure it was Delorme who was killed?"

He shrugged his shoulders. The papers in the breast pocket of the corpse were those of Delorme.

"Did Noisan resemble Delorme?"

He thought back. Of that, he said at last, he couldn't be sure. Delorme had a pointed black beard and Noisan was clean-shaven, but the face of the corpse was badly charred by the fire. The papers would have been still more badly charred, too, if they hadn't been in a leather case. And he himself hadn't seen everything. What with putting out the fire and getting out the body and trying to search what was left of the room and going through the rooms above, the place had been like an ant-hill.

I asked if the two men had been of the same height and build. He didn't know. Voiset said his impressions were that Delorme was the taller and that the two were the same build. I wanted to know what had happened to the body. Fourgeon once more shrugged his shoulders. One of his men had been left with it till the authorities—whoever they might be—arrived. He and his group had had other work to do. Dead collaborators hadn't mattered.

His general impressions were those of Stanning: that Noisan had bolted and Delorme had been killed by the Germans or by the collaborator on the upper floor. Or even, for some reason, by Noisan.

"Noisan vanished," Voiset said. "Never a trace of him from that day to this. We did receive an anonymous letter saying he was in Spain, but at that time the Spanish authorities weren't inclined to be helpful. There was a copy of it in the dossier."

There seemed nothing else to be learned from Fourgeon. Voiset asked to use the telephone. Ten minutes later we were driving across Paris towards Neuilly.

The local police had unearthed a Mme Durau, who had been for many years in the service of Albert Noisan at the Neuilly house. Our way actually led by the house itself—an imposing, rather pretentious-looking place in extensive grounds. Albert Noisan, Voiset told me, had been a very wealthy man.

Mme Durau occupied with a widowed daughter a small apartment that overlooked the river. She was almost eighty and had retired from the service of the Noisans just before the war because of arthritic knees. Her French was deliberate and remarkably clear, so that I hardly needed Voiset as interpreter. She gave us a long account of the Noisan house in its heyday between the wars, and we hadn't the heart to stop her. It was when she began telling us about Auguste that I learned that the mother had been a German. If I'd had time to go thoroughly through that enormous dossier that fact would doubtless have been there.

And so to the question of Morse. It was not till I mentioned the Christian name that she remembered him and how he had come more than once to the house. She forgot when it was that she had seen him last, but she recalled that his French then was very good. She thought it was about 1926.

That was the year when Auguste's only sister, Berthe, had become a *réligieuse*. Berthe had been a Noisan, she said: Auguste had taken after his mother. I judged from the way she had made that last remark that she had been well aware of his collaboration with the Germans.

"You've never heard of him or from him?" Voiset asked her.

"Never," she said. "But I keep that picture because it's a kind of souvenir."

It was a small oil of herself, painted by Auguste Noisan towards the end of his student days. There was in it nothing of the crude directness of Sindle: it was light, typically French, if that conveys anything to you, and with much of the wistfulness of a Renoir.

We tried to get her to recall something of the Morse who had been a friend of Auguste those many years ago, but she had been merely a kind of housekeeper and had seen the young Morse and little more.

"You never by any chance saw him since?"

"Never," she said. "Even if I had, how could I have known him? I saw him so little, and one changes as one grows older."

"You never went to the shop in the Rue de Rivoli?"

She explained patiently about her knees. And there had been the occupation. Only once in her life had she been to the shop, and then to do something for Mme Noisan.

There was no point in putting more questions, so we thanked her warmly and left. Voiset told me I ought to be pleased to have found such a confirmation that Noisan and Morse had been friends. What had happened at the *atelier* was now of comparative unimportance. But when we got back to head-quarters we found a backing for what Mme Durau had told us, and for what I'd learned at Brumford from Timson. Morse had been a student at the Ingres during the year 1922. Noisan had therefore been his contemporary for that one year, and that was when the friendship had begun. And after it Morse had made the violent switch from art to medicine. In that he had probably been influenced by Chale and by the fact—as Timson again had told me—that he had the sense to foresee there'd be very little money in art.

I settled down to the Noisan dossier. Voiset felt it his duty to take me out somewhere for dinner.

"You don't happen to know a place at St. Sulpice?" I said. "A friend of mine in England used to work for an art dealer there and he'll be bound to ask me what things were like."

There was the famous Restaurant Letorre, he said, not two hundred metres from the church. While I was tidying up he reserved a table. It was still light when we got there, so we circled round, but there was no sign of an art shop.

I don't know what that meal cost the French taxpayer, but it was definitely superb, and it seemed almost a sacrilege that while we were eating—and drinking—it we should be talking about the case. I was telling Voiset practically all we knew. He didn't seem surprised at the melodrama of it all. Maybe such things were commonplace in France. Perhaps the last thing I told him was that Auguste Noisan, according to the dossier, had apparently partly abandoned painting for business. I'd noted that he'd accompanied his father twice to Italy and once to America. Voiset said he knew about it. That was one thing that made him less likeable, say, than Fourgeon. He was too professional and he hadn't much humour.

M. Letorre, the proprietor, arrived to ask how the meal had gone. He was an elderly man with the very look of a stage *restaurateur*, and he, too, had a hazardous English of which he seemed quite proud. I didn't see why I shouldn't inflict on him some of my French. It was funny, in a way: I at my French and he still sticking to his English. And, just between ourselves, my French isn't really so bad, as I may have deprecatingly led you to think.

"There used to be an art dealer's near here," I told him. "The Paris branch of an English firm of the name of Hedley."

You haven't heard my French and you won't want to hear his English, so I continue to translate.

"Of course!" he said. "I remember. There was a M. Hedley who ate here very frequently. Also he would bring clients. Americans, Italians, English."

"You don't by any chance remember a M. Bintwood? He worked there too. English, of course."

"Bintwood," he said, and shrugged his shoulders and smiled. "English names are very difficult, which is why I should have remembered this M. Bintwood."

"He was of medium height; reddish-faced, rather a flat nose, and eyes a bit narrow. Not Mongolian exactly, but narrow. A quiet, solid sort of man."

He had been frowning. He said perhaps he remembered, but it was a long time ago. It was well before the war when Hedleys had left Paris. Then he was asking if I knew his M. Hedley. Apparently he would have liked to send him his kindest regards.

It was pretty late when we left the restaurant, but I wanted that Noisan dossier out of the way, so I worked on it till after midnight, and, for all that it told me about Morse, I might as well have been in my bed at the Hotel du Lion. But George could be given a verbal synopsis. What the Higher-Ups would think didn't so much matter, except that even they would realise that that Sunday I'd been busier than a beaver. And, in that context, I decided to omit any reference to the Restaurant Letorre.

Next morning I had my *pétit dejeuner* in bed, and as soon as I'd dressed and packed my belongings I called on Voiset to thank him. A man of his drove me to the airport, where I took the plane home. It was a gorgeous morning with everything spread out beneath one like a bright patchwork quilt. But I saw it only now and again. I was too busy trying to piece together a patchwork of my own.

What had I learned? Frankly, I couldn't say. I had to visualise things through three sets of eyes—those of the Higher-Ups, and George Wharton's and my own. And, paradoxically enough, it would be my views that mattered most, and I was abysmally low in that hierarchy. The onus was on me, and what I wrote in my report I should have to justify. That was why I tried to avoid all wishful thinking and to keep to undoubted facts.

And the facts were these. Morse and Auguste Noisan had been friends during the Paris years of 1922-1926. There had also been ample confirmation of various things that Morse, as president of the Brumford Arts Club, had let fall from time to time to Timson, its secretary. Whether Morse had kept up the friendship by correspondence or during later visits to Paris I didn't know. Timson might recall some mention of a holiday or holidays that Morse had spent there. Indeed it seemed to me essential that Timson should be asked about it, and I made an immediate note.

If—and there I had to be hypothetical—Morse had kept up that friendship, then it wouldn't be too hard to visualise his making for Paris after skipping his bail, and lying low, and, at what he judged the right moment, getting into touch with Noisan, with a suitable story. It was even possible that Morse had some kind of hold over Noisan. That he became a partner in an important business at the very first moment seemed to me an unlikely thing. My idea was that Noisan found a use for him in the business, and that it had been Morse's idea to get German protection at the time of the occupation. That had brought him a full partnership.

And so to the time when the Allies were rapidly nearing Paris. What could I say about that? Nothing except to give Fourgeon's own story and refer to certain observations I had already made about the coincidence of the two fires and the handiness of Morse's English passport and the supposed Delorme's papers. And that left wide open the one really vital matter. *Who* had killed someone was of little consequence. What mattered was who had been killed.

But there it seemed to me that Noisan had no reason for killing Morse-Delorme. What could he tell the authorities or the resistance that they didn't already know? On the other hand, Morse-Delorme had every reason to kill Noisan, and to do that killing in such a way that the body would be taken for his own was a master-stroke. If, on the strength of that passport, the English police were informed of Morse's death, then that old affair at Brumford could be regarded as closed, and Morse would be free to return to England under another name. Passports and papers didn't matter. In Lisbon or elsewhere those things could be had at a price. Take Sindle, for instance. If he were Morse, then from somewhere he had obtained an identity card and a ration book, and, as I know, with comparative ease.

But I didn't harp on that in the report I was appending to my abstract of the Noisan dossier. I merely inferred and left it to others to do the theorising. And as an appendix to an appendix I was proposing to suggest certain things that we or the French police might do. The traces of Morse, for instance, might be picked up at Lisbon. There might have been a real Vandyke Sindle from whom Morse had obtained his papers, and we ought to have a photostat of that anonymous letter written from Spain and hinting that Noisan was still alive. That would have been a shrewd bit of camouflage on the part of Morse-Delorme, and a kind of proof—if the Paris police had ever had doubts—that it was definitely Delorme who had been killed.

There seemed a certain amount of proof, too, in the fact that the Belgian police had known nothing about a Jules Delorme. To pose as a Belgian would have been another excellent stroke by Morse, for it might account for any imperfections in his French. A foreigner never really speaks French, however good a mastered if limited vocabulary. You don't believe that? Then ask yourself what Wharton once asked me. Could you really get angry in French? Could you spot and cope with dialect? Could you say the same thing in different ways to different social strata? You could in English, but could you in French?

The motor-coach took me back to town, and I took a taxi to the Yard. Wharton had been told the time of the plane and he was in his room, and Matthews was there too. And never did I have such a homecoming. Matthews gave me a smile and a wink, but George was positively taciturn. George never is demonstrative, but I'd expected a spate of questions.

"You've got back then?" was what he said, and at once I was having twinges of conscience. Ought I to have returned the previous night? I didn't recall any instructions to that effect.

"Looks like it," I said, and maybe a bit flippantly. I added that I hadn't expected the fatted calf, but why all the gloom?

"Take a look at this," he said, and handed me a clip of papers. "That Paris business seems to have been a waste of time. And all that blether about Morse being Sindle."

I think I must have flushed, but I let that pass. I had a look at the clip of papers. It was a letter, sheet after sheet of it, and then I turned back to the very last sheet. The name at the bottom was *Vandyke Sindle*.

CHAPTER XIV
YET ANOTHER START

DEAR SIRS, (if that is the way to address you)

By the time you receive this I shall be well out of the country. I do not propose to add, and for reasons that will be only too obvious to yourselves, either where I am going or how. But it will not be under the name of Vandyke Sindle.

What my real name is I also have no intention of telling you, and I doubt if you will trace it from the little that I shall be forced to tell you. Unless you have the extraordinary good fortune to discover it soon, it will be much too late. In any case, what does it matter? You are much more anxious at this moment to know why this letter was written. The main answer to that is simply this. I wanted you to know that *I did not kill Dr. Chale.*

You will not credit that, but I hope, nevertheless, to convince you. I may even begin to convince you by admitting at once that I did kill the Wolde woman, though about that there were extenuating circumstances and gross provocation which might have made the charge against me one of manslaughter, and not murder. But even that would have meant a term of imprisonment and all the ghoulish, sniggling publicity of the yellow press.

But about myself, at least as much as I dare truthfully tell you. I was once a painter with a growing reputation. I had a small private income inherited from an aunt, and that allowed me to work when I liked and only at what I wanted. There was no need for me to be at the mercy of swindling dealers or venal critics or the revolting tastes of the public herd. To say more might be dangerous, but there is no harm in adding that I was bullied at school and never gregarious, and, because of some latent sexual aberration, entirely allergic to women. I can also say safely that I neither studied nor lived in London.

Then I had a serious illness followed by an operation, and it was that which, according to Dr. Chale, brought those latent sexual aberrations into the open. In any case I don't propose to whine about it. Suffice it to say that I received a prison sentence for an offence. Fortunately for me, it was committed well away from my then habitat and the conviction was under a false name. Some months after my release I was again convicted and given a longer term.

That was when I tried to take stock of myself. I knew, as you know, that only the monumental asininity of English law makes sexual aberrations a penal offence. Mental deformities can never be cured by rigorous confinement within prison walls. That is why, on the recommendation of a man who was still something of a friend, I consulted Dr. Chale. I had realised what remained of my investments and I hoped that I should have enough to pay his fee. As it happened I had enough, but very little more.

I was frank with him. He learned things about me which you will never know, and he ended by giving me hope. I use that expression, slushy and sentimental though it now reads, because it is assumed that perverts like myself revel in the perversion and that the last thing we long for is a cure. But in my case there was something else. After that term of imprisonment I found to my horror that I could no longer paint. I was like an author or composer whose inspiration has suddenly gone, and in my case it was some lack of co-ordination between brain and hand. But Dr. Chale gave me a new faith. Since most of my money had gone it was vital for me to earn a living, and it was he who obtained that studio for me and tried to force me to paint.

But for him I would never have lived in that studio. I always hated the proximity of so-called neighbours, and in that building there was one of the dealer tribe and a bourgeois portraitist and some hangers-on to the fringes of the arty kind of art. But I determined to keep myself to myself. I arrived with no ostentation, and I avoided as far as possible even the sight of the other tenants. I also began spasmodically to paint. Co-ordination came slowly back and something of the old touch. Little of the old assuredness perhaps, but enough to give me hope. Dr. Chale was very pleased with me.

And then I began to hate that studio and the building and everyone who was in it. Only one of them ever regarded me as anything human. Not that that matters. What really matters is that I had a kind of *idée fixe*. I was convinced that my cure would never be completed in that horrible house, and that it was essential for me to leave London and get back to the country. Dr. Chale tried to induce me not to leave London. Then, just before his death, I told him that I'd already obtained a room away from Borden Walk, and that I should stay there till I could find something better. There is no harm in telling you that that room was near Waterloo Station—No. 37 Wellbank Street, to be precise. That is not gratuitous information. It is something that will convince you, I trust, that what follows is logical and true. But to return to Dr. Chale. He objected to that neighbour-hood and told me that if I'd had patience there would have been no need to obtain that room, and that there was a place in the country which he hoped at once to secure for me. I told him how I stood financially and he insisted on helping, and I was to repay at some suitable time. That was on the Saturday, and he arranged to see me at the studio on the Monday afternoon.

Why he should have wished to come there I cannot say, unless it was to see something of the place and learn professionally, if you know what I mean, what there might have been about it to create in myself so strong a revulsion. But about that incredible Monday. I had been in the City that morning and had intended to be home by three o'clock. He had given me the impression that he would be coming at the time vaguely known as tea-time, which I interpreted as four o'clock. Various things delayed me and I didn't get back till three-thirty or thereabouts. I opened the door with my key, and there was Dr. Chale, face downwards just inside the door. It didn't occur to me that he had no key and therefore couldn't possibly have entered. What did naturally occur to me was that he'd had some sort of seizure, and then I saw that he'd been stabbed in the back. There wasn't a knife, but the slit was there and the blood.

You find that hard to believe? But put it to yourselves. Why should I of all people kill Dr. Chale? I think I would rather have killed myself sooner than Chale. And why should I kill him at the very time when he was going out of his way to help a man like myself who had no claim on his time or his money?

I went through his pockets, and I found the money he had evidently intended me to have. I made up my mind quickly as to what I had to do. I could never go to the police. With a record known as unsavoury I should have stood no chance of being believed. So I did what I did. I tried to make it appear that it was I who had been killed. I didn't altogether succeed, but I gained time in which to alter my appearance and buy clothes. It was fortunate that I had that place in Wellbank Street to which to retire. They had no suspicions of me there, and I might have been there till everything had died down.

It was Wolde whom I underestimated, in fact I didn't consider her at all. I couldn't conceive that a man like Dr. Chale could make her a confidante—a smooth, tight-lipped creature with a veneer of suburban gentility. But on Wednesday evening there was a knock at my door and I opened it, thinking it was the landlady, and there was Wolde. At first she was merely inquisitive and wanting to know what had happened. Then she turned nasty. She refused to believe me. I had killed Chale for the sake of the money. She asked for that money back and another two hundred and fifty with it: if not, she was going straight to the police.

What could I do but temporise? It was not till the morning that I could possibly obtain the money, but I promised to bring it to Meriton Gardens before midday. She said I needn't think of any evasions, as she'd already been in touch with a detective agency and a man of theirs was watching the house, even if he had no idea whatever of the real identity of the man he had to watch. But I knew that for a bluff, and as soon as she'd gone I also was out of the house.

I took a taxi to just short of Meriton Gardens and let myself in with Dr. Chale's keys. I stood behind that heavy curtain at the door, and as soon as she entered I struck her down and gripped her throat till she was dead. I had no compunctions. She was unfit to live. Then I took her up to what I found was her bedroom, undressed her and put her into the bed. Why did I do that? Frankly I don't know. Perhaps I was still in the midst of a brainstorm, or I might have hoped to confuse the police. But I began in that room and went methodically through the whole house. I had her keys and Dr. Chale's and everything was open to me, and I destroyed every record and scrap of paper that might have contained my name or given a hint as to my real identity. It was two in the morning when I got back to Wellbank Street.

There is no time to tell you more, even if there are scores of things that I ought to have more fully explained. But the general sense is there, and in any case it matters very little now. Either you will have accepted this letter as true or else it will be a concoction of lies. The addition of more evidence in my favour would not help, and it might be dangerous for myself. Perhaps if all goes well I shall tell you very much more some months from now. The name I sign, and again you may believe it or disbelieve it, is that of an acquaintance of my student days, long since dead.

VANDYKE SINDLE

I looked up to find Wharton's eyes on me.

"Well?" he said. "What do you make of it?"

"Don't know," I said. "It's a bit of a facer. Where was it posted from?"

"Southampton. On Saturday morning. We didn't get it till first thing this morning."

I had another quick look at that letter.

"Written with the left hand—or isn't it?"

"With the left hand," he said. "We had Sidwell round here at once and that's his verdict. Written very methodically too."

"You mean as if he didn't usually write with the left hand?"

"Might have been," he said. "But we know that Sindle painted chiefly with the left hand, so why shouldn't he write that way?"

"No reason at all," I said. "And what about Wellbank Street?"

"Everything perfect. I went there myself with Matthews. He booked that room on the Thursday before the murder and paid a week in advance and said he didn't know exactly when he'd be able to move in. He told the woman he was an actor and engaged on a picture at Denham, and shortly going to be employed at the Old Vic."

"Why on earth did he do that?"

"Well, we think it was to account for his rather queer appearance, and for taking a room in the Old Vic neighbourhood. If so, it was lucky for him, because when he turned up to take the room over he was clean-shaven and looking quite a professional man. That was on the Monday evening early."

"I don't like it," I said. "Surely it strikes you that by spinning that movie-actor yarn on the Thursday he was preparing for something—murder shall we say—that would make him change his appearance when he took over that room?"

"He wasn't going to paint there," Wharton said. "He couldn't have. It was just a smallish bed-sitting-room, and he had to make up some yarn about himself. The whole letter shows how secretive he was. And cussed too. If she'd asked if he was an artist he'd have sworn blind he wasn't. He hated his affairs being pried into." He waved a dismissing hand. "But there it is. He took over the room on the Monday evening, and he had a couple of bags—bought second-hand obviously—and just the things a man would have. He left everything open, and the landlady happened to see everything, as she put it. He left, ostensibly to begin work rehearsing at the Old Vic, first thing on Thursday morning, and he insisted on paying a week's rent in lieu of notice. Said he couldn't stay because a friend wanted him to stay with him."

"What about the actual street?"

"Highly respectable. Ordinary rooming-house but quite clean. A decent sort of woman. The rooms never empty long, so she said. Sindle's room was already occupied again. So long as they pay their money and behave themselves, that's all she requires. No meals provided—just the room or rooms. If a tenant wants it, she sees to the cleaning."

"That stroke of luck, sir," Matthews reminded him.

"Oh yes," Wharton said. "The landlady heard Sindle come in on that Thursday morning. She has a couple of rooms on the ground floor and she has a pet Peke and he growled. It was at about a quarter to three. That means he probably walked from Meriton Gardens. The name he'd given, by the way, was Charles Nimms."

I told him that it rather looked as if what he'd said about my trip to Paris was true—that it had been wasted time.

"All the same," I said, "I'd like to give you a very brief synopsis. After that, if you're still interested, you can read the full report some time."

I gave them that synopsis, and it took less than ten minutes.

"It's useful," George said. "It bears out the letter to this extent. Nobody's in the slightest degree sure that Morse wasn't killed. You can't prove yourself, can you, that Morse was actually Delorme and that he killed Noisan and made a getaway?"

I said frankly that I couldn't. Any evidence that pointed that way was circumstantial and even mere conjecture.

"But there is just this," I said, "and I've got to get it off my chest. The decisions have got to be yours, but I shan't feel happy unless I unburden my mind. What I have to call your attention to is the queer similarity of sequences. You've heard most of it before: each case had a fire for the purposes of concealing identities. There's no doubt about that, in my mind at least. And now there's another coincidence—Sindle's letter. I admit that the letter the Paris police had about Noisan was anonymous, but it did try to establish that he was still alive, and therefore that Delorme was dead. And I get back here and find you've had a letter trying to establish certain things in Sindle's favour! Can you wonder if I'm just a bit sceptical?"

"I fail to see the similarity," he told me. "One letter was anonymous and this one's at first hand." He rapped it with his knuckles. "It's a confession and a disclaimer, and so far it's been proved to be true."

"Good enough," I told him amiably. "But may I take it that you're assuming from now on that Morse is dead?"

"You're jumping too far ahead," he told me. "What I am assuming for the moment is that Morse couldn't have been Sindle."

"That brings us to the jack-pot question," I said. "After studying that letter, do you think Sindle really had no hand in killing Chale?"

"Don't rush me," he said testily. "I'm not going to be rushed. I've taken certain precautions at Southampton and so on, and Sindle's new description's being put out. We've got to be prepared for anything."

Then he was glancing up at the clock, and I guessed he was due for a conference.

"You'll want to be getting along home," he said. "Leave that report and I'll run through it. Get back here, if you can, at three o'clock."

I was back at three o'clock, and I had a quarter of an hour to wait. There'd been a conference as I'd thought. Wharton sat down heavily in his usual chair and lugged out his pipe and pouch.

"Well, we've decided on a course of action," he told me. "Both possibilities have to be taken into account—that Sindle told the truth and that he didn't. What it boils down to is that he killed Chale himself, or he didn't. We have to work on parallel assumptions. You might almost call it a couple of independent enquiries. If Sindle didn't kill Chale, then who did?"

"You read my report?"

"I got the gist of it," he said. "I don't think it's going to help." Then he waved a placatory hand. "A very well drawn-up report, mind you, for all that. But what I'd like you and me to do is to get our teeth into Sindle's letter. See if we can read into it any sort of clues that slipped his notice."

But first we went into the matter of the Southampton postmark. I thought it might indicate a slipping across to the Channel Islands and so surreptitiously to France. Wharton thought it merely a blind. His hunch was that Sindle had gone to Northern Ireland, from where it would be child's play to slip across the border into Eire.

We settled down to an examination of that letter. We each had a typed copy. And it occurs to me now that you yourself have a copy. Perhaps you might care to glance through it again to check your findings with ours. And just one piece of reassurance. I'm not proposing to give you pages of long-winded argument. What follow now are the things that occurred to us, and in their order as we came to them in the letter. I might also add that the original letter had no fingerprints, and that none likely to belong to Sindle were found in the room in Wellbank Street.

(a) Sindle's claim to have been convicted for an offence under another name. But the police would at least have made an investigation, and there would have been unusual elements that should make fairly easy a tracing of the charge and conviction. Wharton made a note for immediate insertion in the *Police Gazette*.

(b) "Only one of them ever regarded me as anything human." Something about that was hardly in keeping. Why should Sindle, the avowed misanthrope, look back with that faint tinge of gratitude for the one of his fellow tenants who appeared to have been unrebuffed by his churlishness?

And who could that one be? Everyone had openly expressed a loathing for the man. But then again there was the matter of that nude study of Viola Vetch.

"We've put that off too long," Wharton told me. "That's a job for you. You'll have to confront her with it and watch her reactions."

(c) Virtually a free gift of £250 by Chale. Surely there was something wrong about that? Could professional interest go so far as to become post-treatment philanthropy? Could Sindle conceivably have had any hold on Chale?

How could we possibly find out? All records had gone, and only appeals could bring information about similar charities from ex-patients. And yet one fact was unanswerable. Chale had been sufficiently interested in Sindle to obtain that studio.

(d) Why should Chale go to Borden Walk? Sindle could only give an opinion, and it was one that carried little conviction. Sindle ought to have guessed, as we guessed, that Chale had inspected that studio before he'd approached Mrs. Oddfort. It was *before* the occupation that he should have checked up on whether it was likely to suit his patient.

(e) Wolde's mention of a detective agency. That seemed to confirm Wharton's obstinate opinion that it had been she who had rung the Broad Street Detective Agency. In other words, Sindle's letter there had another bolstering of truth.

(f) The claim that Vandyke Sindle had been the name of a fellow student, now dead. Wharton made a note for the *Police Gazette*. Enquiries would be made at once at every School of Art in London and the provinces.

There was just one other thing arising out of the two convictions for sexual offences—the pansy-looking youth whom Ferndale had seen one day with Sindle. Surely that indicated a backsliding on the part of Sindle? And yet he spoke of himself as on the way to a complete cure. Or did that word *cure* mean to him only one thing—the ability once more to paint.

"Wouldn't do any harm," Wharton said, "if you saw Ferndale again. And that Mrs. Oddfort. Chale was only a nephew by marriage, but that murder ought to have shaken her a bit. Maybe she'll have remembered something else Chale said about Sindle when he was asking for that studio."

"You're abandoning entirely the idea that Morse had anything whatever to do with all this?" I said.

"Not exactly," he told me. "The Higher-Ups seem taken with the idea."

I reminded him about asking Timson about Morse's possible holidays in France. And the photostat of that anonymous letter from Spain.

That was the end of our conference. Wharton bustled out and I began making my appointments. Ferndale wasn't at his flat, but I ran him to earth at Knightsbridge, where he was having tea with Mrs. Solness. He wasn't staying long, he said, so I arranged to meet him at five-thirty at Swan and Edgar's corner. Mrs. Oddfort was in, and I arranged to see her at six o'clock. So much for the double coating of sugar: after it would come the pill. I didn't give a sign to Wharton, but it was an exceedingly unhappy Travers who faced the inevitability of that interview with Viola Vetch.

Chapter XV
THUNDERCLAP

FERNDALE'S taxi slewed round into Regent Street. I'd caught a glimpse of him, and I was at the door as he got out. He seemed quite pleased to see me.

"What's it all about?" he said.

"You tell me which way you're going and then I'll surprise you," I said.

"As a matter of fact," he said, "I'm going no farther than across the road to the Café Royal. Fixing up about a small party I'm throwing on Wednesday night."

"Good lord!" I was suddenly remembering. "You're getting married on Thursday."

"What about it?" he said, and smiled.

"Nothing, really. This is a good opportunity, though, to wish you luck. Or isn't that the right word?"

He chuckled.

"Tell you in a few weeks' time. But what's this surprise of yours?"

"That in one minute you can be on your way," I said. "I'm telling you in strict confidence that we've an idea that Sindle was a sexual pervert. That makes it important for you to think back again and see if you can tell us any more about that pansy you spotted him with."

He frowned.

"Don't remember what I did tell you. He was about twenty, I'd say, and had that sort of simpering look and walk."

"Anything else?"

"Not a thing," he said. "I just gave a casual glance. I was trying to avoid Sindle."

"Sindle was actually with him?"

"Now that's something," he said, and frowned again. "My impressions are that the pansy was a bit ahead. I'd say it was as if they'd parted and one was going one way and the other the other."

I thought quickly, then held out my hand.

"That's all then. And take things easy on Wednesday night. Don't forget there's going to be a Thursday morning."

He laughed.

"My dear fellow, I'd make a pretty good bet I'd drink you under the table any day."

I told him I'd never give him the chance. Then a farewell smile and a wave of the hand and we were on our way. I took a bus for Westminster and then another for Millbank. I was dead on time when Mrs. Oddfort opened the door of her flat.

Wharton had made a bad guess about her being shaken by Chale's death, for she was looking as bright-eyed and alert as ever. When I mentioned what I called the tragedy she agreed that it had been a very dreadful business, and then was adding a kind of rider to the effect that she'd never really known Chale at all.

"You'll think me a horrid old woman," she said, "but, to tell the truth, I never had any patience with this psychiatry stuff. I think it's nothing but a lot of quackery. In my young days people weren't supposed to have any nerves, and we weren't any the worse for it."

I said there couldn't be a better example than herself as proof of all that. I added with a sententious rider of my own that it took all sorts to make a world.

"But about your—what shall I call him—nephew-in-law. We seem to think he did a very great deal for this man Sindle, beyond the actual treatment. What was your experience of him? Would you have called him a generous man, from the little you know?"

Her impressions were that he was rather close in money matters.

"I can't tell you any more," she said, "but I do know that my husband was of the same opinion. Something to do with a loan—a gift really—when we were in England."

"And have you remembered anything else about the request Dr. Chale made you about that studio for Sindle?"

She raised her hands in a kind of horror.

"Don't for goodness' sake mention that," she said. "It only reminds me of that letter that Pamela Maine wrote me."

"The one complaining about Sindle?"

"Yes. And it makes me feel so guilty. I simply daren't ever look Pamela in the face again—not after what happened."

She had been speaking with a kind of humorous consternation. Then she was leaning forward in her chair.

"Do you think she was gifted with second sight?"

"Heaven knows," I said. "But isn't that a curious question from someone who doesn't believe in psychiatry?"

She gave her little chuckle of a laugh.

"You're too clever for me. But about Dr. Chale's request that I should let that man Sindle have the studio. You were asking me about that when you were here last, so it's no use asking me again. I can only tell you what I told you then, that he rang me, and I said of course he could have the studio."

"Dr. Chale touched your heart, if I may say so. He said he wanted to do a good turn for an ex-patient."

"That's right," she said, and quite triumphantly.

"And nothing else? Nothing about that ex-patient's financial difficulties?"

"Wait a minute," she said. "He didn't actually mention that, but he did say I need have no worries about the rent. Then I told him I'd ring the agents and he could fix everything up with them."

"It never struck you at any time that Dr. Chale himself might have paid the rent?"

"But why should I think such a thing?"

"I don't know," I said. "I just wondered if you might have had that impression."

It was no use questioning her further. I couldn't even think of a flanking movement to lure her unawares into some half-forgotten admission. So I got up to go, and then she was asking me if I wouldn't have a sherry. I promptly said I would.

"This rather looks like bribery and corruption," I told her as she placed the tray on the table by my chair.

"Of course it is," she said gaily. "And you're to promise me you'll never mention my name to Pamela Maine. I'm simply living in dread of another letter."

I waited for a bus to Sloane Square or Howe Street. I'd spun out the time, and at any moment I'd be on my way to Viola Vetch. A bus for Howe Street drew up and the inevitable was almost at hand. I went on top and tried to do some thinking.

It would be half-past seven when I got to Borden Walk, I told myself, and the two girls would probably be at their meal. Maybe I ought to go on to the Harriers and have a drink and then drop in soon after eight o'clock. Or perhaps the two had gone out for a meal and it might be better to call bright and early in the morning. Then all I need do was see Gulver and find out if he had discovered anything about Pamela Maine. Then the feel of that portfolio I was clutching and the feel of that picture inside it made me suddenly screw my courage to the sticking point. It was like one of those heroic moments when one finally determines to see the dentist. And that much done, I could take my thoughts from Viola Vetch.

In fact I found myself thinking about Pamela Maine. I couldn't do otherwise when I remembered that mock horror on the face of Mrs. Oddfort. And all at once I had a curious idea. It was something that might have occurred to me long before if we hadn't been so positive that Sindle, and Sindle alone, had killed Chale.

There was Wharton's proposition: if Sindle's letter was that much true and he'd found Chale dead, then who had killed him? *And Pamela Maine had suddenly seemed one sort of answer.*

Could she have killed Chale? I saw no reason why not. She might have seen him from her room and followed him up the stairs, and he would have had no reason to wonder why she was close behind him. As for a weapon, there had been a sharp-looking knife with a wooden handle on her trestle table, the one that she used, no doubt, for trimming parchment. And no particular force would have been needed for the blow. It was true that

Cave had said there'd been two blows, but even he couldn't prove that the first hadn't been fatal. So I told myself again that she *could* have killed Chale. If so, she struck twice with that knife just as he opened the door. Then she closed the door and went down to her room.

The bus dropped me at the far end of Howe Street, and as I walked towards Borden Walk I began probing more deeply into that theory. I thought of Pamela Maine, a woman who was as sane as the sanest except about her dead daughter and the man she'd accused of killing her. I went back to that scene with Bintwood in her room, and the strange mad look of her when she told us—or herself—that she *had* seen Chale. Had she been trying to remember what had happened on that Monday afternoon? Was the statement that Chale was trying to hide from her only some tragic link or hint of recollection—of the dead Chale behind that closed door? Just that? Her last sight of him as he fell, and then Chale, as it were, sealed in that room? Had she been up there since when the house was empty of everyone except herself, trying to find him in that burnt-out studio? I didn't know, and somehow I hated to know. There was something almost frightening to try to put one's self inside that tortured and tortuous mind.

Then my thoughts began almost instinctively to swing away. If she had killed Chale, then we would never be able to prove it, and, as I knew that, I was asking myself another question. If she had killed Chale, why did she raise that cry of 'Fire!'? Wouldn't the sight of the smoke that poured from that room have recalled to her what lay behind its door? Or was it, as Matthews had pointed out in quite another context, that there could be no accounting for the actions of those whose minds are even slightly unstable?

And that made me think of something else: something that had been too lightly slurred over when Wharton and I had gone through Sindle's letter—the question that Sindle ought to have asked himself after he had lighted that fire. Obviously Sindle had not provided Chale with a key, so how had Chale been able to let himself into that studio? Sindle had been anxious to get back in order to let Chale in. Where, then, had the key come from? Not from Mrs. Oddfort, or she would have mentioned it. Not from the agents, or Wharton would have discovered the fact when he'd asked them about Sindle.

I found no answer. I doubt if I'd have found one even if I'd had all the time in the world. But there wasn't time. I was at the door of No. 7.

A light was on in Ferndale's studio. I listened shamelessly and could just faintly hear his voice and Gulver's. I went up the stairs and quietly approached Pamela Maine's door. Inside, the wireless was fairly strong. A man was singing, and beneath the voice was the sudden surge of the orchestra. An opera, and in Italian, and rather like Puccini.

There was no sound from Bintwood's room. I went up to the top landing. I listened to the two voices and knew somehow that Bintwood wasn't there. I rapped on the door. Viola opened it, and at once I was making frantic gestures for silence.

"The Harriers? In ten minutes?"

She nodded, eyes a bit staring. The door closed and I tiptoed down the stairs. I walked a few yards towards Howe Street and waited in the shelter of a doorway. It was almost the ten minutes before she appeared, and she gave a little gasp as I suddenly stepped out.

"You gave me a regular shock," she said. "And you do make me tell some lies. I had to make out I'd forgotten an appointment."

"Helena believed you?"

"I don't know," she said. "I don't care if she didn't. You can't always be tied to someone's apron strings."

I had that portfolio of mine under the arm that was nearer to her, but she grabbed the arm all the same. She'd had her meal, she said, but she said it in a way that didn't preclude the ability to confront a dinner. I sidled away from that by asking about Pamela Maine.

"I haven't been able to learn a thing," she said. "If you ask me, she's forgotten all about it. Was that what you wanted me for?"

There seemed something tricky about that question. Luckily we were practically at the pub, and that meant crossing the road. It was fairly early and still not dark and the saloon bar was almost empty. She had a creme de menthe and I had my usual beer, and we found a table in the far corner by ourselves. I took the header straight away.

"I've been given a most unpleasant job," I said. "Why they should pick on me I don't know, unless they thought I knew you. It's about a picture that was found in Sindle's studio."

The eyes looking at me over the green of the glass were widening with surprise.

"In fact it's this," I said, and produced the picture. "Don't ask me about it. I know nothing. I wondered if you might know."

"Why, it's me!" she said. "It's my face."

Then she was gaping. The eyes opened wider.

"You say this was found in his room!"

"So I'm told."

Her face flushed. Remember what I told myself once about sex? It was just that sudden thought of herself and Sindle that brought the flush.

"It couldn't!" she said. "It's a lie. It couldn't have been there."

"I'm sorry, but it was. That's a certainty. But you never sat for it?"

She was getting to her feet. My long arm went across the table and gently held her down.

"I know you're angry," I said. "I hoped you'd be angry. I couldn't conceive of your ever having sat to him."

"To *him*?" she said. "I wouldn't have come within a mile of him. I hated the sight of him."

"Then how'd he come to paint it? From memory?"

She made a gesture of disgust.

"Besides, it isn't me—only the face."

"How do you know?"

The look was almost a glare.

"I know myself, don't I? The flesh tints are all wrong. It's just anybody. It's just a daub."

I put it back in the portfolio.

"That's what I wanted to hear," I said. "All the same, I didn't want Helena to see it. I wanted to keep it just between me and you."

I think she felt a small gratitude for that, even if she told me defiantly that she didn't mind who saw it. I said that we'd still keep it between the two of us.

"I know you're telling the truth," I said, "and that only makes it more of a puzzle. Sindle didn't see you half a dozen times, and yet his memory was so good that he could get your face."

"Someone else did it," she said. "He couldn't have done."

"Did you ever do that particular pose for anyone?"

"Never," she said. "Besides, it isn't me at all. It's just somebody or other with my head stuck on."

"Forget it," I said. "I'll report that you know nothing about it and that'll be the last we hear of it."

"Yes, but how did it get in his room?"

"Lord knows," I said. "Forget it. Have another drink." She said she didn't feel like another. She felt like going home—if she hadn't told Helena she'd be away for at least an hour.

"Let's take a bus ride," I said. "Round by the Park and through the West End."

We took a bus and we sat in the back seat on top, but she didn't take my arm. Getting her to talk was like drawing an elephant's teeth with tweezers. It was only after a second bus dropped us at Sloane Square that she began to come round.

"Sorry I've been so filthy tempered. But wouldn't you have been?"

I said I certainly would. That was when she took my arm.

"And you won't say anything to anyone after all?"

"Not to a soul. Just make a confidential report and that's all."

My arm had a squeeze.

"I wish I hadn't been like I was. You're ever so nice, really."

I forget what we talked about then, but I do remember we were just at Borden Walk when she remembered something. That picture must have been at the back of her mind all the time she'd been talking.

"I wonder," she said, and after a moment or so: "But it couldn't be."

"What couldn't be?"

"Well, you're never to say a word to anyone, but one afternoon when I happened to be in I saw Walter Bintwood and Gulver going into that studio."

"They must have had some reason," I said. "I can't imagine either of them planting that picture there."

"Silly!" she said. "As if they would."

But she was frowning all the same. And then we were at No. 7.

"Why don't you come in?" she said. "I can always say we just happened to meet."

"Not tonight," I said. "Some other time, and we'll have that dinner."

She craned up, and I thought she wanted to whisper something. What she gave me was a quick kiss, then she whisked through the door. I was feeling a bit sheepish as I heard the patter of her heels on the stairs. Then I wiped my cheek and went through the door myself. There had been a light in Gulver's window. I tapped on the door. A moment or two and he was letting me in.

I tried to look official. I took the grandfather chair he drew up for me, but I didn't take off my hat and I was clutching that portfolio.

"This is a very confidential call," I told him. "What I'm going to ask you is on no account to be repeated."

"If it's about Miss Maine," he said, "then I haven't been able to do anything for you, sir."

"It's not that," I said. "Scotland Yard has many ways of finding things out, and we've found something out. That one afternoon you and Mr. Bintwood were in Sindle's studio. I have to ask you to explain."

"Oh, that, sir." He shuffled in his chair and he wouldn't meet my eyes. "It wasn't anything, really, sir. Just what you might call natural curiosity."

Early one afternoon when he'd been coming back from town he'd seen Sindle take a bus at Howe Street. Just as he got home he saw Bintwood, who occasionally dropped in at lunch-time, and Gulver mentioned Sindle. Bintwood wondered what sort of stuff he painted, being interested, as Gulver said, in any kind of bargain. Gulver said it would be easy to find out, so the two had gone upstairs, and Gulver had opened the door with his master-key and Bintwood had had a quick look.

"He wasn't in more'n a couple of minutes, sir. Nothing there but a lot of junk was what he said."

"And when was this?"

"Be about a fortnight after he got here."

I told him it should have been reported. I warned him what might happen if he dared to mention a word to Bintwood, or any other living soul. I added that for my part I wouldn't mention the matter to Mrs. Oddfort, but even then he was a badly scared man when I left him.

It was then about half-past nine. Somehow I felt like walk-ing, so I turned back towards Sloane Square, and I was thinking about all sorts of things. In spite of that farewell peck of a kiss I was sure that Viola Vetch had told me nothing but the truth. Nor did that kiss mean anything beyond a kind of gratitude. She was like that, and that was just her way.

As for what she had told me about Bintwood, and in conjunction with what I'd heard from Gulver, that was strik-ing me as something reasonably natural. A man like Bintwood would always be on the lookout for a bargain: something like that Gauguin drawing he'd picked up once in Paris. Sindle might have been good and some of his stuff well worth an investment. And naturally Bintwood hadn't said a word to Wharton or myself—even on the murder night when he'd seen those pictures in Sindle's room—for fear of incriminating Gulver. And who was I pharisaically to condemn a man's curiosity? I could even twist that famous remark of John Bradford and tell myself that there, but for the grace of God, went Ludovic Travers.

I looked round to see a bus overtaking me, so I lengthened my stride and caught it at the stop. It was just after ten o'clock when I got to the Yard, and I was realising that it was a good many hours since I'd had a meal. Then just as I was thinking of leaving a note for Wharton he happened to come in. It was a quarter-past ten.

I opened my mouth. I closed it again as the buzzer went. Wharton moved across to his chair, sat down heavily and picked up the receiver.

"Wharton here."

A couple of seconds and I knew something had happened.

"My God, no!" was what he had said, and had followed it up with a: "Keep him there. I'll be along."

He slapped the receiver back and gave me a look.

"Know what that was?"

I shrugged my shoulders. I was too tired for parlour games.

"That Pamela Maine," he said, and got to his feet. "Someone's tried to do her in."

Chapter XVI
A TELEPHONE BOX

We were in Brackley Street; quiet, not too well lighted, and leading round to the south end of Borden Walk. Just where we stood a passage cut back to a warehouse and yard from which another passage came out not far from the Tabby Cat. Gulver was there and Matthews with him.

"This is the spot?" Wharton said.

"Right where you're standing, sir. Whoever did it must have slipped back along this passage."

"How'd you happen to be here, Gulver?"

Gulver explained. Maybe if I hadn't had reason an hour before to give him something of a dressing-down he'd have been telling things which I wasn't too anxious for Wharton to hear. I knew myself involved, and more than emotionally, in what had happened to Pamela Maine.

"Well, sir, I saw her go out, and I've been keeping an eye on her lately. She's not so strong as she used to be, you know, sir, so I just went along behind and smoked my pipe until we got just short of here at the bend of the road. I had to hold back a bit because she wouldn't have liked it if she'd have known, and then, when I came round the corner here, there she was. I thought she'd had a fit or something."

"And then?"

"Well, sir, then I saw a taxi coming, and I stopped it and got him to telephone for the ambulance. I could have picked her up myself, sir, but something told me not to do it, she was breathing so heavy."

We walked on the few yards to that bend in the road where Gulver had been when he'd lost sight of her.

"Tonight's was one of her usual walks?" Wharton wanted to know.

"She practically never takes any other," he said. "Down Warberry Street and round into Meriton Gardens, and then back home round here. About a quarter of an hour, the rate she usually walked."

"Any idea why she should want to walk at night?"

"Oh, yes. She told me herself, sir. That was when she was always most alive, sir, if you know what I mean: being an actress, you know, sir. And she liked to get some fresh air before going to bed."

We went back to where she'd been struck down.

"Everything bone dry," Wharton said. "Hopeless to look for footmarks. Better go through this passage in the morning, though, as soon as it's light. You get along home, Gulver, and you go through her room, Matthews, before you seal it. Not that I'm expecting you to find anything there."

They moved off. Gulver turned back.

"How *is* the lady, sir?—if you don't mind me asking."

"Still unconscious," Wharton said. "Just a chance of her pulling through."

The two moved off again. Wharton still stood there.

"Who was he?" he asked me. "Some young hooligan waiting here with a cosh on the off-chance?"

"I don't think so," I said. "It was light enough for him to see that she hadn't a handbag. What could he hope to get?"

"Yes," he said, and pursed his lips. "More in it than that. Let's get back to the Yard."

We went on to the car and neither of us did any talking. As I said, I was more than emotionally involved in the affairs of Pamela Maine, and, as I was beginning to see what lay behind this latest development, I knew that it was I and no other who was really responsible for that night's work. As soon as I stepped into Wharton's room I knew I had to get it off my mind. I told him how I'd hoped she might confide to someone what it was that she might have seen at Meriton Gardens.

"I know," he told me testily. "You had something about that in a report."

"Yes, but if I hadn't spread the news round at No. 7 that she probably did know something, then she wouldn't have been attacked tonight."

"So you're coming to it at last," he said, and gave a snort. "That's why someone struck her down tonight. If it hadn't been for that old-fashioned hat she was wearing and that Gulver was fairly close behind, that'd have been the end of her. But that isn't half of it. You see what the whole thing implies?"

I wished that I didn't. What it implied was that Sindle had never left the country after all and that that part of his letter had been bluff.

We talked about that for a minute or two, and then George was suddenly swerving away.

"No use taking too much for granted," he told me. "After all, it may have been just an ordinary coshing. In any case there's nothing we can do now. Better sleep on it. I don't know about you, but I've had a pretty long day."

That suited my book, and I didn't stand on the order of my going. I was too tired mentally to think of eating and I wondered if I should be able to sleep. And then, just before midnight, when I did fall asleep my brain gave a last spasmodic kick.

"Why should Sindle attempt to kill Pamela Maine?" That was what I was asking myself. Sindle didn't have to worry. What did

it matter to him what she might have seen at Meriton Gardens? He'd already frankly confessed that he'd killed Hermione Wolde!

In the morning I was bright and early at the Yard, and that was the question I immediately fired at Wharton.

"Just what I've been thinking myself," he said, and gave a nod or two. "You know, Travers, this is a pretty complicated case. A dam' sight too much so for my liking."

When George gets confidentially friendly like that it's a sure sign he's floundering.

"If he didn't do it," I said, "then we have to consider the question of a confederate. And that's only making it even more complicated."

"Suppose he did kill Chale and she saw him?" Then he was shaking his head. "No sense in that either. He'll be hanged for killing Wolde, so why worry about Chale."

I asked him about Pamela Maine. She'd recovered consciousness and a man was ready to take a statement, but that wouldn't be yet. It probably wouldn't be for a day or two.

The talk hung fire again. I hadn't had time to write the previous night's report, so I told him about Bintwood and Gulver and that surreptitious peep into Sindle's room. At once he was breathing out threatenings and slaughter. I tried to convince him that it was merely a natural, if somewhat mercenary, curiosity.

"Yet butter wouldn't have melted in his mouth when he saw those pictures on the Monday night," he said. "And what about his prints?"

Then he gaped. He had the same idea as myself. Bintwood had left prints on that surreptitious visit, but they'd been camouflaged by his second handling on the Monday night.

"I don't know," he said, and was giving the second of those Colosseum smiles—the one when the lion had pounced on and missed the plump Christian. "I'd like to know a whole lot more about that chap Bintwood. Get to work on him this morning and see what you can find out."

Before I could ask for suggestions he was going on.

"Why should he be living there at all? He isn't an artist, is he?"

"They're nice rooms," I said, "and rooms aren't easy to come by. And they're handy for his work. Useful, too, to be living in the neighbourhood of arty people."

Wharton grunted.

"One thing can put him in the clear," I said. "You get hold of him now and ask for his alibi for ten o'clock last night."

He rang down for the number.

"That photostat coming?" I said.

"The first plane this morning," he told me.

"And just one other little thing. Why not let the backroom boys get to work on Sindle's letter—the ink, I mean—and find out when it was written?"

"What's the point of that?"

I said I didn't exactly know, but I had a hunch it ought to be done. Then the call came through. Wharton picked up the receiver.

I couldn't gather what it was all about, though I did hear him say it would have to be checked. There'd also been the eyewash about red-tape and only the guilty objecting to giving alibis.

"There we are," he said when he'd rung off. "He was at his sister's. Didn't leave till after ten o'clock. I'll have it checked. You get along and see what you can find out all the same."

He didn't suggest how and I didn't ask. But I had an idea, and I thought I'd walk through to Old Bond Street. But I couldn't help wondering just what had been at the back of Wharton's mind. Could it be possible he was reverting to that Morse theory and thinking that Bintwood might somehow be Morse? It seemed fantastic to me, and yet somehow I didn't know. Bintwood was the right height and, according to Viola, his French was fluent. As to any surgical work on his face, there was that curiously squat nose of his. Morse's nose in that *Gazette* picture had been rather of the Roman kind, but a cartilege might have been removed. Then there were his somewhat slanting eyes, and those again might be different from what God gave him. And he had come to Borden Walk at somewhere about the time when Morse might have returned to England.

But it was a waste of time to speculate, and in a few minutes I hoped I should know. And when I got to the neighbourhood of the old Hedley place I began looking for a picture dealer. I found one not a hundred yards from the bombed space. A fine Dutch still-life of flowers and fruit was in the window and a couple of Morland prints with the bloom as fresh as a butterfly's wing.

I walked in. A rather dapper, middle-aged man appeared from somewhere in the back regions. I showed him my warrant card. His eyebrows were raised as he handed it back.

"Not stolen property?"

"Nothing like it," I said. "You're Mr. Drewson?"

"Yes," he said. "Mark Drewson."

"You been here long?"

"Most of my life," he said. "Forty years or thereabouts."

"You used to know Hedleys?"

He knew Hedleys. He knew Bintwood. He didn't remember the exact dates, but he knew Bintwood had been in the Paris branch and had come back well before the war. After that he knew Bintwood had been there continually till the place had been bombed to the ground in 1942.

"A nice sort of chap," he said, and gave me an enquiring look. "I'd be sorry to hear anything was wrong with him."

I assured him that Bintwood's good name was as immaculate as ever. Mine was merely a cross-checking of statements connected with a third party. He didn't follow that—how could he?—but he tried to look as if he did. All that remained was to thank him and impress on him the need for secrecy.

"Isn't he with Markov now?" he asked me as we went towards the door.

I said he was, but that didn't make the matter any less confidential. That rather puzzled him again. As I moved off towards Piccadilly I was wondering if he'd succumb to curiosity and ring Bintwood. Not that I was worrying even about that.

I didn't hurry back to the Yard. After all the chatter of the previous day I was feeling a bit allergic to more and more theorising, so I took my time over the coffee in a restaurant and stoked up against a possible loss of lunch with a couple of cakes.

I smoked a pipe and took my time as I walked down through Whitehall to the Yard. It was about half-past eleven when I got there. I heard voices as I opened the door, and there was Sidwell, the handwriting expert. He and Wharton were peering at something on Wharton's desk. It looked as if that photostat had arrived.

"At first glance," Sidwell was saying, "I'd say it was the same hand. What's the difference in age, did you say?"

"Six years or so," Wharton told him.

Sidwell frowned. He said he'd like a thorough test.

"Can't afford the time," Wharton said. "You get to work over there. There's a good light and here's my glass."

Sidwell settled down at the table by the window. Wharton and I did our talking in little more than whispers. I said if Sidwell's first guess was right, then my morning had been wasted. In any case Bintwood was definitely not Morse. Drewson could swear that Bintwood had been with Hedleys off Old Bond Street from well before the war till 1942.

Wharton had yet another look over at where Sidwell was working. He told me Bintwood's alibi had been tested and was absolutely right.

"Looks as if we've got to fall back on Sindle," he said, and then he couldn't restrain himself and was going across to Sidwell.

"How's it coming along?"

Sidwell still thought the handwriting the same.

"And you'd be prepared to go into the witness-box?"

"Not at the moment." He got to his feet. "The quickest way, you know, would be for me to take these home and really get down to it."

"Right," Wharton said. "Just sign a couple of receipts and that'll be that. But don't forget I want your report by five o'clock at the latest."

Sidwell said unconcernedly that he'd see what he could do. Like the rest of us he was used to Wharton.

"What's your considered opinion at the moment?" Wharton had to ask him at the door.

"Don't know," Sidwell said. "An even-money chance they're the same? Or three to two on?"

"But isn't that good enough?"

"Wishful thinking won't hang this chap Sindle," Sidwell told him dryly. "You just possess your soul in patience. It has to end up at a thousand to one on."

Wharton came back to his chair. He gave a dour nod or two.

"Three to two on. That ought to be good enough. No use waiting for certainties."

I said I supposed an expert ought to be sure. But what could we do? If those two letters were by the same hand, then Sindle was Morse. And then what?

"Dammit, what's the good of being pessimistic!" He let out a breath after that explosion. "It throws a new light on everything, doesn't it? It means that Chale knew he was Morse. It explains why Chale went to Borden Walk."

"Granted," I said. "It might even explain why Sindle killed him. They knew too much about each other and Sindle struck first."

"Then why did Sindle tell us he didn't kill Chale?" He snorted exasperatedly. "He admitted killing Wolde, didn't he? He knew he'd swing for it, so why shouldn't he own up to killing Chale as well?"

I said it might be like one of those riddles where something's put in to make it more difficult.

"But don't you see this, George. If Sindle is Morse, then all that screed of a letter is nothing but deliberate lies, put down to obscure the issue. There're only two things in it on which we can rely—that Chale did get the studio for him and that he killed Hermione Wolde."

Wharton got up. His eye went to the clock.

"The night brings counsel," he told me. "That's what they say. I'm going to see what a square meal'll do."

I said he wouldn't want me on his tail, so I'd do the same. And after it I thought I might see Gulver.

"Nothing found in Miss Maine's room?"

"Not that's any help," he said. "You might see Gulver, though. You can handle him better than Matthews."

I had a meal at my club and rang Gulver from there, and I didn't tell him why I wanted to see him. For a good reason, perhaps: that I had nothing at the moment in my mind, but was hoping with some dim optimism or other that something might turn up.

It was about a quarter-past two when I got off the bus at Howe Street, and a rather amusing thing happened as I walked along. A couple of cockney children—a boy of about seven and a girl a bit older—had apparently been eating an orange, and the two of them had cut a section of the rind to imitate a set of teeth.

"Look, mister!" the girl said.

Her brother had that orange rind in his mouth and she was laughing. I had to smile, and not only at the grotesqueness of the face.

"Your own orange?" I said.

"No, mister, we found some skin."

I felt in my pocket and out came a shilling.

"Here you are," I said. "Go and buy yourselves an orange each."

She looked at me, then the sticky hand grabbed the shilling.

"Coo!" she said. The boy spat the peel from his mouth and she grabbed his hand. I moved on. The girl had remembered her manners, as my old nurse used to say, and was calling her thanks. I gave them a wave and a smile. I'd had good value for a shilling. At my age it's good to recapture even a moment of what has ineluctably gone, and those two urchins had sent me back to my boyhood and how I'd once tried to scare my nurse with one of those sets of orange teeth.

And then I think I stopped smiling. Orange teeth: false teeth, as it were, for children: teeth that altered a face and pushed out one's lips and even altered one's voice. Rabbit teeth one called them when a human mouth was built that way. And Sindle's mouth had been something like that.

But I was actually walking past the door of No. 7. I turned the few paces back and went in. Gulver's door was ajar and I looked in and he was there.

"Come in, sir," he said. "Just been tidying up a bit."

He shook the homely cushion on the chair. I took off my hat and sat down. I offered him a cigarette. I had one myself.

"Miss Maine's going to recover," I told him.

"I'm glad of that, sir. I'd never have forgiven myself if she hadn't."

"And that reminds me," I said. "Just whom did you speak to about what you and I were talking about? You remember. Getting her to say what she might have seen round at Meriton Gardens."

"I had a word with the girls, sir, but they found nothing out. I didn't say nothing to Mr. Bintwood because you told me not to, but I did have a word with Mr. Ferndale and he gave me a ticking off. Reckoned it'd be criminal to go worrying her considering what she was like."

"Well, he wasn't far wrong," I said. "Mr. Ferndale was here yesterday afternoon, wasn't he?"

"Just come to see about some of his things," he said. "Painting things and such-like. He's going to do some work, as he calls it, when he's on his honeymoon."

"Of course," I said. "I keep forgetting he's getting married."

"Day after tomorrow, sir. Taking his car over by the afternoon boat and going to Italy. Mrs. Solness has a sister there."

"Very nice too," I said. "I wouldn't mind a few weeks of Italy myself."

"Never was there," he said. "They tell me it's a very nice country, though."

We talked about it for a minute or two. It was mechanical on my part, for I was trying to think of vastly different things. I'd come to that room with a vague and flatulent hope, and nothing whatever had emerged. The best thing I could do was try to find inspiration elsewhere. I might, for instance, make the latest news about Pamela Maine an excuse for a chat with Bintwood.

"A funny sort o' place it'll be here now, sir," Gulver was saying, "what with poor Miss Maine in the hospital and now Mr.

Ferndale away. May be gone for some weeks, he was telling me. All sorts of jobs I used to do for him and Mrs. Solness, and for Miss Maine if it comes to that."

I wondered suddenly if he were angling for a tip; then I guessed he was only relieving his mind.

"Might I use your telephone?"

"Of course, sir. This way, sir."

We went out to the hall and on to a kind of cubby-hole under the stairs. There was just a stand for the telephone and a shelf for the directories, and on a nail hung a book for the entry of calls.

"You trust a lot to people's honesty?" I said.

"Everyone's all right here, sir," he told me. "They just come down and phone when they like. They can't take a call, of course, not unless they happen to be here. Or I'm here myself."

I think I must have stared at him. I know that my fingers were all at once fumbling with my glasses.

"I don't think I need telephone after all," I said, and stepped back to the hall again. "Sorry to have bothered you, Gulver."

"That's all right, sir," he was saying, but I was already at the door.

But I wasn't making for Sloane Square and Bintwood. I wanted to get somewhere quiet; somewhere where I could think; somewhere where I could answer just one question—*did I now know, or didn't I, just who it was that had killed Chale?*

Chapter XVII

NEARING THE END

I WENT past the Tabby Cat, through Meriton Gardens and on to the river. I looked up at the block of flats by the Tate and wondered idly if Mrs. Oddfort were in. And having got that far I went on to Westminster and a teashop. I was there for about half an hour, and then I went through to the Yard. And I still hadn't found the answer to that question. Or perhaps I had. I knew, or I almost knew, who had killed Chale. What I couldn't do was prove it. Too many fantastic things reared themselves in the way: things which it would take more than one of Wharton's square meals to clear from the path of lucidity and logic.

That was why I decided to say nothing to Wharton. He was in his room and, by the fug, at his sixth or seventh pipe. He looked up and gave me a grunt. I was merely an obtrusion between himself and thought.

"Anything new?" I asked him.

"Yes," he said, and the irony was far too heavy. "We've found the people who moved Sindle's things. The place he bought them at. Matthews is round there now. All we've got to do now is find Sindle."

"Nothing from Sidwell?"

"Not that I know of."

I hung up my hat and sat down. I lighted a cigarette and looked out of the window. The buzzer went.

Sidwell was on the line. I could guess what he was saying long before Wharton rang off.

"He's certain," he told me.

The quick excitement went. He shrugged his shoulders and leaned back in his chair.

"Maybe the Higher-Ups can think of something," he said. "I've thought till I can't think any more."

He talked about the bad luck of everything. He even brought up my ineptitude in not grabbing Hermione Wolde on that Monday night. She, the one who might have spilled the beans, was dead. Chale was dead. The records were burnt. I was feeling as if I had murdered Chale myself.

"What can we do? Sindle, or Morse—call him what you like—has gone to earth. If he's got half the sense he showed over those murders, then we'll never clap a hand on him."

"One thing I wish you would do," I said. "I mentioned it before. Get that letter of Sindle's round to the backroom boys. Collect it from Sidwell and tell them it's a rush job. Say we've got to know just when that letter was written."

"What's the point of it?"

"Don't know," I said. "But it's the biggest hunch I ever had. Let's suppose something. Suppose that letter was written before Wolde was killed."

"Optimistic, aren't you?"

I pointed out that everything was supposition. I'd used that by way of illustration. And it still didn't make the hunch any less insistent. And we'd played hunches before and they'd never done us any harm.

"All right," he said heavily. "You know what you're doing. I'll get to work on it."

"Anything else for me now?"

He said there wasn't. He said it as if it was the worst day in his life when he'd first clapped eyes on me.

"Well, you'll know where to find me," I said. "If you can get that letter business rushed through, you might give me a ring. Or why not get this room off your mind and drop in on me."

He wouldn't hear of it, so I went back to the flat. Bernice was in and we had a domestic evening. I did my couple of crossword puzzles and she went on knitting the pullover which I wasn't supposed to know was for my birthday. We had a service meal, and all the time the thoughts were seeping through my mind like water through a filter. Each time they came out just a little clearer. I could tell myself that I knew who killed Chale and Wolde. What I still couldn't do was prove it.

I could prove it to myself, mind you, but that's far from convincing a public prosecutor or those twelve people in a jury-box. I had to have unshakeable proof: proof that would stand a grilling by counsel. And there was something else. Paradoxically enough, I saw how I might get that proof; but, if I got it, then we wouldn't get the one who had murdered Chale. *I had to have both murderer and proof at one and the same time.*

The evening wore on, and now there wasn't even need to think. It was just short of ten o'clock and I was thinking of making up for lost sleep when the telephone rang. Wharton was on the line.

"That idea of ours," he said. "It was plumb right."

Ours, mind you.

"You mean the letter?"

"That's right," he said. "It was written a week ago. Not less than seven days ago and not more than a fortnight. Probably the day after Chale was killed. They can't get nearer than that."

I didn't say a word. I was wondering just how I could tell him what I now knew.

"Well?" he was saying. "What about it now? Like to talk it over?"

I said I would. In a quarter of an hour I'd be at the Yard.

It was a fine, clear night and I walked, not because I had to shake off a sleepiness but to get ideas in order before I saw Wharton. We were on to something big, and in less than twenty-four hours the case should be virtually closed. It had to be. We had just that margin of time, and no more. One bad slip and we might be in for a spell of trouble.

George was waiting for me and he was literally rubbing his hands. He even passed me his tobacco pouch.

"Well, we've had some lucky guesses in our time," he said, "but not many so lucky as this."

The hunch was still apparently ours. I didn't mind. I doubt if there was even irony in my smile. I'd long got past the stage of worrying about George's little whims and stratagems and tantrums. I was Travers, who snapped his fingers at filthy lucre and sleuthed for the fun of it—almost. Or wasn't that irony?

"You saw the implications?" I said.

"Straight away," he said. "Wolde's murder was planned before it took place."

"I meant that other implication, to do with that perversion business."

"I spotted that all right," he told me. "Just one last push and the boat's out. This time tomorrow we ought to have our hands on Sindle."

I suppose it was a bit unpardonable of me to be so happy about telling him he was wrong. I had to prove that we needed several pushes, and that a push too strong might be just that one too much.

"Well, what comes first?" he said.

"Morse's fingerprints. Everything's got to revolve round that."

"His prints?" he said. "But Brumford never did have his prints."

"They're in Brumford," I said. "They ought to be somewhere on that portrait he painted of Timson. Nobody should have handled the actual canvas but himself. A reputable artist buys a suitable frame and does the framing himself. The prints on the frame will have been dusted off long ago, but they still ought to be on the canvas if it's never been removed. If it was removed after a year, say, for varnishing, then it was Morse who did the varnishing."

He said a bit dubiously that the prints would be stale.

"Maybe," I said, "but with the special treatment they ought to come up. You ring Brumford in the morning to fix up about Timson and I'll take Sergeant Wells. If anyone can get those prints, he will."

"We've got a man down there," the inspector told us, "and they're doing everything they can. We're trying to find out the daughter's name from here."

"What about the *Gazette* files?" I said. "She'll have been married from Brumford."

He'd said they'd just thought of that. But it would take time. The neighbour, who had seen her, thought she was about forty, and that would mean hunting through hundreds of daily files. I could have mentioned the Arts Club, but I didn't. After all, we had plenty of time. What I said was that we'd get ourselves a meal and report back between one and two.

We had our meal and reported back, and there was still nothing. Then it emerged that they'd taken things too much for granted. Since Timson hadn't been in when they rang, they'd waited with the hope he might be back. It was eleven o'clock before they'd found out about Sulliford.

We waited and waited, and it was after two o'clock when the *Gazette* sent that married name. And since it was the not uncommon one of Black, that would mean a longer hunt at the Sulliford end. I rang the Yard and said there was just a chance we might not be back at six as arranged. Then, at a quarter to three, we heard that Timson had been located and was on his way. It was a quarter past when he got out of the police car at his gate. Then there had to be explanations, and it was another five minutes before Wells could get to work.

Morse, as I had thought, had selected the frame and fitted it. Timson had papered the back to keep out the dust. I didn't want him hovering round in the way of Wells, so he and I went into the living-room. I didn't give much away. I said the fingerprints would be a help and we hoped they'd run Morse to earth. He was talking about the excitement in Brumford if he really was apprehended, and he was wanting to know if that old blackmail case would be reopened. I had to say I didn't know, but he could certainly be arrested for estreating his bail.

While I was talking I was taking surreptitious peeps at my watch. It was half-past three when Wells came in.

"I think we've got what we want," he told me. "There's only one thing. I'd rather have the photographing done at the Yard if Mr. Timson doesn't mind."

Timson was agreeable, so I wrote a quick receipt. Then I had to use his telephone to get hold of Wharton. I said that with the best will in the world I couldn't get back till half-past six at the earliest, and then there'd be the prints to check. That meant a quick reorganisation of plans, but it was well after four o'clock when we finally got away.

I made the driver shift over and handled that car myself. If I'm going to land up in a hospital I'd like to be the one responsible, but I changed the route slightly to avoid the heavy traffic, and the three of us were still whole when we came into the Edgware Road at soon after six. Even then it was nearer half-past when we turned in at the Yard. And it was after half-past when I walked into Wharton's room.

I don't care too much for flashbacks, but maybe you'd like to know what Wharton had to do.

From the first thing in the morning there had been a tail on each of the tenants of No. 7, Borden Walk and their movements had been reported during the day. Wharton had had an easy time. All he had had to do was to sit in his room, smoke his pipe, eat his meals and listen to what was happening.

During the afternoon a report came in from the hospital. Pamela Maine had been able to shed no light on that attack. She had seen nothing and heard nothing. Wharton wasn't worried. He'd expected nothing else.

Towards five o'clock the pace quickened. Matthews was near Borden Walk in a patrol car. Viola Vetch came home at soon after five, Helena Grace at five-fifteen, and Bintwood at just short of five-thirty. Gulver had been out during the morning, but he hadn't budged in the afternoon. Matthews saw the four of them. It was in connection, he said, with that attack on Pamela Maine, and he'd like them to pay a quick visit to the Yard. A car would take them there and bring them back, and he'd like them to be ready to move off at six-fifteen. Gulver and Bintwood were quite amenable. Helena Grace seemed a bit uneasy and Viola Vetch was a bit flippant.

"We *are* coming home, then," was what she said to Matthews. "Sure you aren't going to arrest us? I'd rather like to spend a night at Holloway."

"I'll take you there some time," Matthews told her, and he probably gave her a wink.

That much reported, Wharton himself saw Ferndale at his flat. Chief-Inspector Jewle was with him, and they went in two separate cars. Ferndale was just about to dress for that evening at the Cafe Royal. Wharton told him that something was in the wind about that attack on Pamela Maine, and that the tenants of No. 7 would be at the Yard at six-thirty.

"I'd like to help," Ferndale said, "but I'm sure I know nothing. Besides, I have to be at the Cafe Royal by seven at the latest."

Wharton said he'd used Ferndale's name to influence the others. And he could promise that proceedings at the Yard would be over in time for Ferndale to get back to Regent Street.

"You do your dressing now," he said, "and I'll wait. Then when everything's over you can go straight to the Café Royal."

At a quarter-past six Ferndale was ready. He and Wharton went out together.

"See you in a few minutes," Wharton told him as he showed him into Jewle's car. "This is Chief-Inspector Jewle. He'll take you up to my room at the Yard. I've got to see a man about a dog."

Jewle's car moved off towards the Yard. Wharton's moved off far more rapidly, and in the direction of Knightsbridge. At five and twenty to seven he was ringing the Yard and telling Matthews to hold the fort as arranged. It was just as Matthews hung up that I walked into the room. Matthews gave me a grin.

"Everything all right, sir?"

"Wells thinks so," I said. "What's happened to Wharton?"

He told me. Ferndale had taken longer over his dressing than he'd thought. Wharton, in fact, had expected to find him dressed for the evening.

"Hadn't you better be getting 'em in?"

"Do 'em no harm to wait," he said. "The balloon can't go up till the Super gets back."

But he rang down all the same. A moment or two and the five were coming in. Gulver and Bintwood looked somewhat stolidly about them, Helena looked a bit nervous, and Viola gave me a queer look that began as a grin and ended as I didn't know what. Ferndale was annoyed.

"You're here, Travers," he said testily. "Can't you do something to hurry things up? It was distinctly promised I should get back before seven o'clock."

"If it was promised, then you'll be back," I said. "The whole thing's little more than a formality and just to save us time. Perhaps you'd like to ring the Café Royal just in case you're a minute or so late."

"That's all right," he said. "I just wanted to be there a bit early, to see to things, you know. Make sure everything was right. Where do I sit?"

Matthews was setting out the chairs. Ferndale hadn't done a lot of dressing for that party of his; in fact he was wearing much the same clothes as on that Monday night when I'd first seen him, and when he'd also had a party. Gulver and Bintwood were in what one might call their ordinary best. Helena was dressed to kill, with a stylish, fur-collared coat and a perky hat. Viola just looked herself. She wore no hat, and that reddish hair of hers and the *gamine* look kept one somehow from noticing her clothes.

Matthews cleared his throat.

"Well, ladies and gentlemen, you've been good enough to come here and help us over that attack on Miss Maine. We're strongly of the opinion that it wasn't just an ordinary cosh attack for purposes of robbery. We think, in fact, that someone was trying to close her mouth in case she might let out something she saw in connection with the two murders, of Dr. Chale and Miss Wolde. Or it might have been something she knew about the missing Sindle."

He looked round to watch the effect. Then the door opened and Wharton came in.

It was a first-class entry. Matthews got to his feet. I thought I'd better rise too. Everyone else thought he'd better rise. It was like the entry of Mr. Speaker. And Wharton was looking his most impressive. There's six feet of him, though one wouldn't think it, and a back like the end of a barge, and when he chooses to look magisterial he makes a good hand of the job.

"Sit down, ladies and gentlemen, please."

He settled down in the chair which Matthews had vacated, and laid on the desk the papers he'd been carrying. Those, I judged, were for effect. Ten minutes at the very least were needed, and he took his time at adjusting the old-fashioned spectacles.

"I'm sorry you've been kept like this. Especially you, Mr. Ferndale. I took the liberty of ringing the manager and saying you mightn't arrive till a bit after seven. He said I was to assure you that everything was in hand."

There was a whispered word or two with Matthews. Then he leaned forward, and he peered at us over the spectacle tops. I'd often thought that little trick of his was rather funny; it didn't seem funny then.

"Sergeant Matthews has told you what we think about that attempt to kill Miss Maine. Please regard this as a kind of family party. There's nothing here to overawe anyone, so I'd like you to speak your minds. First of all, did you discuss those two murders with anyone? You, Miss Vetch?"

"I suppose I did," she said. "I didn't see any harm, and everyone knew where I lived."

"That's all right." He raised a placatory hand. "You, Miss Grace?"

"Not outside the building," she said.

"Naturally that's what I meant," Wharton told her. "It was only natural that you should talk about it yourselves. But why didn't you talk about it outside?"

"Well," she said, "it was an order, really. Mr. Durance—that's my boss—said I wasn't even to mention where I lived. He was very strict about it. He said what happened would be the wrong kind of publicity."

"I see. And you, Mr. Ferndale?"

Ferndale shrugged his shoulders.

"I think I talked about it quite a lot—or, rather, I had to. Everyone who knew where my studio was would naturally mention it."

"And you, Mr. Bintwood?"

"I don't remember talking it over with anyone except Mr. Markov." He gave a dry little smile. "If you don't mind me saying so, pictures and murders don't go very well together."

Wharton thought that worth a smile of his own. Somehow it made a little stir of relief. People moved in their seats.

"And you, Mr. Gulver?"

"Well, sir, I did," he said. "I don't know as I'm interested in murders more than most, but this was something special, as you might say, being on our own premises."

"Right," Wharton said briskly. "Now the vital question. I'd like just a plain yes or no. Did any of you mention Miss Maine's name to a single soul outside the building? You, Miss Vetch?"

"No. Not ever."

"Miss Grace?"

“Never.”

“Mr. Ferndale?”

“Never. Why on earth should I?”

“Mr. Bintwood?”

“Never. Except to my sister and her husband.”

“Mr. Gulver?”

“No, sir. I was very strict about that after what Mr. Travers told me.”

“That’s that, then,” Wharton said, and let out a disappointed breath. “But just one other question, and it’s really the last. Did anyone try to question *you* about the murder at Borden Walk? Show an undue interest, I mean, or try to get you to divulge anything of what the police were doing. Miss Vetch?”

“No one did.”

“Miss Grace?”

“No one.”

“Mr. Ferndale?”

“Not to my knowledge.”

And that was when the buzzer went.

“Pardon me,” Wharton said, and picked up the receiver. “Wharton here. . . . I see. . . . That’s capital. I don’t think there’s any need to keep anyone any longer.”

The receiver went back. People had been on their company manners, looking away as if that would stop them from listening. Now they were looking at Wharton again. His smile made everyone smile.

“Well, ladies and gentlemen, you’ll be glad to hear we think we’ve got the one who attacked Miss Maine. That means I needn’t keep you any longer.”

His hand went up as he glanced at the clock. It was just after five minutes past seven.

“I’d just like one quick word with you, Mr. Gulver. Perhaps you wouldn’t mind waiting a minute outside. And just one little personal matter with you, Mr. Ferndale.”

He went to the door himself, like a kirk elder with a departing congregation.

"Good night. Miss Vetch. Good night, Miss Grace, and thank you. Good night, Mr. Bintwood, and thank you for what you've done. I'll see you in a minute, Mr. Gulver. Wait just there, will you?"

The door closed and he came slowly back. There was a curious sort of smile on his face, and for some reason or other my heart began to beat too quickly. His hand fell on Ferndale's shoulder.

Ferndale smiled. Maybe he thought it was a clap on the back. Then he looked at Wharton, and Wharton wasn't smiling. I saw the fingers tighten on Ferndale's shoulder.

"Colin Morse, I have a warrant for your arrest for estreating your bail at Brumford on May the 20th, 1939, and I'm taking you into custody. I have to warn you . . ."

CHAPTER XVIII
WHYS AND WHEREFORES

THAT was the holding charge. And the evidence? Only the fact that Morse's prints were those of Ferndale. There had been no need that night at the Yard for us to indulge in any hocus-pocus like making people write down this and that. Besides, we had the prints of everyone but Ferndale, and when Wharton went to his flat that night he simply pocketed that day's issue of *The Times* while Ferndale was dressing. But, as I was saying, it was a holding charge. No bail could be granted, and we'd have time to amass all the evidence and be ready, when the graver charges came, to present a water-tight case.

I'm writing at the time when that case was on the eve of presentation. A certain amount of evidence had to be circumstantial and suggestive, but it merely gave weight to what was undeniable fact. It would be a longish case, too, with a good many witnesses, including those from France. And the simple story— it wasn't necessary for us to establish all of it—was this.

Morse and Chale were both involved in that Brumford blackmail. Morse bolted because it was easier for him to find a perfect hidey-hole, and I doubt if he anticipated a very long exile. Chale paid the couple who'd gone bail and so whitewashed himself. There was nothing that summer of 1939 to stop his going to France. He probably saw Morse there and arranged about finances.

Morse got in touch at the right moment with his friend of the *atelier* Ingres. Every bit of evidence we'd had about him was that he was a 'clever devil'; a man of ubiquity, charm and adaptability. It brought him a partnership with Noisan and it gave him the trust of the Nazi higher-ups. It brought him abundant money: enough, when the first sign of a Nazi cracking was to be discerned, to have a cache in Spain and maybe another in Portugal. Maybe, too, that association with the Nazis added a ruthlessness to his make-up. Life wasn't of too much account in those occupation years.

Then came the allied landings and the break-through. Morse had to make a getaway, and Noisan represented a possible confession and incrimination. So Noisan was killed and Morse bolted to Spain. Later he wrote that letter to the Paris police from a restaurant in the Puerta del Sol in Madrid. He didn't know it was a letter that would hang him. He couldn't possibly conceive that it would ever be under scrutiny by Scotland Yard.

After the German collapse he made his way to England, but at Lisbon—for a price—he could have provided himself with what papers he needed. We could find no reason, by the way, why he chose the name of Gordon Ferndale. And in England he would get in touch with Chale.

Did Chale, the surgeon, operate in any way on his face? We doubted it. Morse had got very much thinner. The longish, artistic hair and the little side-whiskers would make someone very different from the full-faced professional man of the Brumford days. And that Brumford case was dead and forgotten. It had been a local affair, and who in London would ever recognise Morse? And if the million-to-one chance eventuated, there was Chale to swear a denial.

But it must have been the influence of Chale with Mrs. Oddfort that obtained that fine studio for him. Mrs. Oddfort, when questioned, just remembered it and no more; and in a letter, for she'd been out of England at the time. So Morse took up painting. There was a mutual scratching of backs. Chale could casually recommend Morse to his suitable women patients, and, when Morse was established, he could give recommendations to Chale. And a very discreet, and highly selective blackmail business was resumed. That would be operated by a gross over-charging of a selected victim's bill. Or Ferndale could have applied pressure from information supplied by Chale. But when there was blackmail there had to be no risk of another Brumford case, and that was why there were so few cases. Chale's few cash payments to his bank proved that. And there wasn't a doubt that when Wolde became established with Chale she was a complete part of things. That little legacy of hers must have long since gone, and a woman doesn't accumulate three thousand pounds as a secretary-receptionist.

And so to a couple of months before the murder. There must have been some sort of a quarrel followed by a definite tension. Maybe some blackmail business had almost brought disaster, and then, in any case, Morse announced his engage-ment to Mrs. Solness and his intention of getting out of things. And each knew the other for a tricky customer. Maybe Chale threatened to break that engagement. My guess was that Mrs. Solness had originally been picked as a blackmail victim. What was certain was that just over a month before the murder Morse began planning.

Everything had to be synchronised. Everything depended on the successful creation of Sindle.

And something there has to be kept in mind. Morse had a month in which to test whether Sindle had really been accepted as the tenant of that upper studio. All the other planning would be going on at the same time, but only if he was dead sure about Sindle would he add the last touch to that murder plan. At any moment he could have withdrawn. Sindle would merely have disappeared. A three days' wonder, and that would have been that.

Chale was the instrument of his own murder. Morse must have known as soon as anyone that that studio was about to fall vacant, and he asked Chale to get it for an old artist friend who had fallen on bad days. The disguise was simplicity itself. If you don't credit that, then do this. Cut yourself a piece of stout, whitish cardboard about the size of a quarter-section of orange peel. Cut it across for the tongue to protrude and then fashion top and bottom to imitate teeth. Put it in your mouth and pad it slightly against the gums so that the teeth protrude above your own. Then look at yourself in the glass. Then, if unconvinced, add a few wispy hairs on the upper lip, a little tuft for the imperial, and the hair fluffed well out round the ears to hide the little side-whiskers. A drop of some harmless irritant reddens the eyes, and any sort of plumpers fill out the cheeks and a touch of colour makes them sallow. Then add glasses for the final touch. And say a few words with those home-made false teeth in your mouth and hear the absolute change in your voice.

Remember something else. Sindle took good care never to be long under observation. Everything he did was quickly done. And he had to establish that gross churlishness. His appearances had to be few but decisive. Even at the Tabby Cat he was there for a few minutes and no more, and at an unpopular time. The studio itself was in keeping and ready for a quick glimpse by anyone who might call. It gave support to that idea of drink and drugs and a kind of penurious hostility. And Sindle wore soft-soled shoes. No one could check his comings and goings by his feet on the stairs. And the tiled floor deadened movements in the room itself.

And so to the alibi. The details of that were obtained from Mrs. Solness, and there I should mention, if you didn't guess it at once, that it was she whom Wharton saw on that Wednesday night when he left Jewle to drive Ferndale to the Yard. He didn't, of course, learn all of it then, but he learned enough.

The portrait was suggested and the pose agreed on. Of those two people, Morse was easily the controlling mind. And he was handling a stupid woman whose brain was always in much of a flutter. When the climax was at hand she came to the studio at about twenty past three. Gulver had been sent on a distant errand by Morse, and there was only the presumably resting Pamela Maine in the building.

Hypnotism? Oh no. It was much simpler. Just a preliminary cup of tea and a slight opiate. And the drowsy warmth of the electric fire.

"What I want is that look of sleep," Morse said. "Close the eyes. I can do them later. To save the strain to the neck I'll pack you round, like this, with these cushions. Then just relax."

She relaxed, and she slept. Morse met Chale at the door.

"Sorry, I forgot I'd be having a sitter. Let's go up to that chap Sindle's room. He always leaves it open for me. Don't make a noise. That Miss Maine is probably asleep."

And that was the end of Chale. Maybe as soon as he was at the opened door he saw those curious preparations on the floor, but then it was too late. Twelve minutes or so later Morse came very quietly downstairs, and with the bundle that was Chale's clothes.

The sleep had been light but enough. Some noise was made to waken the Lady Macbeth.

"Oh dear. I believe I was actually asleep."

"Nonsense, my dear. I was watching you all the time."

"I really think I was."

"If you were, it was only for a second. I ought to know."

And so to the waking of Pamela Maine and the call of 'Fire!' And then Maud Solness was really awake. A word or two later that night convinced her that she had never been asleep.

But the really damning thing was this. Morse had wanted the wedding to take place that following Wednesday, but about that one thing Mrs. Solness had been obstinate. The marriage was at a register office and she had insisted that a certain old friend should be a witness, and that friend wasn't available till the following week. If it had taken place on that Wednesday, Morse would have been out of the country on the Thursday, long—as he would hope—before the police knew the body was that of Chale. But that wasn't all. Once Mrs. Solness was his wife she was lost to the police as a witness. She could never mention that vital nap. Or, as a stupid woman and a probably besotted wife, she'd be only too agreeable to swearing what was necessary to support the alibi.

The realisation of that, of course, was why we had to hurry. Morse had to be given no suspicions or he'd have bolted again. And we daren't question Mrs. Solness till the very last moment, when she could no longer get into touch with him. And if we didn't get those proofs from Brumford by that Wednesday night, then Morse might have been away on his honeymoon. And he had to be given a perfectly credible reason for coming to the Yard.

Why did Chale go to Borden Walk? Almost certainly to bring Morse a share of some unsavoury deal or his final cash settlement. It would have been dangerous for Morse to have gone to Meriton Gardens or Chale to have gone to Morse's flat. It had been essential, in fact, that the two should be utterly unacquainted. Neither could be sure that the Brumford affair was definitely a closed book.

And what about Wolde? Did Morse know how closely she'd become tied to Chale? Certainly he must have regarded her as just as much a danger to his new life with Maud Solness. My idea was that he'd tried to strike some sort of bargain with her after the murder and had decided that she couldn't be trusted in spite of the much he knew. Wharton's idea was that she was scared to death of Morse as soon as she realised that it was Chale, not a someone called Sindle, who must have been murdered. It was Morse, not myself, whom she'd been avoiding. I compromised by saying we could never hope to see into Morse's mind. Morse, satanically clever, utterly ruthless, suavely plausible and so charmingly convincing. Take that matter of the false teeth.

He'd called on a dentist in the small town of R . . . and he'd had the effrontery to present one of Chale's cards. That made him a medical man with every chance of a special pull.

"I'm staying in the town over the week-end," he had said, "and I'd like you to do me a favour. Naturally I'm prepared to pay all costs. Only a crude job, though. We're having a hospital reunion next week and I want to play a trick on my friends. You know the sort of thing: turn up as someone else and then later on take out the false teeth and pull off the wig."

Gum impressions had been taken and a couple of rough sets made up in plastic with porcelain teeth. Morse had collected them on the Monday and had chucklingly paid the small bill. It was a couple of days after the arrest that we heard about that. Why that dentist had read about Chale's murder and had seen no connection with Sindle passes all comprehension. What he told us was that he was too distracted with patients and the filling-up of forms to have much time for reading the newspapers.

Wolde, we now thought, had been killed near her room. Morse had entered the house when she was in bed, and she had heard a sound and had been struck down on the landing when she went to investigate. Whether the rest of the Sindle letter had any truth we had no means of telling. Maybe she had tried to blackmail him and had paid for it. Maybe he had only regarded her killing as a regrettable necessity, and just because she knew far too much. She represented at least a threat to that new, married life of his. As for the burning of all Chale's records and her private papers, that was a double safeguard. In her case it was an assurance that it ought to be some time before the police picked up her former connection with Chale, revived that old blackmail case, and had doubts, maybe, about that Paris killing of Morse.

But I don't think he worried overmuch about his ever being connected with that supposedly dead Morse. The danger was that the police might consider the killing of Chale an inside job and begin an enquiry into the history and antecedents of the tenants of No. 7. And if they did, then how could he account for his own life from, say, 1939 till the time he'd got back to England?

But if Morse was so clever, you may say, in what exactly did he go wrong? I don't admit that he did go wrong: what happened is that things didn't go right. Ought he to have taken seriously into account that anonymous letter he had sent all those years ago to the Paris police from Madrid? I maintain that there was no reason whatever. And doubtless on his arrival in England he took some steps to find out in Brumford if Morse was accepted as dead. He had only to go there for a day and start a conversation in a hotel bar.

Or take the Sindle letter. I still regard it as a model of persuasiveness. Nothing could have been more in keeping with the character he had built up, or, should I say, so deftly sketched. It was reticent where it had to be and informative where it could do no harm. It perpetuated the lost Sindle and kept him in our minds. It was more than a red herring: it was an ambuscade and a trap. But for amazing good luck we should have looked for the vanished Sindle for the rest of our police days.

If he made mistakes at all, it was in being too florid. He did too many things, and I don't refer particularly to that attempt to silence Pamela Maine. But he did scatter too many side-trails in that grim paper-chase, though doubtless he had his reasons. That business of ringing the Broad Street Detective Agency, for instance, was to hint that if the body were ultimately found to be Chare's, then it must have been Sindle, the ex-patient, who'd killed him. And by quoting an appointment in North London at six o'clock, it would have put us on the wrong scent of a possibly missing Chale. Then there were those pictures that he painted with his left hand for Sindle's studio: just the kind of thing that might be done by a man who was trying to find again his true *genre*. Then he had to put in that nude of Viola Vetch as another false trail. Wharton thought that picture had never been intended to be there but had been left by mistake. That was why, in the Sindle letter, he made that cryptic allusion to Viola Vetch to cover up the slip. I wasn't so sure. I regarded him as sufficiently self-assured to think we'd never regard her as incapable of sitting even to Sindle. What he did was badly misjudge her real nature.

But we should have gone at once far more thoroughly into the matter of that picture. If Vetch had never sat for it, then it had been painted from memory. And who was more likely to have painted it than the man who'd drawn for us a portrait of the remembered Sindle? That was something we missed and because Ferndale's alibi put him apparently beyond the faintest suspicion. There were other things, but let me mention them in another context. And permit me to say about them what I've often said before about the difficulty of assessing what may or may not be a vital clue. It's the big, showy things that are often of no consequence and the insignificant that may have all the urgency in the world. The problem is how to tell which from which. My name would go down to history with Sherlock Holmes and Lecoq if you could only enlighten me about the way to do that!

There's always something slightly sadistic about Wharton when we come to the end of a case. That night, when Morse had been taken away and he'd had his word with Gulver, he came back to his room and grabbed his hat.

"Let's stand ourselves a meal. Don't know about you, but I reckon we've earned it."

I was willing enough, even if it meant the likelihood of my paying the bill. At any rate we went to a certain restaurant where they know me, and we got a corner table. George had a double Scotch with plenty of soda and I an iced lager while we waited for the meal.

"Well, here's to the rope round Morse's neck," he told me as he took a pull at his glass.

I drank too, but not necessarily to that toast. Once the chase is virtually over my interest is gone. Sometimes it's sentiment that creeps in, and in any case I hate the thought of the rope and the drop. I'm not, as you long ago have gathered, of the stuff of which he-detectives are made.

"That Mrs. Solness is going to have the very hell of a shock," he was telling me later. "He'd got round her absolutely proper. I reckon she'll tell us all we want to know, out of sheer vindictiveness."

"No. 7's going to have a nine days' wonder," was what I said. "I'm sorry, in a way, about not going round there again. It had got to be almost like home."

We'd finished the meal and were almost through the coffee when he began the patting on the back—his own back as well as mine.

"I don't know, George," I said. "I don't think somehow, I'd like the whole story to get out. If we're going to keep our reputations there're some things we've got to slur over remarkably lightly."

"What d'you mean?" he was asking indignantly.

"Well, take the Sindle letter. The very moment we got it we ought to have spotted something. It purported to be the history of a sexual pervert. And who was the only one at No. 7 who was supposed to see Sindle as that kind of pervert? Ferndale—when he told us about that pansy. That's why we ought to have concentrated at once on Ferndale."

"I did spot it later on, didn't I?" he snorted. "You're expecting too much. We can't all be perfect."

That hit about perfection was aimed at me. I had nothing to throw back except an old tag of mine.

"If the prophet had bid thee do some great thing, George, wouldst thou not have done it?" He'd heard that before, but it didn't keep back the question.

"And what're you getting at there?"

"Just the simplicity of things," I said. "What looks unimportant, and isn't. Take, for instance, the soup."

"What soup?"

"The soup, and the soup alone, that Sindle had at the Tabby Cat. We thought he couldn't afford a square meal. But it wasn't that."

"Oh?" he said. "And what was it?"

"The fact," I said, "that the teeth he was wearing were only for show. He couldn't have eaten a steak if you'd given it free and thrown in a bottle of Burgundy. All he could manage with those dummy teeth of his was soup with bread soaked in it."

"Yes," he said, and tried hard to chuckle. "Pretty good, that."

"And there's one other thing that makes me kick myself when I think of it," I said. "We missed the simplest thing of all—the telephone at No. 7."

He frowned, and he was trying to make time.

"Just a minute," he said. "You mentioned that the other night. And you dragged in Sherlock Holmes and the dog."

"Got the answer yet?"

"A fat lot of time I've had for riddles," he told me. "Still, I reckon you've got the answer."

"Maybe I have," I said. "But as I was telling you that other afternoon, nothing was wrong with the telephone except that it *was* a telephone. Got it now?"

"Carry on," he told me gruffly.

"Well, there was a telephone at No. 7. But Ferndale went all the way to Howe Street to a fire alarm when all he had to do was dial 999 from where he was. In other words, he wanted that fire to go on burning for as long as he could make it. The last thing he wanted was to put it out."

"Yes," he said. "You're right enough there. Funny you should miss a thing like that."

I had to laugh, and for various reasons. George can be stridently aware of my shortcomings and so serenely oblivious of his own. And I supposed I'd asked for that comment of his. There's often more than a touch of boastfulness about humility and apologetics.

"That sketch he did of Sindle," he suddenly said. "Wasn't he supposed to give it to you?"

I said that was so. Then he was getting up, ostensibly for repairs, though I guessed he was hoping that in his absence I'd settle the bill. But I was thinking about that sketch. Clever enough, but I had no use for it now. Maybe I'd give it to Bintwood, who could cash in on its notoriety value. I'd get him to spend the money on No. 7. A dinner, say, at the Tabby Cat. But, for reasons of his own, no Ludovic Travers. After all, one never knew who might appear suddenly around even the darkest corners.

THE END

www.ingramcontent.com/pod-product-compliance
Lightning Source LLC
Chambersburg PA
CBHW031015190726
48286CB00003BA/862